The Done Thing

Tracy Manaster

TYRUS
BOOKS

Published by
TYRUS BOOKS
an imprint of F+W Media, Inc.
10151 Carver Road, Suite 200
Blue Ash, OH 45242. U.S.A.
www.tyrusbooks.com

ISBN 10: 1-4405-9672-7
ISBN 13: 978-1-4405-9672-8
eISBN 10: 1-4405-9673-5
eISBN 13: 978-1-4405-9673-5

Printed in the United States of America.

10 9 8 7 6 5 4 3 2 1

Library of Congress Cataloging-in-Publication Data
Manaster, Tracy, author.
The done thing / Tracy Manaster.
Blue Ash, OH: Tyrus Books, 2016.
LCCN 2016012028 (print) | LCCN 2016018552 (ebook) | ISBN 9781440596728 (hc) |
ISBN 1440596727 (hc) | ISBN 9781440596735 (ebook) | ISBN 1440596735 (ebook)
LCSH: Murder victims' families--Fiction. | Interpersonal relations--Fiction. | Prisoners--Fiction.
| Pen pals--Fiction. | BISAC: FICTION / Contemporary Women. | FICTION / Family Life.
LCC PS3613.A527 D66 2016 (print) | LCC PS3613.A527 (ebook) | DDC 813/.6--dc23
LC record available at https://lccn.loc.gov/2016012028

Cover design by Sylvia McArdle.
Cover images © iStockphoto.com/AlexanderZam; iStockphoto.com/Ken Brown;
iStockphoto.com/michaelgzc; iStockphoto.com/raclro; iStockphoto.com/narloch-liberra;
iStockphoto.com/Boryan.

This book is available at quantity discounts for bulk purchases.
For information, please call 1-800-289-0963.

For my parents,
Steve and B.J. Manaster, upon whom
no characters in this book are based.

1.

The State of Arizona conducted its executions at dawn and had for the past several years, a policy change from midnight for which no explanation had been offered. I liked to keep abreast of such things. I had the *Daily Star* delivered to my St. Louis home, days late and at no small cost. For nearly two decades I'd collected clippings and taken notes on legal pads. I ran calculations and so I knew: forty-eight percent of inmates took breakfast as their final meals. Maybe they sought grounding, one last moment in step with the breakfasting rest of the world. The eggs, though, threw me. Thirty-four percent of prisoners—even some slated for electrocution—demanded fried eggs. Breakfast any mother might serve: the buttery stuff of hurried kitchens, pan to plate in under ten minutes. Kiddie food, and cheap. I'd read the studies. Few inmates in Intensive Supervision Unit-Stemble came from privilege. Maybe they ate and thought of their first eggs and the hands that brought them. Mothering of some persuasion, over- or under-, it was all just rhetoric. I read those articles, too. Every execution had its editorializing. Never mind justice. He grew up hard. Blame the mothers. The mothers will do.

Or, worse, the alternative: maternal address to camera and court. Rote permutations: I know what my son did, please don't take my son, my son knows what it is to take, please, my son knows what is to be taken. While inside and over the wall he chewed his eggs, the fear and grease shunting them down to loose bowels. I

5

hoped the cooks couldn't get an egg right. I hoped shells snuck in and startled, crunching like bones.

I wanted to see him.

I wanted to hear him complain about the grub.

He would, too, if it was nasty stuff. Or he'd explain the eggs. "See here. The food's so foul a fried egg's the only thing they can't screw up." He used to have this way of speaking, leaning forward, pitch lilting like he was letting the world in on a private joke. "Maybe we just like eggs. It doesn't have to mean a thing."

It didn't have to be nostalgia. Eggs fry up quick. They're easy to spice. Fodder for the self-sufficient. Bachelor food.

I knew my statistics. Clarence Lusk was lucky to be white. Lucky Clarence, to have his mother out there funneling her retirement into his defense. A little darker, a little poorer, and he'd be long buried.

For eighteen years and four appeals I'd waited. I tried to visit. Each April I petitioned, miserable annual paperwork, right on the heel of taxes. He invariably denied me. "Understand this," my lawyer said, "few things remain that he has the power to refuse."

I wanted to see his face. He'd be older now, too. Everybody was, with certain, notable exceptions. When we put my sister in the ground, her hair had haloed around her face, a cropped, unruly mess of curls. Layered. The fashion of the day, archaic now. She looked like a dandelion gone to seed. Hair grew postmortem. Nails too. In the bitter months between funeral and verdict I remember finding comfort in this. My underground sister continued to change. She grew wild out of sight.

Clarence appeared at trial with his hair shorn close. This was no longer mandatory—some prisoners' rights lawsuit—so it had to be strategy. Before, he'd let it go shaggy. Maybe he thought the cut would make him respectable.

It wouldn't. Nothing would again. And I hoped it wasn't strategy. I hoped it was lice.

My husband Frank, God bless, used to stop me from running away with myself. Lida, he'd say, what good can thinking like that do? Frank was a gentleman, in the sense that the word is the sum of *gentle* and of *man*. He knew there was no peace to be had from a certain vein of thought. How I loved him. As he did me, even when I was frayed, even when I loosed the shrill, full honesty: it wasn't actually peace I wanted. I wanted to be sure Clarence Lusk wouldn't find any. I could say that sort of thing to Frank, and that was a measure of the soundness of our marriage. And this was as well: I did not often say such things to Frank. I saw how it made him feel helpless.

Our Pamela had grown up measured and very sweet, like Frank. A confident, lovely girl, except when I mentioned Clarence. Her father, locked far away. Her father, who had put her mother underground. She said I looked absolutely hawkish when I spoke of him. And so I didn't do it much. The way it knit her face together. Three times a year we let him write Pam. When she was just a little thing and young enough to forget.

Clarence didn't have the right to deny me anything.

And so I had no one, really, to talk to about the eggs. Thirty-four percent. I'd triple checked. I used a calculator. Why eggs, why fried, I couldn't figure. Eggs were bizarrely optimistic. Eggs were a beginning. Yellow. Cheerful. Though fried, of course, they'd never grow.

Someone should conduct a study. *Shattered Eggshells: A Comprehensive Analysis of Proteins, Lipids and the Murdering Mind.* The data could make a difference. Waitresses could phone a hotline after taking orders. Barbra would have appreciated that line of thought. She always got this impish look when she guessed I was thinking something terrible. Barbra would've had her own theory. Everyone knows breakfast's the most important meal of the day. The condemned have high pressure mornings ahead. Better load up on protein. But my sister never said anything of the sort. She had no reason to. I only learned my statistics after. Almost twenty years gone now. Frank dead, Pammie out of the nest and married. But Clarence. Clarence lingered, unshakable as the phantom weight a watch leaves on a naked wrist. Once he died I could find new thoughts. I wanted that. I wanted it desperately. I wanted to fly to Arizona. I wanted to fry him an egg.

2.

Sixty-four years ago, I was born Lida Helen Haas, daughter of Tate and Renate Haas. Like my parents, I've passed my life in the orbit of St. Louis, near the cola-colored confluence of two great rivers. The family orchard Barbra and I grew up on was a half hour outside the city. It had been generations in Ma's family, a rich, black-earthed holding that upon inheriting I—despite the impulse of sentimentality—subdivided at good profit. My earliest memories were orchard ones: me and Ma making do, putting up cherries. Red half-moons built up beneath my fingernails. A splinter pierced my foot as I bore jars into the dank basement, tentative on slatted steps.

"We'll be lucky in winter," Ma said. "The cherries will be a godsend. A little sweetness to do us good." But we only opened jars when sweetness was redundant. When the war in Europe was done. When the Japanese surrendered. When we learned my father was slated to return. He stepped out of the picture on the mantel, then out of his uniform, then off the orchard and onto the floor of Haas Home & Pharmacy.

"Fruit trees are small scale, Lidalee. Farm's fine for living, but the store keeps us all in shoe leather." A car followed. A refrigerator. A washer. A dryer. One thing and then the next, clicking into place like abacus beads.

For fifty-four years I have been a sister. Ma called Barbra and me her sandwich girls. Two sturdy children, sound as bread, with the war the meat between us. As a child my parents encouraged me to make do. Barbra, child of peace and plenty, they encouraged to do her best. To my lasting shame, we were not close as children. She was always getting into my things, spoiling them. Barbra Barbarian, I used to call her. The words shared a root. *Barbaros*: one who isn't Greek. A stranger.

At twenty-five I married Francis Stearl. We saved up for a down payment and bought a Dutch Colonial on a broad street with fine trees. We held Memorial Day barbecues and in December I baked our neighbors pfeffernüsse. Just after our twentieth anniversary, well in advance of current fads, my Frank took up running. He was nearing fifty and I accused him of vanity. "I intend to stick around, that's all," he said. "For you and Pammie." He met each dawn with a dedicated hour's jog. I seldom joined him. I kept trim swimming laps at the club, and, though Frank was invariably patient when I did tag along, I didn't want the back of his neck to become the patch of skin I knew best. I bought him sweatbands, an erratic pedometer, and, in case he ever ran too far, Nikes with a pocket for a payphone quarter. I began to linger over my morning coffee and the *Post-Dispatch*. In yellow highlighter I marked headlines my returning husband would find of interest. In the four years since his death I haven't been able to shake the habit.

Before my retirement at sixty, I practiced as an orthodontist. The discipline has extraordinary grace, interlacing bands, subtle tugging, and time almost always adding up to perfection. And that was the joy of my long career: with teeth at least, anything wrong I could make right. I enjoyed my job, even in the mid-eighties, when we'd all had to relearn the feel of it. I donned latex gloves a good year before they were compulsory; doctors back then knew so little about transmission and I had Pamela to think about, and Frank. I made a careful study of teeth beneath gloves. Brackets, glue, wire, enamel: everything was so much duller dry, and I finally got the sense of what those boys—that boy, really, Martin Dorsey, singular, the only one before Frank—had gone on about. Plain truth. You don't feel as much through rubber.

For twenty-three years I had been an aunt. Pamela Clare came into the world slippery, prune-faced, and squalling, with whorls of fine down on her head. I flew to Arizona to meet her the day she came home from the hospital. Her name surprised me. I had expected some permutation of Barbra; every doll my sister owned she had named after herself. "Clarence talked me out of using a palindrome," Barbra said. "I wanted Anna, Eve, Nan. A girl who's the same backwards and forwards. Steady. True like an equation. Do you want to hold her?"

"Who the hell talks like that?" Clarence asked, before I could answer. Yes, I wanted to hold the baby.

I laughed though. He was right; my sister was nothing if not loquacious.

We were all so happy; Barbra was laughing, too. "The next one will be a boy. And I'm calling him Bob." She stuck out an impish tongue at Clarence.

"We're lucky she didn't want to name this one pi," he said. Barbra taught high school mathematics.

"*Pamela* isn't a palindrome," I reminded them. "Now let me meet my niece properly."

"No one loves a know-it-all," said Barbra, and she settled the warm weight of Pam into my arms.

Clarence chuckled. "And *Pam* backwards is *map*. That's something. Baby's going places." He bent low over his daughter. His lips upon her forehead.

Five years later, that baby was mine.

It was easier to get through taking it fact after simple fact: At 1:30 P.M. on Monday, October 25th, 1982, Barbra never showed up to teach her fifth-period calculus class. One of her students notified the front office. The vice-principal, who usually served as emergency sub, couldn't be located either. The receptionist posted a sign directing Barbra's remaining three classes to the library for study hall and left a message on the Lusks' answering machine. Midway through the afternoon, a freshman set off the fire alarm. For the balance of the day faculty and staff worked distracted, and no one troubled much over Barbra's absence or that of vice-principal Lawrence Ring.

On the morning of Tuesday, October 26th, when neither reported to work, the phone chain began: the receptionist left another message at Barbra's home and a second at Lawrence Ring's. Nothing. She found Ring's Rolodex and in it the number of his cleaning lady. The cleaning lady straightened his place Mondays anyhow. She agreed to stop by sooner rather than later. It was the cleaning lady who dialed 911. Her quick inspection yielded a kitchen, one upturned chair, two crumpled bodies, and a brown and slippery floor.

The police pieced together the scene with little trouble. The assailant fired first on Barbra's friend. Lawrence Richard Ring. Barbra fell next, split apart by four bullets, two more than had bored into— the couple's state left little question—her lover. Chest wounds and stomach. They had been eating Chinese takeout. Pamela's school reported that her father had picked her up early on the previous afternoon. He had told them she had a dentist appointment. He said his wife must have forgotten to let them know.

At around six o'clock Tuesday evening, a policeman identified Clarence's plates and Clarence pulled over. But only briefly. He sped into the approaching uniform, in panic, maybe, or thinking that one more death made little difference, or perhaps as final, wild resistance to whatever future he had left. Georg Ring—no *e*, no middle name, no relation to Vice-Principal Lawrence R.—died ten and a half hours later, having never regained consciousness. He was a muscular, strong-featured, handsome man, in whose obituary smile I could sense that the praise of his colleagues was well-earned. He had founded an after-school baseball program to keep kids out of trouble. He'd been saving for a Hawaiian vacation, a second honeymoon with his wife of fifteen years, the mother of his three children. I wrote annual checks to the foundation established in his name.

The arresting officer found Clarence just ten miles down the highway. He'd parked on the road's shoulder and was waiting, seatbelt buckled, hands on the steering wheel. Pamela sat in the backseat, strapped safe to her plastic chair. Her fist was full of crayons. She asked to take the picture she was working on with her. She said please.

"Tell me about your drawing," her social worker said.

"It's a chickie-bird. She just invented Popsicles."

Bright, her file read, *imaginative*. *Resilient*, underlined three times.

Such are the small things I never expected to be grateful for.

I had done absolutely right by Pamela. On the days when my retirement didn't suit me, when I felt as effective and lively as a tin of beef, the thought of her warded off self-pity. I had marshaled to radiant adulthood a woman who knew to never carry a bag that cost more than her shoes or eat oysters in a month spelled without *r*s. Pamela flossed. She hand-washed bras. Her thank-you notes arrived promptly. She kept receipts and bought the warranty. Applied perfume sparingly, as I did, with an atomizer, spraying in front of her four times and stepping into the mist. She always wore sunscreen, SPF 30 or higher. She drove with her sunshade fully up or fully down. I had warned her and she listened; this world was perilous. Crash with it angled and pay with an eye. Whenever I missed her I brushed my teeth. I knew she brushed as I did. Recite the preamble to the Constitution once for each quadrant, once for the gums, once for the tongue, and once for the roof of the mouth. That's how to know you've made a proper job of it.

3.

On the occasion of my sixty-third birthday, Pamela took me computer shopping. The excursion was more for Pam than it was for me; she had been after me about the computer for some time. I went along with it though. It was October of 2001. Everyone was humoring the people they loved. Pamela and I met at the store she had pre-selected. Its doors opened for us with an electronic whoosh and she guided me toward the display.

"Pamela Clare, I hope you're not about to push one of those matchmaker sites." My circle meant well, and their suggestions had been coming thick of late: did I know about suchandsuch a swing dance club? Or that soandso had a widower cousin to whom I could be introduced? It had been three years, and barely that.

"Oh please," Pam said. "You're matchless." Pammie had a way with words that I doubted most people noticed. She liked to pause before rebutting, measuring precisely, and that built the illusion of soft-spokenness.

I gave a theatrical bow. "I really don't need any of this," I said, indicating the machines. They were so small now. "I hardly use the one at home," I reminded Pam. The one she had written her high school essays on. Frank had been so excited buying it. He was mildly dyslexic and here was a machine that knew how to spell.

"That thing?" Pam grinned. "A shoebox has as much oomph."

"It's only ten years old."

Pamela, luckily, did not inherit her mother's barking laugh; hers trilled.

Together, we selected a computer.

At the register, I attempted to pay. Pamela rolled her eyes—the strange and green-flecked blue of vacation brochure oceans—and for a moment that made her look about twelve.

"It's your birthday, Lida. We want to do this for you." Every present is a kind of reflection, laying bare the giver's hopes. So this was Pam's payback for the flute, the oil pastels, the microscope, the chemistry set. At least she believed me up for it, never one of those tizzy widows, unequal to the challenge of setting a digital clock. Pamela carried the box to the car. She set the machine up at my desk. I was amazed. She only consulted the manual a handful of times. She taught me. This is how you fire it up. This is how you go online. We met her husband downtown for dinner. They didn't let me pay for that either.

And then the evening found me—overfull of starch and chocolate—alone again in the townhouse. How absurd that I was the sole occupant of these six rooms, that I'd chosen the paint myself, that I had neighbors on either side instead of our vast yard where Frank had waged war on dandelions. But I'd been right to situate myself here. There was something to be said for a thriving neighborhood. On good days it felt a very fine thing to navigate the boutiques and cafés; on bad, the noise meant I was less alone. I stowed the Styrofoam shell of leftover paella in the fridge and went online so I could tell Pammie tomorrow that I had used her gift. I hunt-and-pecked my own name. We're a shallow species. Everyone tries their own names first when they're learning to type. Shallow, but not wholly egomaniacal. With a foreign language, *I love you* is the first phrase we need.

I clicked and waited. The screen changed.

I'd once heard that a woman's name should appear in print only three times: on the occasions of her birth, her marriage, and her death.

Even Ma had pshawed that one. But I understood the principle. Anonymity was the sign of a life cleanly lived. I was relieved when my name yielded few results. My position on the board of Pamela's high school. An out-of-date listing of area orthodontists.

I typed in my husband's name. A bow hunter in Idaho, apparently, shared it and offered guide services. My own Frank, the Internet noted, had placed ninth in his age group in a half marathon five years ago. I re-read his obituary. A photo topped it, taken ages before diagnosis. His favorite red shirt. Hair two weeks overdue for the barber. Cancer of the stomach. In lieu of flowers, donations. Survived by his wife, his beloved niece. And that was all. No hint of his unshakable calm, no lists of the nonsensical sayings he used to avoid swearing. The way he placed his hands wrong for dancing. So much for new technology.

I made sure to capitalize Pamela's name. One dated link appeared for Pamela Lusk, listing her as co-chair of Washington University's French Conversation Hour. Onscreen, a prompt inquired if perhaps I meant Pamela *Luck*.

Pamela Claverie. She'd taken Blue's name.

And there they were in the *Post-Dispatch*: Pamela and Blue dressed for their wedding, grinning in oversized matching sunglasses. And that horrid headline. *Love Is Blind*. Appalling taste on the part of the reporter; I'd written to the editor and got not a peep by way of response. To just say it folksy like that, local blind man weds guide dog trainer, like it was a joke, like Blue hadn't made a tremendous success of himself as a lawyer, like Pam didn't graduate *magna cum laude*. For that matter, the girl I'd hired to take the wedding pictures had done a much better job of it than the pro from the *Dispatch*, even if I didn't crack the album often. It had been a hard day—happy, yes, but hard. What to do about the aisle walking with Frank gone. Our family pew so sparse. And I was lousy at the small talk after. The whole time terrified I'd accidentally say something to

Blue along the lines of *You look fantastic, dear* or *I'll see you after the honeymoon.*

I didn't search for Barbra. I chose not to. It was my birthday, and I simply wasn't equal to the work of seeing how thoroughly she had vanished.

Instead, Clarence. I didn't know what I was hoping for. A clock, maybe, counting down. A diagram of his eventual end. See this prisoner. This is who he killed. This is how. This is a needle. This is sodium thiopental, this pancuronium bromide, this potassium chloride. My mouth felt dry as crackers. His name on my screen, unbounded by cell bars. Clarence Lusk, Clarence Lusk. My mouse hovered.

Some sorrow-sap society for prisoners' rights designed the page. Words marched backwards across the top, from right to left: Be a Penfriend. It's the Write Thing. Be a Candle to Those in Darkness. Periodically, the tops of each letter burst into flame. A U.S. map. Prisons labeled with black dots. I could probably recite the address. Intensive Supervision Unit, Stemble Complex, Arizona State Prison, Judith, Arizona. He'd negotiated for three letters to Pamela a year; I'd acquiesced, knowing from my clients' gummed-up sticky smiles the binges brought on by prohibition. I never wanted Pamela curious about him. I clicked on "Arizona," and then on "Stemble." An alphabetized list of inmates loaded. I had to scroll down to the *L*s. The page loaded. Inmate 58344.

Hello out there.

I would like to hear from you, whoever you are.

I'll answer every letter I get unless you've found religion and want me to find it too. I get a lot of that here. If you aren't on some mission I can't guess why you would choose to read this, but I thank you for doing it. I've been on death row almost twenty years for my mistakes. It's everything you'd think. Mixed bag boring, lonely and, truth be told, scary. You can't do anything about that last bit, but letters are company and company passes time. Time's not something I've got a lot of left, just so you know. I'm running low on appeals and hope. So write. You're likely to get me for life without having to promise the same. I'm a good correspondent. I hope you can see I still have a sense of humor. I've got to have something, right? And I just admitted I am afraid, so you know I am honest at least. I'll never claim I didn't do the things I've done. I won't ever ask you for more than letters. I have paper. I get stamps through commissary. Just send words.

    —C. Lusk

Of course I wasn't going to write him. What could I possibly say? Any letter I sent, he'd shred as soon as he saw my name.

Dear Inmate.

    I'm glad you're bored, glad you're lonely, glad you're scared.

From this chair I can see two pictures of your wife. There she is, moon-faced, cradling your newborn daughter, their wrists still encircled with identification bracelets. And there: Barbra garlanded and serene in wedding white, and I look so young beside her. She smiles. The moles on her cheekbone and below her lips give the expression an air of frozen asymmetry. Sometimes I turn that snapshot face down. She doesn't know what she's marrying and I can't stand the grin.

    I won't tell you about the pictures of Pamela we have framed. You don't have the right.

    I caught her once cutting into candids. The pictures I could never display because you were in them too. Pamela excised you.

Scissors flashed. She skimmed Barbra's silhouette. Little Pam made neat work of it. And I had to stop her; not because you were a human father, but because on film you touched my sister. Waist, shoulders, belly. You never could let her alone.

"He had long fingers," Pammie asked, "didn't he?"

"I hadn't noticed." I lied to Pamela, Clarence. Not for your sake, but because her own fingers were long. Girlish like yours, but without the roughness at the knuckles. Still are. You'd have no way to know.

"And he bit his nails," Pam said.

So did she. Frank and I had painted hers with foul shellac, but no use. That day, she stopped. Your daughter has lovely hands. She visits a manicurist weekly.

Her manicurist knows what you did.

Pamela tells everyone. I raised her to. No good comes from keeping it secret and it isn't us who should be ashamed.

Her husband knows. Blue. You should see how he loves her. And he's a courteous man, intelligent. When we first met he said I sounded like the kind of person who would know the names of stars and constellations. I don't. He pretended to be impressed by my elementary school mnemonic.

"My very energetic mother just served us nine pizzas. Mercury, Venus, Earth, Mars, Jupiter, Saturn, Uranus, Neptune, Pluto."

"But Pluto might not be a planet anymore," Blue said. "Don't they think it's an asteroid?" That's the kind of person he is. He knows about stars, he thinks about them, even though he'll never in his life see one.

And I bet you never knew that about Pluto, how much the universe has changed since you've been locked away from it. One whole planet less. I'm grateful for it.

And I'm grateful for Pamela. God, am I ever grateful. She works outside. Muck and dog hair all over. Every day to get to work, Pam crosses state lines. She calls me sometimes if there's traffic on the bridge.

"Guess what state I'm in, Lida."

"I bet you're above the Mississippi. I bet you're neither here nor there." It's not much of a joke, but it feels like one by dint of repetition.

Clarence, you will never joke with her. You will never cross another state line. I know your case; one more appeal and you'll die in Arizona.

And before you meet the needle, know this: for years Pam wore tinted contacts that hid the strange blue eyes she inherited from you. You should know what she says when asked about her father.

He isn't a factor in my life.

You killed a math teacher. Perhaps you remember the basics. This is how you multiply: factor, factor, product. You are nothing that made her. You should know she grew up quiet. You should know she sleeps with blankets curled around her, burrito-style, and that it's not you, but dark birds, that plague her dreamscape. You should know that she speaks French and reads Braille; that she swims laps daily; that she's allergic to ketchup and can't abide the taste of cough syrup; you should know that for two Halloweens running I dressed her as blind Justice.

4.

I am one of those women who sleep deeply and well. A rare thing, I am given to understand.

My Frank was a restless sleeper, always fussing with his pillows. Pammie too. And they both dreamed, regularly, as I seldom did. At breakfast they swapped night-narratives, Pamela's dark, swooping birds, Frank's missed appointments in cities with origami skylines. It seemed a sorry sort of conversation, more verbal tennis than proper connection, her dream volleyed and his lobbed back. But I held my tongue. I had nothing to contribute. As I've mentioned: I rarely dream.

(About Pammie's recurring birds: I consulted a dream dictionary about them once, at the public library on my lunch hour. Birds as the harbingers of freedom, as a call to listen to one's own sacred self. The book's pages had the cheap feel of newsprint and I hoped that no one spied me consulting that piffle.)

I mention all this because I *did* dream on the night of my sixty-third. I dreamed that I had somehow forgotten to remove Pam's braces. She came to the townhouse, carrying the graduation briefcase I had given her, the briefcase she never needed for her job outdoors with the dogs. She spoke the names of my tools lovingly, *scalar, Mathieu pliers*. She had an Italian accent. What she lifted from the case didn't match her words. An old hex key. A typewriter ribbon. She lay her head in my lap and opened wide. I didn't have

my gloves. Pam's brackets peeled away like Band-Aids and then—
the instant before I woke—my finger slipped through her incisor.

It was still dark out. I turned on my bedside lamp and cinched
my thick, spongy robe. I have always invested in good cotton.
Robes, yes, and sheets. Frank liked to tease. Spendthrift, he called
me, and sensualist. But he understood, my Frank. When bad nights
came, my small, safe luxuries could sometimes help absorb them.
I smiled. In Stemble, there would be no robes. And sheets. Your
sheets must be rough as shingles. I cinched my robe against the
thought, Clarence. It wouldn't do to dwell.

I ducked into the master bathroom, the one I'd had outfitted
with good lighting and an antique tub. I'd hung the matching
medicine cabinet myself, damned if I was going to be one of those
widows who dithered at the prospect of opening their husbands'
tool chests. I opened its mirrored door and stood on tiptoe to reach
the top shelf. Of course I'd fixed Pam's teeth. They were lovely
now. I had kept the plaster molds. Yes, there they were, the flawed
set—upper centrals bucking, a cuspid descending askew—and the
perfect one. I sat on the edge of the bathtub and held a mold in each
hand, bookends of a job well done.

I had a third set of teeth. Up there on the shelf, all alone. The
unpaired Before of Maisie Keller, pronounced underbite, cusps
jagged as a saw. The mold highlighted her interproximal gaps;
only her molars had grown in fully flush. Maisie Keller was a little
Korean girl, an adoptee whose mother worked with Frank at Wash
U. There'd have been good money in those teeth, but I couldn't.
I couldn't. She'd been in my chair getting her initial impressions
made when the phone rang that terrible Tuesday about Arizona. I
referred her to a colleague for treatment. Now *here* was an insomniac
thought: Maisie Keller was out there somewhere. I could have
looked *her* up. Instead of—I shuddered. I ran a finger along the
smooth, chalky bow of Pam's mouth-mold. Her gums had bled, a

little, in my dream. And in my waking life, when I first set in the wires. What a mind I had. I returned the mouths to their shelves. I clicked the hinged mirror shut. It threw back my static-wild hair. Pouches beneath my eyes, the color of dirty fingernails.

There'd be no more sleep tonight. I made toast. I was running low on bread, and added it to the list beside the fridge, reminders to return library books, purchase decaf, pay the phone bill, re-attach a blouse button. I had time now, a blank, unrolling skein of it. I had begun to ration errands.

The microwave clock turned from 2:47 to 2:48. The oven clock read 2:48 too. A simultaneous switchover. I have always liked catching little moments like that. There's a cleanness; the world feels briefly tidied. I stood sleepless and glazed beside the clocks. 3:00. 3:01. If all the clocks in my house aligned, I was doing okay.

If all my clocks aligned, I would allow myself to write you.

Just a thought. A preposterous little bet with myself. I was wide awake now though. No. *Wild* awake.

The cherry wood grandfather that dominated the front room read 3:01. The living room VCR agreed. Beside my bed, the alarm clock I no longer bothered to set read 3:01. My silver wristwatch's hands—digital watches were for children; I liked the revolving grace of a proper clock—seemed close enough, as did my two office clocks, one red plastic and wall-mounted, the other Frank's old desk set, a barometer and timepiece in one. As Pam had taught me, the computer was off for the night and surge-protected. It would take a good five minutes to fire up; an exception could be made. I was grinning now. I felt it in my cheeks.

But. There. On the guest room end table, Pamela's old clock radio blinked and blinked. Twelve o'clock. Midnight, noon, midnight. I jerked the cord from the socket. Ages ago, Pam had covered the radio almost entirely with stickers. It was a wonder any sound came through. So very very Pamela. At the onset of her awkward age, she'd layered stickers over everything—we'd had to sand and refinish her entire bedroom set. It was the same when she learned to write her name. For weeks we couldn't allow her permanent markers. All through the house her name appeared in colored pencil. Pamela, Pammie, Pam; this is mine, and this, and this.

I turned the radio against the wall. What kind of woman makes decisions based on clocks? It was irresponsible, flopping about. The way Frank would have teased. Lida, he'd say, you've got a sharp mind and more guts than the village gut-monger. Just decide.

If I wrote you, I'd be sending a piece of myself; and you had no right to that.

And yet: you had no right to shrink from me.

Anything that came to you in my name you'd shred. I knew how things went with you. I didn't know why. I didn't know enough.

For most of my adult life I'd had a system to help make up my mind. When in doubt, I always opted for *no*. *No* required less fuss. No time. No expenditure. This process had always served me well. It was useful in its pure arbitrariness: any relief or regret in the wake of *no* hinted at my true desires. Even if I couldn't articulate them, even if they were terrible to acknowledge, a gut response meant they could no longer hide. Which brought to light another feature of *no*. Unlike *yes, no* was simple to reverse.

5.

Sleep makes grapes of raisins. That was one of my mother's sayings; she'd doled them out for big woes and small, easy as acetaminophen. And Ma was right. Sleepless, I felt dry and fully shriveled, old as Ma herself, eight years dead come December. We'd cremated her. Frank too. Everyone after Barbra, I cremated. The thought of another body in the ground. Still and wet, getting wetter. My horrible mind. I should have *willed* myself to sleep. There were tricks for it. Back in the day, we'd had an expert work through them with Pam. Too late for all that though. Instead, I took careful time with my face and my hair. I selected a shirt with a flattering cut. I was exhausted, yes, but I'd be flayed and fried before I'd look it in front of Kath Claverie.

Kath was Blue's mother. We walked on Monday mornings. Her idea. *You'll have to show me the* real *neighborhood, Lida.* The Claveries lived out in Ladue. Frank and I could certainly have afforded to, but he'd enjoyed walking to work and—I don't like saying this; it sounds ugly and self-congratulatory—we couldn't see raising Pam so the only black people she met were the ones cutting grass.

Kath Claverie knocked precisely at ten; Kath Claverie was always on time. I had an unkind theory about that—not about Kath, specifically, who I did like, but about her brand of woman, the ones who'd managed homes instead of careers. They tend to make a grand thing of punctuality. It's a way of showing that *their* time also matters. I hollered for her to come in.

"You don't lock your door?" Autumnal light spilled in with Kath, followed by her subtle bloom of expensive scent. Some women—and I feared sometimes I was one of them—figured out what worked on them makeup-wise very young and then altered their faces very little from one decade to the next. Not so Kath Claverie. She looked current and put together but never actively done up.

"I *unlocked* it, Kath," I said. "I knew you were coming." There was a border when it came to makeup, a one-way crossing. We used it to make ourselves look older and then we used it to make ourselves look younger. Barbra died right on that border's cusp.

Kath bent to hug me upon entry to the townhouse; the Claveries are a very touchy family. They're all tall too; I stood just at the level of Kath's neck. The usual gold chain encircled it. Eight pendants dangled, running left to right. A tourmaline, an emerald, a topaz, a pearl, a sapphire, another topaz, an opal, and a ruby. One birthstone for each grandchild, strung in order of their arrival. I keep telling the kids to have at it in May, went Kath's favorite joke, purple's my favorite and amethysts are cheap.

I zipped my house key and credit card into a fanny pack. Hideous things, fanny packs, but I'd done my research. The two forms of ID I would need to open a P.O. box were tucked away inside. I had regular mail service, naturally, and I liked that I was the sort of woman who knew my mailman's name. But—and I'm sure you don't need me to spell this out, Clarence; you always were a clever one—I didn't want you knowing where I lived. To Kath, I said, "I'll want us to swing by the post office. I need stamps." Kath gave a cheery thumbs up. She knew I liked tacking errands onto our walks. They felt less frivolous that way. I never told Frank this given his love of running, but motion for motion's sake could seem so silly.

We walked, skirting the park where fall colors—my favorites—were just starting to creep in. I'm not tall, but kept pace with Kath, who carried most of our conversation. She was good at it; some people naturally are. I apologized and told her, truly, that I hadn't slept well. It felt good to be telling her something simple and true. Not that I was questioning myself. I'd made up my mind. Another saying of Ma's who, for all her farm-wife quaintness, hadn't raised her girls to be ditherers: *May bees make no honey.*

Kath and I passed a bakery we'd discovered a few walks previously. I liked the Lida I was with Kath. With Kath, I was a Lida who frequented tucked-away bakeries; under my own steam I'd have grabbed a regular loaf at my regular grocery. "I'm getting a post box too," I told her. "Isn't that silly? But I can't get that white powder out of my head."

"Anthrax." She shuddered. I think it surprised Pam, how well Kath and I got on. But there was a proper spine to Kath Claverie, and a kindred sort of nerviness, though Kath, in all honesty, bore up with more grace than I. There were four Claverie children, three girls and then Blue. I suspected Kath and Bill, God rest, were the sort of old-fashioned couple who'd kept trying till they got their son and heir. And then, his blindness. It took a lot of gumption to carry on in the face of something like that. To get what you dearly want, but in a way that's horribly wrong: Clarence, you know I am no stranger to the scenario.

The post office hummed with industrial light. Everything inside—even the postmen—was linoleum colored, pallid and speckled with bits of brown and gray. Kath and I were their only customers. She paused to inspect the wall of wanted criminals. She was tall and immaculate and wore snazzy workout gear. I remembered that high school era trick of Barbra's. If you're up to something mischievous, do it alongside someone more memorable than yourself.

Discounting Kath, a wall display of stamps was the room's only source of real color. I did have stamps at home, left over from Pam and Blue's wedding, but they were hardly suitable. They were heart shaped. They had doily edges. I couldn't possibly use them for you; I was embarrassed even putting them on bills. I picked up an alternate pack. Illustrated trains burned through rectangular landscape. I couldn't go with those. The energy they provided, the motion, the promise of escape. And you liked trains. I remembered your hand capped over Pamela's on her second Christmas, running a model train around the lip of the table. She tried to mimic your choo-chooing. "No, no, Pammie Clare," you corrected, "it's not a sneeze."

Maybe Fruits of America. You'd had years of industrial kitchens, legally bound to sustain, but laboring under budget constraints. They'd make do with the bounty of cans. These might work. I could have you eager for that last meal, drooling over cancelled postage.

But your letter to Pam on her ninth birthday: You thanked her for sending color to latch onto, and a bit of sky. All she'd sent was a grade school photo. That false cloud background. That fuchsia sweater she'd loved. The hippo ballerina embroidered beside the buttons. The pink curve of her Peter Pan collar.

You didn't deserve the brightness of these fruits.

Nothing was right. A top-hatted, bell-ringing baby honored the turn of the year. A dove drifted across a blue background, commemorating NATO. And then the set commemorating American glassworks, stamps that showed brittle, brilliant, empty vessels. My sister collected vases. Glass ones because she liked that glass was never what it seemed: not solid, but liquid, imperceptibly flowing. I picked up a package. You would remember. My sister, who lined windowsills with vases. In the afternoons her rooms glowed with colored light.

And you were prohibited glass. Your palms must crave the weight of objects, the things your life had once controlled. I hoped you dreamt of shards, liquid fragments that could never flow back into a solid whole. Even the smallest bit could split open a vein. I grabbed a pack.

"I'd like a post box too," I said at the counter. You sped toward your last appeal. "I don't think I'll need it more than six months."

The postman tugged at his collar, letting in a bit of air.

On the forms he gave me, I listed Maisie Keller as a minor child who might also be receiving mail. Just thinking the name pleased me. You wanted letters from a stranger. You'd get them. Letters from that girl in the chair when I heard what you'd done, whose broken smile hid behind my bathroom mirror. I wrote her name clearly and with a deliberate hand. No one was going to give me any trouble. Even with the world ending, minors didn't carry ID. And it was a *modern* world ending. People—people with manners, in any event—knew better than to fuss over families with mismatched surnames. I grinned, turning in the paperwork. In some ways I have a dangerously readable face. Kath, I hoped, would take my expression for relief. Another step removed now from an envelope of white catastrophe. You would know better, Clarence. Barbra's face could be readable in much the same way. The postman gave me my key. It caught the light.

6.

I had never learned to type properly. This was deliberate—the best way to ensure I never wound up a secretary was to be in perpetual need of one. I would write to you by hand. I gathered a notepad, an envelope, and the bouquet of pens that occupied an old soup can that eight-year-old Pammie had pasted over with bits of construction paper. A Mother's Day craft project brought home from school. A hard day, that, and Father's Day too. Every year. But of course we couldn't flounce about and insist Pam's classes ignore it. That bit about the squeaky wheel is true only to a point. *Perpetual* squeaks fade into so much background din.

I set up at the dining room table, where I'd left my purse. Inside it, stamps waited, shining beneath plastic. *Dear Clarence*, I wrote. You'd been twenty years alone. Always so eager to be well thought of, so easy with the charm. You'd go weak at the knees for a girl who called you dear. My script was lovely. In school I'd won penmanship prizes. The narrow bow of the *C* and the *D*'s full-breasted arc seemed to beckon, fragile and alluring, against the notepaper's lines. Prison must be all right angles. How you must long for curves. *I want you to know that in writing you I presume nothing about you. I try to be open and fair in everything and am better at being told things than I am at guessing. I am willing to hear anything you have to say.*

No. Absolutely not. I ran my fingers comb-like through my hair. A new sheet. *Willing to hear* was a phrase from Pamela's adolescence, our girl skulking in past curfew, smudged makeup ringing each eye like a bruise. We're willing to hear your reasons, Pammie, if you have them. Maisie Keller couldn't talk like that. Maisie couldn't have it in her to judge. Not yet. *I am here to listen to whatever you want to say. I will be here if that is what you want. I'm not really sure what prompted me to write a stranger. Maybe it's that my own life is good and that I am happy in it and I thought that if I wrote you I could pass that on in some small way.* My tongue slicked along my teeth, stretching my lip. I looked like any one of my clients after their final visits. Everyone licks their own teeth once the brace is gone. They can't help it; they're not yet accustomed to the absence of restraint. *I am twenty-three and just at the beginning of things, really,* I wrote. Pammie's age, which would gut you. I laughed. The only small advantage of living alone. No one about to pry into a private chuckle. Twenty-three. Only off by forty years.

All my life, I had looked as though, given a year or so, I would turn out beautiful. I'd been a plain, round-cheeked child with wide light eyes, good thick hair, and a smile completely devoid of dental caries. I still had the same full face and even features, now undeniably scored with lines. But I liked my wrinkles. They lent me a new sort of appeal. I still wasn't quite pretty, but now I looked as though I had been once, and not too long ago. A change for the better, without question, now that I was rid of that element of waiting. And maybe I had been, briefly, a looker and never noticed. What an idea.

But Maisie Keller I would make dazzle, and not just by virtue of youth's firm skin and the still-firm bits it encapsulated. She would be another Barbra, face a smooth and near-perfect circle, hair a shining easy mess, limbs quick and bird-boned. Adopted, Korean— why not?—like the real Maisie Keller, that patient in my chair, the last pair of eyes I'd looked into before hearing what you'd done. For Barbra, I would give Maisie Keller high, full breasts. For Barbra at ten, twelve, nineteen, waiting, waiting. Her impatient voice. "I'm such a Patty Pancake. I'll be a Patty Pancake till I die."

Pretty words from pretty Maisie: *I can tell you a little bit about my life if you think it would be of interest. If you decide to write back and let me know what you're really interested in hearing, I promise I won't yammer on about myself so much. When I was little, my parents called me Little Miss Me-Me. My last ex called me something similar (ha ha) but with more adult phrasing (maybe you can imagine).*

My profession gave me some advantage here. I'd dealt with the world's Maisies at their most vulnerable, lying wide-mouthed in my chair while I remade them in subtle, painful increments. They called themselves names before others had a chance to. Railroad tracks, zipperface. The jokes of the young are painful, and not just because they are never as funny as the teller believes them to be.

Maisie continued: *It's strange to share my big major flaw with someone I don't know at all, but maybe that's how a stranger becomes not so much a stranger, and your letter showed your share of vulnerability (which is why I picked it). I bet we could have a good conversation.*

About me: I just moved back to St. Louis (I bet you guessed that from the postmark) after college and am trying to figure out what I want to make of my life. I'm living with my Mom for now and even if she sometimes forgets that I'm no longer her little girl, we're getting on fine. I love her to death. To death. Maisie Keller was young enough to be that kind of callous. In her next letter, she'd see the crassness of it and apologize. You'd like that. *Mom does know I'm writing you and she isn't too thrilled about it. She thinks it's a scam and that if I tell you I'm not sending money or dirty pictures you won't write back. I hope that when I'm old I don't automatically think so badly of people. Anyhow, I promised her I would tell you I am not that kind of girl. So consider yourself informed! She'll still be put out when I send this. But everyone has parents, I guess. If she wasn't upset about this, she'd find something else.*

This letter seems so small and I am sure you'd rather think of bigger things since I guess that's the sort of letter that will stop you from being bored. I'm sending it on anyhow in hopes that bigger things will follow. I am sorry if this seems flakey,—

A word I learned from Pam. Authentically twenty-three.

—I really am. Next time I'll do better. It's just that I have no idea how I'm supposed to go about writing to a stranger.

Which was what you were, Clarence. Even to me. Even when I thought you were family. I felt feverish. Excited too. The paper showed it. By the letter's end my penmanship-prize writing looked harsh. Each character dark, each curve gouged into pulp. I traced the imprints, pen canyons beneath my fingers, like Braille in reverse. I'd have to redo them; Maisie couldn't seem angry just yet. And the perfect script at the letter's start wasn't quite right either. Old-fashioned, it pained me to admit. Even if you didn't recognize my hand, you'd recognize my age. I began to rewrite, making each letter lighter, looser, almost slovenly. I would tack on a postscript, apologizing for the sloppiness. Schools these days offer such cursory instruction in penmanship.

7.

On the anniversary of her mother's death, Pammie and I met for lunch. Her idea. She didn't mention the occasion when we made our plans, but the twenty-fifth fell on a Thursday that year and Pamela worked full time. Pamela has always been one to take her responsibilities seriously; she wouldn't take time off without reason.

She beat me to the restaurant; I'd had a horrible time finding street parking. She stood outside, blowing into her hands. She'd turned out precisely as I always expected: not pretty enough to cause trouble, not plain enough to be troubled by it. She spied me and walked my way. She hadn't put on makeup and had abandoned her usual ponytail; her hair fell loose and thick beyond her shoulders, crackling silvery blond in the wind. She approached with purpose, her arms pumping, her strides loping and precise. This precision was nothing new. She'd had it as a child, though back then she took timid steps, elbows glued to ribs, shoulders rounded down. I shook my head. Astounding how that long-ago Pamela, who tried to move unseen from one interval of stillness to another, had become this approaching woman, erect, confident, the easy swing of her arms slicing through the air between us.

"Pammie!" I called.

"Here I am," she said. No one uses the word *merry* anymore, not outside of Christmas, but it was the apt one for her smile. I'd done such a good job with her teeth.

"Yes," I said. "Here you are." We hugged. She'd changed shampoos. This new brand had lavender in it. I stood on tiptoe to kiss her forehead. The freckles I'd assured her would fade—as Barbra's had—I now had to admit never would. Your eyes in her sockets glittered. She offered my hand a quick squeeze.

"Cold," I said, and gave an exaggerated shiver; I didn't let go of her though. "I should give you my driving gloves. The Saab's steering wheel never gets as chilly as the old—what?"

"If my life were a drinking game, we'd all have to do shots every time you started solving problems that weren't even problems."

"You shouldn't be drinking, Miss. Not till you're forty."

"Root beer only, cross my heart."

"Or coffee," I said. Her preferred vice.

"Been cutting back, actually."

"Heaven forefend."

"Thought you'd be thrilled. Good for the teeth and all." She tapped her incisors lightly.

"Wise woman. But aren't you tired?" She looked it, actually.

A shrug.

"You look a little pale."

"There's a cold going round the center."

"I've got oranges at home. Organic ones. I'll save some out for you." The oranges were from Green Mother Grocery, a neighborhood gem I'd happened on while out and about with Kath, where the fruit had never been in the vicinity of pesticides and looked more curated than actually for sale. My regular checker knew me by name. She was a year out of college, taking Mandarin classes part-time, and saving for a China trip in hopes of tracking down her birth mother. She'd dyed her hair the most electric pink and always stood birdlike on one foot. In my own head, I called her Flamingo.

Pam said, "You know that's not worth the extra money, right? An orange is an orange. I'm just tired. We're swamped at the center, that's all."

All that work. All day, outside. Dog hair clung to her coat sleeve. And I couldn't see how Blue would be much help by night. No wonder she was run down. We reached the restaurant. I made sure to hold the door. "I'm sorry Blue couldn't join us," I said, though I had no idea how he'd have got himself here. Pamela'd done wonders with his dog, of course, but there were limits.

"Blue wasn't invited," said Pam, hip-checking me. "Just us girls. You can flirt with him at linner." *Linner* was a Kath Claverie word. She held them every Saturday. Any family, she liked to say, can have brunch. It takes a Claverie to have a linner.

"Pamela Clare. I don't flirt."

"Heaven forefend." She was an adroit mimic. Her voice sounded like my own. Not as it does to my own ears, but the tinny Lida on the townhouse's answering machine.

Our hostess wore a square-necked shirt. Her collarbones stood out. Pamela unzipped her windbreaker and folded it over the back of her chair. Chunky, irregular ceramic beads hung from her neck on a leather cord. She worried her fingers over the lowest one.

"I have a bowl that color at home." I sat, pointing.

"Kath gave it to me." Pam gave the necklace a brief, affectionate pat.

"Very attractive." And it was. Kath had a good eye. If I'd been shopping for Pam, I'd have gravitated toward something delicate that would never have looked quite right. Tucked away in my purse, I had a Ziploc bag of twist ties. Pam had mentioned that she used them for Blue, matching his outfits at the turn of each season, banding them together at the hanger's necks. I'd been squirreling them away for weeks, but I could wait. Give it a few days and the offering wouldn't suffer by comparison.

Pam ordered a chipotle club sandwich. Everywhere she went, she ordered club sandwiches.

"It'll be spicy," I said.

"I know. I know chipotles. Lida." She said *Lida* like Frank had when there was something of importance to follow.

Nothing did.

"Of course you know chipotles. My foot's really in it today. I bet you even know habaneros." I was relatively sure I'd pronounced *habaneros* properly.

"It's fine, Li." There was laughter in her voice, yes, but also exasperation. Pamela was a forthright girl, but that didn't mean she was an uncomplicated one.

"How's Blue?" I asked, knowing that I'd brought him up already, knowing that in all probability I was being a trifle annoying. But it was either that or simply sit there. When she first came into our care, Pam's social worker said to follow her lead on the hard conversations, the ones that tackled you, tackled Barbra. Barbra, who died nineteen years ago to the day. I stopped myself from yammering. Pamela was the one who arranged this lunch; Pamela had something to say. The best thing I could do was give her the space to say it.

"Blue's wonderful," she said, sounding muzzy and entirely besotted. I remembered how it was with Frank. Those first plummy years, the newlywed intoxication of just us. Early on, Frank said we should fake a hobby, something so time-consuming we could decline most invites and so obscure none of our acquaintanceship would take it up. We claimed we were bird watchers. I got him a pair of binoculars for our tenth anniversary, small ones to show I remembered, not the fancy kind for watching real birds.

Our plates arrived. Extra mayonnaise on the side for Pam, who liked it on French fries. I'd be hard pressed to think of something less palatable, but she'd picked up a taste for it visiting Belgium.

"This looks good," I said, of my own French onion soup.

Pam dipped a fry, raised it as if to toast. "Here's to days off."

"Days off?"

She chuckled. "That's how I know you're well and truly retired. It's a workday for us nine-to-fivers." She popped the French fry in her mouth.

"Yes. It's Thursday. The twenty-fifth. I know."

A wide palmed gesture as if to say, *ta-da*. She'd painted her nails an unexpected orange. A quiet lunch to mark her mother's passing was no occasion for *ta-da*, and it wasn't like Pam to be careless of such things, or cruel. She must have simply forgotten. I hissed without meaning to. Concern scudded across her face. "Hot," I said, indicating the soup. I tapped my spoon against the thick lid of cheese. The essential person-ness of being a person is that we are capable of *assigning* meaning. I could choose to label Pam as heartless, sloughing off the heft of today. Or I could opt for hale, whole, happy, to have stepped out from its long shadow. My spoon broke through the cheese. "Center closed today?" I made my voice mild. It may surprise you, Clarence, but I can be very good at that.

Pam pointed at her mouth: wait for me to chew.

"Some kind of holiday?" I guessed. "Helen Keller's birthday?" A frisson with the two syllables of *Keller*. Maisie was a Keller too. My letter is on its way to Arizona. Today, tomorrow, soon.

I hadn't forgotten, Clarence.

Pamela swallowed. "Lida. That's not funny."

"What?"

"Do you have any idea how many Helen Keller jokes Blue heard growing up?"

"Yes. No. I mean, I can't imagine. But I was asking. As in just—actually asking."

A sigh.

"I'm sorry, Pam. I shouldn't be let out of the house today." I'll admit it. I gave a little extra weight to that *today*.

"Lida. You should get out of the house *more*."

"I walked with Kath just Monday. And I'm here with you. Today." Again the lean on *today*. Nineteen years. Three thousand, nine hundred, and thirty-five days.

Pam picked up a fork and jabbed another fry. She put it down again without bringing it to her lips. "I worry," she said.

"You shouldn't worry. It's not your job to worry. I'm the one whose job it is to worry."

"We've just said *worry* so much it doesn't even make sense as a word anymore." A smile from Pam, one that almost reached her eyes. All that time working out of doors meant they'd line earlier than mine had. Her mother's never really had a chance to pucker. A smear of chipotle lingered in the corner of her mouth, just a speck. I fingered the spot on my own face. She did nothing. I dipped my napkin in the glass and dabbed my lips. Still nothing.

"I've joined a bird-watching club," I said, and continued to daub the spot. "We get up at an ungodly hour."

"Good. Great. That's really good. Because, Lida?" She pushed away the plate. She had only managed half the sandwich. That chipotle was a touch too spicy after all.

"What is it?"

"Nothing."

I knew my Pam. It wasn't nothing. Not when her voice shrank like that. I waited.

"I've been thinking about him. A lot."

The human heart is the size of a human fist. Mine clenched. *Him*, she said, not *her*. And today of all days. I drew a steadying breath. All of this was roughest on Pam. Credit me with this much, Clarence: I tried not to lose sight of that. She'd lost her mother, yes, but also, she'd lost you. I spoke the only words I could manage: "Oh, Pammie."

"Kind of, all the time. More even than over the holidays. More than at the wedding. Just about every day, I can't turn it off. When I'm home at night, with Blue. I just wonder. How he might be today, how much easier things would be on you."

Again that fist in my chest. Tighter and tighter.

"I don't need things easy," I reminded her. "And it's no burden, it never was."

"I wish he had a chance to meet Blue. It's been keeping me awake." Small hollows appeared beneath her cheekbones. Inside her mouth, I knew, her molars staked down a slick roll of cheek flesh. Pam's bottling-up expression; whenever she lay open-mouthed in my dental chair I noted the raw patches in her buccal tissue. The smoothness of our relationship and the circumference of the abrasions were inversely proportional. "I miss him," she said, and she sounded very young.

My heart felt smaller than a fist. Small as a peach pit. The hardest parts of raising her were times like this. When she said she missed you. I remembered seven-year-old Pam at our kitchen table, responding to your end-of-school letter. I miss you more than you would miss recess if they cancelled it, you wrote, I miss you like you would miss your toys. Already she was lost to you, a generic stand-in, half a foot taller than she'd been at her mother's funeral. You never learned from me that she stood quiet and alone at recess, that she had to be cajoled into games. You'd had no way to know that her favorite plaything was Good Puppy, a stuffed dog with plastic goggle eyes who had come with a certificate thanking Pam for redeeming him from the pound. Good Puppy lay belly up beneath her chair as she worked on her letter. A jump rope linked Pam and her toy, knotted at his neck and her wrist. "How do you spell *miss*?" Pam asked.

And I told her, Clarence. I didn't say, remember that he killed your mother. I didn't say, Pamela Clare, how could you possibly? *M*, I said, *I, S, S*. I didn't even make her sound it out.

"Lida," Pam was saying. "Lida, I didn't mean to—" Her voice cracked. She looked at me. I was Barbra's sister. I shared her lousy poker face.

Again, I said, "Oh, Pammie," and then, composing myself, "It's fine. Of course you do. Really. It's fine."

A sniff from Pam. She really did have a cold coming on. "Please don't *oh Pammie it's fine* me. I didn't mean to bring you down."

"It's fine," I said again. "I'm grand. And you've got some sauce right there."

"Sure you're fine." Pam daubed the spot. "I *can* actually see your face, you know."

I pulled an elaborate monkey one; crossed eyes and lolling tongue. When she was small, we could sometimes jolly her out of a mood.

Pamela mirrored my monkey face. "Look at us," she said. "Spaghetti and goofballs."

"Your uncle used to say that." Whenever he came upon us being particularly silly.

"I know," Pam said, and her eyes shone. "I hate that I never asked him who was who." Another sniff, and then a firecracker of feeling. Frank, Clarence. Pamela missed *Frank*. Not you. Frank, who was so much the reason she had grown into this extraordinary Pam, for whom today was just another day in a string of autumn days. Oh, Clarence. Things were going to come so easy for Maisie. You'd be hungry. There was no one in the world save me who ever even thought of you.

8.

Every day I checked the post box. Nothing. Nothing. Sunday. Nothing. A mis-delivered issue of *Self* magazine. Nothing. Nothing. And then. There. Your letter. Its white edge cut apart the dark.

I hesitated. First moment since my birthday. Your hand had touched that envelope. Your hand. You used to have a callus on your ring finger from holding your pencil wrong, and all through your trial that finger still bore its wedding ring. I wondered if Stemble let you keep it. I didn't know—I had never wanted to—what Ma did with Barbra's matching one.

I let the post box door snap shut, and then I fled. That's really the only honest verb for it. Back to the townhouse, where I rooted through drawers. My good winter gloves, leather and lined with rabbit fur, were much too stiff to deal with envelopes. I snapped on a pair of medical gloves, remnants of my practice; encased, my hands looked like my hands again, useful. Useful, but suspect. It wouldn't do to call attention to myself. I peeled them off and pitched them straight in the trash. I layered paper towels over them, wasteful but even so. They'd held their shape. Before the towels covered them they'd been shocking against the refuse, puffy and plaintive, like actual hands.

A final pair of gloves waited in my bedroom closet, their flat box bound up with twine. Even well-dressed women these days seldom wore such gloves. Wrist length, like I'd had at Easter as a girl, but black where I'd once worn white, banded in matte satin and secured with Tahitian pearl. I struggled with the box strings. My hands had been much nimbler when I first did up this package, double-, no triple-, knotted tight against early use. Tissue crinkled. The department store smell of entirely too many perfumes had nearly faded. I pulled on the gloves. When they last sheathed my hands, my skin had been smooth as milk. I pressed them before me, inspecting. Nothing like lambskin to make me feel expensive. I drew a finger to my lip. *Shhhh.*

These gloves were meant to go with my execution suit. I'd had to buy three over the years; fashion moves swifter than justice. They hung in zippered garment bags, a sachet in the bottom of each. Together, they made a stylish timeline: here were the bold shoulders of the nineteen eighties purchased—in an impatient burst—on the occasion of your sentencing, here a peplum jacket that marked the early nineties and two appeals down, here the notched neckline of just last year, bought after the execution of Alonzo Nuz bumped yours next in line. All were black; the gloves would go with whichever one I picked. The gloves would keep me dignified. No one would know if my knuckles whitened, involuntarily—because you were the one who taught me a splash of Worcestershire's was the trick to a perfect burger—or with anger—because Barbra would never study glass-blowing or see Antarctica—or in fear that this wouldn't come off, that you'd stumble onto a last minute reprieve.

I felt safe in those gloves, and sneaky. A child who's pinched a drugstore sweet. The whole walk back to the post office, I couldn't stop peeking at them, my fingers dark and sleek and trim. Thin enough that they didn't trip me up any, unlocking the box once more, substantial enough to turn your letter back to paper, detritus of some dead tree. Still, I didn't want to read it in my townhouse. Not in the place I called home. I walked to a nearby bakery, your letter between my finger and my thumb. The bakery was a Kath discovery, thanks to our weekly wanders, warm with that yeasty smell that is supposed to mean solace. I purchased a wedge of zucchini bread and claimed a table. Your penmanship had not improved. You included your inmate number on the return address. The red word *inspected* was rubber-stamped across the flap.

Dear Maisie,

I thank you kindly for your letter. It made today different than yesterday and the day that came before.

Please, don't you apologize for your handwriting, not until you've seen mine at least. I don't have a pen to write you, just one of those wobbly cylinders that's inside a real pen. It's too skinny to get a good grip on and the ink's not much good. But a real pen could be just right for soft spots, the eyes or nostrils that no one realizes until it's too late link up straight to the brain. I don't say this to disturb you and I am sorry if it does. I am not the kind of man who thinks such things. Or I wasn't that kind of man before. But when you find out you can't have a real pen, you get to thinking why.

For a while we got pencils, but not real ones. The mini kind that golfers use in the world. They didn't say why they changed them up for pens and it didn't make a difference to me anyhow. Those pencils were the same as pens anyhow. No erasers. They aren't big on the idea that mistakes can be corrected in here, right? Besides, those pencils got me thinking about golf. I never played it before, but hell, the idea of it now. A whole game that's based on walking around in the open, and that goes on slow, like a golfer's got all the time there is.

Anyhow, don't go saying sorry. If anything, bad handwriting takes longer to read so your words last a while.

I'd guess that happens a lot, a person thinking something about them's bad when really it's good. It goes the other way too, if you think about it, and I do think about it (I spend a lot of time thinking). What seems good at first can turn out pretty bad.

At least I know that's true in my case (and after all these years my case is probably the only thing I really know). For men like me, the state runs tabs on our mitigating and aggravating circumstances. At the end, the judge checks them against one another and decides what's next. Trouble with me is the same facts that land me on one list land me on the other. I'm a father. After my mistakes, I ran. I took my child with me. Believe you me, I did everything I could to keep her safe. My lawyer says this can make me seem well-meaning, even in my worst moments. When they caught me she was done up safe in her car seat. She wasn't dehydrated or anything like that. But the prosecution says she was with me in the first place when I was arrested. Car seat and juice boxes be damned. (My language doesn't offend, right? You probably expect it. Especially considering my note says no religious wackhammers.) We were only twenty minutes from Mexico. That's abduction. You see how it works. I was (I am) a gentle man. Not one prior. Should be a mitigating circumstance, right? Not unless they point out that to land in here I used a gun that I went out and bought the week before the incidents. They say that's premeditation.

Another fine way to begin. But maybe mentioning the rough stuff at the start is the best way to go. And I know I promised to write the truth. If that truth's going to stop you from writing, I'd rather know it now. I'm not going to cross out a word of this. No erasing. The guards that read this over before sending it along will sure be proud. Those of them that can actually <u>read</u>, that is.

But I'm wandering off into ugliness. Let's try again. Please write back (you wouldn't believe all the one or two time onlies I get in here). Chatter on about St. Louis. I swear I've spent more time imagining that town than anyone alive. I visited a few times when I was in the world. Your arch was really disappointing. Sorry. It should have at least gone over the Mississippi. My wife's people are from there and she had this story about convincing a busload of tourists that at sunset the thing sank down into the earth. She could really make you laugh with that story. Or she'd get you feeling sorry for those dumb people who believed her. Whatever she wanted—

The letter puckered in my grip. A territorial flash, or the echo of a long ago one: that story with the arch was mine. Barbra was always stealing. And upgrading. It had only been one elderly couple. No meanness about it. They'd asked when, not if, and I was young; I hadn't learned to work around my shyness. It had seemed rude not to name an hour. A pulse of longing. I wanted to call my sister. I wanted to call, just to call her *on* it. Barbra took casually, she lied casually, and for the first half of my life our squabbles came regular as rain clouds. Funny how I missed that. Playing chicken with the telephone. Wanting *her* to be the one to apologize this time around. I breathed in the brûléed bakery air and forced calm. I turned to a new page. You'd folded down the corner. No staples in Intensive Supervision Unit-Stemble. No tiny, glinting, metal teeth.

—you to buy, you bought. She could make anyone believe anything.

My daughter grew up in St. Louis (if you've just finished college, you're probably about her age). She still lives thereabouts. My mother moved up there too, or near enough. She's in O'Fallon. She visited Stemble just a handful of times. Everyone back home knew how I landed myself here and even if she didn't say much about it, them knowing wasn't easy on her. I said get away from it since you're lucky enough to be able to. Just up and pick a place. She felt guilty leaving me, but I told her she chose right.

Because strange as it sounds, I don't much like visitors. Forty-five minutes with a guard and glass between us, with strip down before and after. I see people much clearer in my mind. They stick around longer that way too. There's no guard. No screen or searches. And I don't feel closed in all over again when they get to leave and I have to stay put.

The hardest visits are the lawyer ones. He's got so old and fat, which shows how much time's gone by. And it's the kind of fat that makes his sorry old face easy to read. Things are not going well for me. He's been with me since the start, and I think it'll hit him hard when I go. It's coming, Maisie Keller, and I hope it doesn't put you off any when I mention it. I've been thinking that if there is an After it may be some place like St. Louis, an okay enough city full of everyone I've ever known, split down the middle into the good part and the bad. In life there are bridges that span the water. I hope that part stays the same.

This is probably too much philosophy for a first time letter, but I can't help it if my thoughts go all over. My thoughts are the only things that <u>can</u> move around in here, and boy do they ever. Just now I began to think about you and about my daughter, because maybe you passed her on the street today and none of us will ever know it. Nothing is ever random like that in here.

You know that game little kids play, hot lava? Where they jump from place to place and the rules are you can't ever touch the ground? My daughter loved it. She jumped and scrambled like she had no clue it would hurt to fall. Until I caught her one time halfway up a bookshelf, screaming her pretty head off. She'd forgot it was just a game and she'd forgot how she got to where she was. That's how it gets sometimes inside my head. I make these crazy leaps trying not to touch what's always beneath. So I do a bit of hot lava myself. Just to slow my mind down. With every new thought I touch something in my cell. If I tie my thoughts to something real, I'll be able to retrace them. I'll never get stuck somewhere and panic. (I touch my sleeve as I write this.) Most of the day I spend touching things. Things, but never walls. This would only get me pacing. Two appeals ago, I decided to stop pacing.

I'm coming to the end of this sheet and if I start another I'll feel obliged to finish it. I think (I hope) that we will be friends, even if I threw too much at you right away. Maybe that's why so many people stop writing after a letter or so. I don't know what they expect. Gratitude? For pages on end? All I have is my thoughts. If they're not what you want to hear, I won't apologize. What's the point of just hearing what you want to? I hope you run with it and that you will write back. I'll finish up these last few lines and wait for an officer to come and collect it. They'll read it (well, maybe not the big words) and seal it and it will make its way to you in my daughter's city and we will see what happens next.

Yours,

Clarence Lusk

This is what I did, Clarence. Right there in the bakery: I took a last bite of zucchini bread and I took the ceramic plate in my hand. A pretty thing, fragile, a painted rooster in its center. I held it at arm's length and released it to shatter on the concrete floor. Of the pair of us, Barbra was the sister prone to drama. I was very much borrowing her sort of gesture; sisters share. Because I needed the sound, Clarence. The crash of something breaking that wasn't me. You were so pleasant in your letter. So forthright, so affable. Well. Barbra always said you could charm the stripes from bees.

The counter staff scurried with their brooms and were very kind. I apologized. It felt good to be saying sorry—not quite a balm, but—a Band-Aid for the way I'd *liked* you when Barbra first introduced us, how I told Frank she was trading up after a series of duds. Rooster shards clattered in the dustpan, the sound of irrevocably broken things. One of the last times we talked, Barbra told me you broke one of her vases, the marbled one Frank and I brought back from our honeymoon. I wondered, after, if she'd been trying to get me to ask how. If she'd have told me you'd been fighting and that the vase broke in anger. If that had been my one chance to tell her: I'm on your side. Trust your gut. Grab Pammie, get out. Instead, I assumed you were simply clumsy, Clarence; I hadn't yet learned to think more terrible things.

I tipped well and left the café, crossing into Forest Park, which was all dormant flower beds and stripped elms. In the distance, the turnoff for the zoo, where Pamela once asked me what the animals had done to be put in cages. A pair of groundskeepers struggled with a fat spool of Christmas lights, and it still weeks from Thanksgiving. Our father bought Ma perfume one Christmas. Even before we knew it smelled good Barbra said she wanted to live inside that cut-glass bottle.

But this was all drift and sentiment. What I had to do was *think*. I walked on, gloved, pumping my arms as Kath Claverie had instructed to maximize aerobic effect. You could charm stripes from bees, from zebras even, from highway lanes, from work-gang jumpsuits, but that wouldn't change what you'd let slip: Marjorie Lusk was close by.

In the past few decades we orthodontists had begun to use a new sort of arch wire. NASA perfected it first, a heat-activated nickel-titanium alloy they use for solar panels. This wire bends supple at room temperature. Once affixed to the teeth, it loses pliancy. The warmth of the mouth hardens it; it begins to exude pressure, its long, slow work of setting things to rights. As you, Clarence, had warmed to Maisie Keller. Sure and steady as mouth-warmth, and faster than I had expected, trusting her—right away, how lonely you must be—with something I could bring to bear against you. Your mother in O'Fallon. At most a river away.

9.

I'm lousy in front of crowds, but nevertheless had been the one to speak at Barbra's funeral. Ma was a slack balloon of shakes and tranquilizers, unequal to the task. Frank was wonderful but not blood. I still had my speech in the top drawer of my desk, a set of paper-clipped three-by-fives, more scraps of paper I couldn't bring myself to discard.

"On the day she graduated college, my sister explained why she loved mathematics. She said, 'It has to do with everything.' I scoffed and she wrote something right on the back of her diploma and then read it aloud. I found that diploma last night and re-read her words: 'If you have a process that is the accumulation of random outcomes infinitely summed, and if on average you don't know if the numbers you are adding are positive or negative, and if the process goes on forever, every number that you establish as a boundary will eventually be crossed.' She always knew things like that, right off the top of her head. You all know how smart she was. Of course I had no idea what she was talking about. Maybe some of her students today do. She often spoke of how bright you all are. And even if you don't know, what you do know is Barbra's willingness to answer questions. When I asked her, she explained. Barbra said: 'It's simple enough. All it means is that if you live long enough there's no line that you won't cross.'"

Frank and I had packed for Arizona in a rush. My dress hadn't traveled well. There was a run in my stockings, a sorry ladder to nowhere. I'd discovered it at the motel that morning. I'd had plenty of time to buy another pair. Even the Safeway stocked them. But I'd stood numb and indecisive before the display, working my way through the thick fan of samples, laying one hue and then another over my forearm. The color of my flesh was no longer familiar. Fifteen minutes passed before I chose. The wrong size, but I wouldn't know that till too late. At the checkout, I added a box of animal crackers for Pamela. They'd be good to have on hand. She was our little girl now. I didn't yet know what she ate, or at what intervals.

"I am appalled today at the line that's been crossed and what that has caused us to lose. I am shocked because Barbra, who was bright and courageous and curious, is gone. She has no more lines to cross and I can't bear it."

The air was close with the heat and scent of too many mourners. Memorials for the young were always well attended. "A novelty gig," Barbra might have said, drawing a hand over her mouth as if she could scoop the words back inside. "That was meaner spirited than I meant it."

"You never mean it," I would have replied.

And Barbra would have justified. "It's all math anyhow. Young or old, the same percentage of acquaintances show up. It's just a larger sample size. More people above ground."

All Barbra's students wore purple and black. I'd wondered if they'd phoned one another to coordinate, unsure what to wear for a funeral. The first for most of them. Or the second. Lawrence Ring's burial took place the day before. Eleven solid rows of students. Some gawkers, no question. I should've made them prove they'd been Barbra's, present calculus midterms corrected in the green ink my sister used because she thought red looked hostile.

I should've insisted they pipe in better music.

And scrapped the lilies. They always made Barbra sneeze.

And I should've tasked someone with keeping an eye out for Marjorie Lusk. Posted a thick-necked second cousin with her picture by the door. Oh yes, I saw her, skulking back there.

At least we'd had sense enough to bar reporters.

"Barbra has left us in an impossible situation," I continued. "We remember her, her passion and her energy, and so we miss her. That isn't even the word for it. We long. We have all these little lines that make up our lives, and they're approaching and they'll keep on coming. We'll have to cross them because that's how time works, but we can't because that means leaving Barbra behind. The only way to bring her with us is to remember. She'd want us to do that. To be brave like she'd be. To be honest. Always."

Marjorie Lusk leaned against the sanctuary door. I couldn't imagine my words had bowled her over. It wasn't a very good speech; my sister deserved better.

Only when I was through speaking could I look at the front row. Frank and Ma in tears. Pamela between them, eyes dry, upper lip luminous with snot. She'd managed to lose a shoe. Her tights were worn at the heel. A few stitches had popped at the tip and a single toe peeked through. Clearly, these last few months Barbra's mind hadn't been entirely on her daughter.

I would have to buy new socks. Probably shoes as well.

I would get us through this if I thought in lists: offices to contact, appointments to reshuffle, attorneys to telephone. I needed to find the right kindergarten. I needed a pediatrician. A psychologist too, more likely than not.

Frank said I could slow down. No one expected me to do everything at once. These things take time. He didn't understand. I couldn't afford to ever be slow again. Not since I looked up from the open mouth of Maisie Keller to see my receptionist dawdling toward me, a strange sick look on her face, on the verge of disproving the axiom that bad news travels swiftly.

People lingered after the service. Strangers. They ate clammy cold cuts, limp crudités, gingersnaps, with coffee and punch. Ma never could hostess without pressing food on her guests.

Purple and black, it turned out, were Folsom High's colors.

"It was the student council's idea," a rabbity senior explained. "We want to show our support."

"Like a pep rally?"

Barbra would have laughed.

"No, no." He bowed each time he spoke the word. "No, no, no. We didn't mean it like that." He extended his hand. "I'm Terry Pelhs, from her fifth period calc."

I didn't want to lift my hand from the top of Pammie's head. She kept busy with her crackers, seeking out the lions she liked best. She crunched them headfirst and without enthusiasm. I had no idea if this brutality was standard or post-traumatic.

"Thank you, for coming," I said. "And please thank your friends for the colors."

"We did it yesterday for Dr. R. too." Terry blushed. I knew teenagers. I straightened their teeth. This kid was yet-to-bloom, but smart. He knew enough details. They all did. At some point everyone here must have imagined the lovers entwined. Barbra knew pi to fifty-seven digits. She could convert to metric in her head. A college boyfriend tore up her midterm because she'd beat his grade by two percent and Barbra had the sense to dump him on the spot. How could she have been so stupid?

One of Ma's cousins drove her back to our hotel. Frank and I were last to leave. We walked with Pamela between us, like we would walk from now on, hand in hand in hand.

Marjorie Lusk was waiting in the parking lot. Had been there a long time, from the looks of it. Sweat marred her blouse. Her face was glossy, overripe, and less wrinkled than Ma's. Cuff bracelets hung loose on her wrists, reflecting afternoon sun. She held herself still, crackling with the presence of a larger, younger woman. She made no move to touch Pam.

"Lida, Lida, I've been waiting. I know enough to guess you didn't want me inside."

I stared beyond Marjorie at the adobe houses across the street. So wisely designed, those interior, protected courtyards. "No," I said, "You aren't welcome."

"I'm here to say it's tragic. I'm just shocked."

"*Just* shocked? We're leveled. We're mourning."

"That isn't what I meant."

"We're angry."

That woman never blinked.

"Angry," I repeated.

Marjorie Lusk bowed her head. And then: "You don't know what it is to be a mother. I'm grieving, but the things you'd think were unforgivable . . ."

"Look at me and say that."

She had Pamela's eyes. That strange blue. Her son's. "You don't know what it is to be a mother."

"Or you a sister."

Frank broke in. "Marjorie, you said yourself you shouldn't be here."

"Frank's right. Please leave."

"Just know I came with condolences. I wish Barbra were still alive."

"For your own sake. For your son's."

"For all ours. For Pammie. Let's not do this."

"Pamela will be fine," said Frank, and he sounded like he believed it.

Pam looked up. Good girl. She hadn't let go of our hands.

"We'll make sure of it," I said.

"I'm surprised you brought her here. You don't know what it is to be a mother," Marjorie repeated. That bitch who bore Clarence.

Ma thought it best Pam come. The only opinion she'd had about any of the arrangements. Some of her haze had thinned in giving it, and I'd had my mother again, steady, collected, sure of what was to be done. I held Marjorie's eyes. I echoed Ma. "Pamela needs to understand what happened. We want her to have a proper goodbye."

"A proper goodbye?" Marjorie's face was hopeful, alive with it. So quick-shifting. It's true that people go mad with grief. "Perhaps we could arrange for her to visit . . ."

"I don't think so," Frank said.

"We've explained what happened," I added. "Or, we did our best to."

Marjorie crumpled. It was as though a string had been holding her posture perfect. It was as though that string had been cut. "She's a child. What kind of woman are you?"

"There's no lie in the world that can fix this."

"He's grieving too, Lida."

"I doubt he'd be permitted to see her anyhow," Frank offered.

Don't pander to her. Clarence's mother.

Bitter crone.

No lie in the world can fix this.

An animal look came to Marjorie's eyes. "Pammie, chubchick, I'm your Grandmom Lusk."

"I know." She sounded less scornful than I wanted her to.

"I know you know *now*. I want you to concentrate on remembering."

Pamela's head bobbed up and down.

Marjorie's eyes were on mine once more. Cornered animals, the both of us, and the parking lot open and meadow-wide. "You're going to tell her everything, then?"

I nodded.

"Tell your truth then. Keep telling it. And sooner or later you'll bump into the mess her mother made and the fact my son's a feeling father no matter what's been done. There's no truth that will leave that out. I'm going to kiss her now."

Marjorie's lips came to rest on Pamela's forehead.

She turned away without another word. A smear of lipstick marked Pammie's freckled brow. On either side of our niece, Frank and I drew closer, pressing tight against her as if she were some shattered bone we were meant to splint.

10.

There were two O'Fallons in spitting distance, the one in Missouri and the one in Illinois. Home again, I re-read your letter. No hint as to east of the Mississippi or west. You'd been so careful, Clarence. I noticed—I appreciated; full credit to you—that you didn't give Maisie Pamela's name. It was 1982 when you went away. The last computer you'd have seen would have been a fat-mouthed floppy eater. I went to my desk. You had no proper sense of how easy things came out here.

Click. m a r j o r i e l u s k was your mother and I didn't waste the capital letters. I waited. Nothing. I clicked again, hoping for the Illinois O'Fallon. Not because of the state line, exactly. Just squiggles on a map. But this particular squiggle was the Mississippi River. We'd wronged each other terribly, Marjorie and I, and any strategist knows it's best to keep deep water between home fires and enemies. Nothing onscreen. I clicked again; no change. I pressed my hands to either side of the monitor as if that could force results. Marjorie with her over-rouged lips and your blue eyes. When she'd bent to kiss Pam those eyes had looked like bits of sky, falling.

Still nothing. Black words in the white query box. I highlighted them and their colors reversed. Backspace. A single keystroke winked them out. The words flashed their brief onscreen after-ghost, white on white: m a r j o r i e l u s k.

No space. That's all. Pure sloppiness. I tried again, properly this time. The Internet bolded the words I'd asked for.

. . . encourages prison visits for at-risk youths. To critics, **Marjorie Lusk** rebuts, "Of course it scares them. That's our intent." **Lusk**, whose interest in the project . . .

. . . her address Monday at Clark High, **Marjorie Lusk** began, "I remember my son at your age. A program like this might've changed his future." Since 1982, **Lusk's** . . .

. . . raffle winner **Marjorie Lusk** looks forward to the trip. All auction proceeds go to Families Across Bars, a volunteer group dedicated to easing the frustrations of . . .

. . . It is with great regret that I take over for **Marjorie Lusk**, who has been our recording secretary for over ten years. Her drive and organization will be missed. As . . .

I clicked that last link. Families Across Bars, an organization that sounded like so much mush. The page took an age loading. The minutes of the Illinois chapter; O'Fallon, Illinois then. The clench around my throat let go. The Mississippi between me and Marjorie. As it should be. Natural and right, that deep silted space between us.

Your mother's replacement as secretary was singularly unforthcoming with details. She only noted that doctors remained cautiously optimistic in the aftermath of Marjorie's stroke, before recapitulating FAB's successes with the statewide visit day carpool system and its ambitions for a Mother-Daughter Girl Scout Troop at Logan Correctional. Respectfully submitted, Leigh Hopper. She didn't even list visiting information; no one must have asked. These people, Clarence. I don't know why I was surprised. Such altruism, serving prison families; never mind that they *were* the families. Selfishness tarted up as a 501(c)(3).

Bad blood shows. Obviously, I don't buy into that nonsense. Look at Pamela, Clarence, and then look at you. Nevertheless, I thought it there at the computer, reading on. A heartbeat thrum to the phrase: bad blood, bad blood, bad blood. The Internet said your mother cut a compelling figure. Marjorie up on stage while her bad blood congealed. A clot one-eighth of one-eighth of one-eighth of one pinhead. Look at this: her heart beats and bears the clot up; it pulses brain-bound on oxygenated blood. It happens slowly. The crowd applauds. No one notices. The clot floats along. Passages narrow. The way before it bifurcates, bifurcates again.

You wrote that you see people clearest in your mind. That moments there can last forever. I know how that works. Every time Pam shrieked or snitted or pouted, your mother was there. Her voice: *you don't know what it is to be a mother.* She knew just what to say to keep me up nights. The two of you. I hope you see this, Clarence. She stands at the edge of a driveway. Bracelets clatter as she reaches into her mailbox. Her hand emerges with grocery circulars. Her fingers feel swollen, her skin prickly, her guts dark and gummy, like blackberry preserves. This feeling, this lack of feeling, spreads up her arm. She grips at the post box. Steady. She wonders if she can raise her leg. She examines the circular. Texas Toast, two for five dollars. *Coupon*, she thinks. *Coupon*, she tries to say. The word comes out: *capon. Capstone. Corningware.* In her hands the paper, the whatsit, the flat smear of color blurs. She lowers her foot, slowly. She thinks it could miss the ground. A flash. A split down her brain, something clattering inside, some battering ram building for release. Some buttering churn.

Picture it. She falls.

In another life is a game for fools; Clarence, you and I know we only ever get the one. Nevertheless: in another life Marjorie and I might have kept in tenuous touch. She might have been granted the occasional visit. Family was important, essential, and Pam didn't have much of it left. Only she came to us raw in the funeral home parking lot. Only she opened her mouth and let loose those terrible things.

Pamela cried most nights those first months.

I'd never tell Blue—or anyone—this, but she wet the bed.

Well into her teens she stiffened when she saw cop cars on the highway.

Before we took custody she had spent exactly one weekend in my care.

And your mother lay in wait outside the funeral.

You know, of course, how badly Frank and I had wanted a child. We tried from the time we first married. It never—none of them ever—took, and that was very painful. Doctors couldn't do then what they do now, what with every third forty-year-old birthing quintuplets. Frank knew the Kellers from work and they referred us to the agency that had brought them Maisie. We gelled with the woman who manned it and read all we could about Korea. We painted the spare room buttercup gold and hung curtains with a Marimekko print. A social worker came and took notes. We answered intrusive questions and wrote enormous checks. You and Barbra penned a letter on our behalf. Mostly you, I'd imagine; you had the better way with words.

Pam had been with us eight weeks when the agency sent the photograph. A face that I will never describe to you, a bow affixed to her not-very-much hair. Hyun-Ay. A name I was sure to botch on the diphthongs. Paperwork in two languages, the English I'd grown up with, the Korean I'd had all best intentions of someday learning.

Its characters looked permanently impenetrable. I let my eyes blur and they turned random, a scattering of pick-up sticks.

We disrupted the adoption. There's a reason that word sounds like *rupture*, and a reason *rupture* is a word so often paired with the heart. Still, it was the right thing to do; Frank and I believed that absolutely. Imagine if we'd gone ahead with it and Pam thought there was a soul in this universe we wanted more than her. We never told her, and that was also the right decision; Pamela has always taken things upon herself unreasonably. Hyun-Ay's picture was in my safety deposit box, though I needed a better plan for it; as things stood, Pam would come across it, baffled, in the event of my sudden demise.

About your mother, Clarence, and the scene she made in the parking lot: I've carried that with me. *You don't know what it is to be a mother.* For the simple fact of saying it, I've sometimes hated her even more than you.

The Internet yielded a comprehensive list: elder care in O'Fallon, Illinois. I composed myself and worked through it calmly, meticulously, in alphabetical order. On the phone, I used Barbra's old trick: if you're ever nervous, pretend you're someone else, an actress, auditioning for Lida Stearl. By the time I came to Riverview, I had perfected my patter. "This is Maisie Keller. I'm trying to find the best time to visit Marjorie Lusk. The best time for her, I mean, because of her treatment schedule." Easy-peasy. Be nice, but don't ask. Instruct. Speak with authority and people cede it.

"Lusk?"

"L-U-S-as-in-Sam-K."

The receptionist put me on hold to check a master schedule. She returned and rattled off visiting hours.

It really was that simple.

Your mother did not need to fill out Form ISU-009v, requesting to place me on her visitor roster.

I needed to neither fill out nor return Form ISU-010v, the application to visit.

Riverview staff would conduct no criminal background check.

At Riverview's threshold I would be subject to no search of person or possessions.

In Marjorie Lusk's room we would be allowed our privacy.

She and I would be permitted to touch.

11.

Dear Clarence,

I never thought about the arch that way (or about it sinking into the earth, what an imagination your wife has!) before. It's supposed to be the gateway to the west. So don't you have to be able to pass through it going west (or east, if you like to do things backwards)? If it bridged the river, you could only go south, unless you wanted to fight a massive current. The St. Louis marathon ends right near the arch. I think it's strange that they didn't put it just a bit farther and put the finish line right under it.

No, I'm not a marathoner. (Don't I wish. I ran a 5K once. Ouch.) My father was and I liked to go and cheer. He passed away last June. I don't think I have to tell you how much I miss him. He's what my mind returns to and I don't think any kind of lava game will help it. He collected electric trains and I always used to tease him that it was an old man's hobby. Now I just wish he got to be an old man. Mom doesn't know this but I've set up a small train set under my bed. At night when I can't sleep, I switch it on. I like to pretend that the train could carry me to a place where I could see him again. But that's not how the world works. I don't have to tell you. The train just goes round and round.

I hope it's not rude to mention death, given your situation. I'm sorry if it is. I imagine it could be like someone lighting up when you're trying to stop smoking. That could have been rude too, if you are an ex-smoker. Or a smoker who feels guilty about it. Are you? Do they even let you? In movies, prisoners smoke all the time. That was rude also. I'm not usually this bad mannered. It's just that when I think of you (and yes, I do think of you) I don't know how to picture you or your life. My mother says I am much too nosey.

There isn't much to say about St. Louis. I hope you are not disappointed in me. St. Louis is St. Louis and this time of year everything turns gray and cold. I work in an organic grocery and it's funny that with fruit and stuff at work I see all the colors that are missing when I walk to there. It's two miles. So that's four miles a day. Maybe I'll wind up a marathoner despite myself. Ha ha. Mom offers to drive, but it's healthier this way and I think that maybe if I'm walking around I'll be the first one to spot signs of spring when they come. What else? Oranges are in season. Those little baby ones without seeds. Clementines. I can peel them in one piece (and that's just about the only party trick I've got). We have a little deli café and some nights I bring dinner home. I can barely fry an egg and Mom wears herself out by being lonely. Even though dinner's a small thing I like to feel I'm helping her.

I guess this means I lied to you in the first letter, when I said that my life was good and that I am happy in it. I didn't know that I would get comfortable enough to share this. I'm kind of surprised that I have. What I should have said is that I know my life can be good and that I am trying to be happy in it.

Mom and I go to movies some nights. I think it's a relief for her to sit and not talk and not notice who <u>isn't</u> around to talk. So even though I would like to talk with her, I try and give her what she needs, which are quiet evenings with somebody else's story. I'd be lying if I said it wasn't nice for me to get lost that way sometimes too.

Look at this. I've gone and written a *pity me* letter. I didn't mean to. What I mean to say is that I enjoy hearing from you and feel that when I write back I am finally, really speaking.

12.

When my mother died she went quickly; my father did too when Barbra and I were young. I had no idea what people wore to nursing homes. I unstacked trousers and blouses, scarves, my good out-in-the-world and working clothes. They'd been shut in drawers, airless, a long time. They smelled it. Pamela used to bring home arts and crafts sachets, bundles of herbs, oranges spiked with cloves. I should have kept them, I suppose, but I never did see what would stop them from rotting. Nothing suited. Not these plain old office clothes. I went to the closet. Execution suits in their garment bag. When your time came I couldn't wear all three. And this way your mother would know me. She'd seen me in black last time around. A bit of a drive, my townhouse to Riverview. The gabardine would wrinkle least. I unzipped the garment bag. I'd stuffed the jacket with tissue paper; even back when I bought it I'd known it would have to hold its shape a while. The tissue inside crunched.

I packed a fat photo album, all Pam's school plays and Halloweens. I'd want them, maybe, if I couldn't think of something to say. I had to use my largest purse. Pam was mugging in some of the photographs, aloof in some, healthy and cared for in all. A long ago feeling I couldn't properly name; shades of sitting on the school bus, homeward bound, a sealed report card in my hand and the knowledge that I had done well. I stopped at Green Mother Grocery for flowers. That darling little checker, Flamingo, steered me toward tulips because they were cheerful. I let her pick a dozen, costly and not yet in season. I put the change in her tip jar. She was saving for that China trip, after all.

Riverview was L shaped and bordered a parking lot. Its awning read *Welcome* in the sort of excessively curly script reserved for Italian restaurants. The river was nowhere in sight and the lobby was heated to the edge of uncomfortable. A television nested in the fireplace, broadcasting the image of an actual fire. A girl, Pam's age or just shy of it, sat at a desk, phone crimped between shoulder and ear. She swiveled her chair and shuffled a file into one of the cabinets behind her. I waved the tulips, a jaunty salute. I made for the double doors. If asked to describe me later, the girl would only remember a yellow blur. A plastic sign announced that this was the Irene P. Cotter Ward.

Marjorie, I'd say. I don't know if you recognize me. It's been a while. I want to tell you that Pamela's brilliant. Perfect. Her mother would be so proud. Her father too if he hadn't—but it doesn't do any kind of good, us getting into that.

But why else had I come here? In my good gabardine.

She was in this building, breathing my same air. In and out of her parking lot lips.

When she kissed Pammie goodbye we had a time scrubbing away that lipstick.

She was your mother.

I should come into her room like thunder.

Nice place you got here, Marjorie. Riverview. I'm sure it's costing you. I'm glad. Less money in the pot for his defense. But, Marjorie, you should know that not a whole lot of it goes to security. No one made a move to stop me. That phone girl didn't ask for my name. But you know me. You know who I—

"Ma'am? Can I help you?" the lobby girl asked. She wore frosted lip gloss.

"I'm visiting." I shook the tulips again, so glad I'd thought to bring them. Cameras were so small now. They could perch anywhere. Catching me at strange angles, squashed or bloated, like a reflection in a spoon.

"Who are—"

"Marjorie Lusk. She's one of your stroke patients."

"Sure. Great. Let's get you signed in." Frostmouth waved a clipboard and gestured to a bouquet of pens, every one of them taped to enormous silk flowers to prevent folks from carrying them off.

"I'm family," I said. And what a thing it was to have a family, I would tell Marjorie. Snarled together like a mess of unbrushed hair. Bound up by Clarence. Nice boy, that son of yours. I'd tell her: If you raised him right he'd be here for you. He'd bring you Pammie. She's so big, Marjorie. I'm learning to be happy about it. You were dead wrong that day. "I called ahead," I told Frostmouth. "One of you people knew that I was coming."

"Name?"

I hesitated. Marjorie *was* your mother. Perhaps they were obliged to alert you with the names of people who dropped by. "Kath Claverie," I said, because after Pam's name, which wouldn't do, and Maisie's which I obviously couldn't use, it was the first that came to me. "Marjorie is my mother," I said, and then, because I couldn't do that to Ma, "In-law. My mother-in-law."

"Well," said Frostmouth. I knew that tone. My brace-tightening voice. There, that wasn't so bad. "Here we go." I took the clipboard from her. *Kath Claverie*, I wrote.

I returned the clipboard. Frostmouth looked over my entry and asked for ID.

"I forgot." I sounded like a patient, talking about a retainer. My mind went rat-ta-tat. ID. We caught Pamela once with a fake one. Maybe she'd tell me where she'd got it. She wouldn't back then, no matter the grounding. I couldn't tell her so then, but I was proud: Barbra wouldn't have ratted either.

Frostmouth eyed my purse.

I made an exaggerated show of rifling through it. "Senior moment," I said, though I hated the term.

"I'm really sorry," said Frostmouth, not quite sounding it. "But I can't—"

"I just want to see her."

"Your mother-in-law?" Her voice was threaded with disbelief.

I nodded, vehemently. Comporting myself like a galumphing puppy, I knew.

"Listen, you're family. So I'm sure you understand how important it is we respect our residents' privacy. And security, right? I mean—" She stopped right there, like she'd run out of script.

"Please. I have to see Marjorie." I had to know. If there were dogs in your childhood and if you tied tin cans to their tails. If she knew then. If neighbor children put their hands a little deeper in their pockets when you passed, touching their nickels or sweets one last time before you took them. If she'd known when you started to bring home girls, spiritless dishrags with bruise-colored eyes. What she'd made of my sister and her spine. Why she never warned her.

"If there's an emergency . . ."

"Please. I just left my ID back at home." I raised the flowers. "I had these to juggle and it slipped my mind."

"I'm sorry. Maybe I can give her the flowers? Say hi and everything."

I surrendered the blooms and Frostmouth told me to drive safe. Sometimes there was a speed trap just after the merge. I didn't want to be pulled over without my license.

A quartet stood just outside. Father, daughter, grandmother, and grandmother's walker. I buckled myself into the car. My gabardine had begun to wrinkle. I waited to start the engine and watched the family hug goodbye. Both father and daughter wore denim and sloppy sweatshirts, like seeing family was roughly as important as yard work. Grandmother shuffled back inside. Father and daughter walked to their car. The girl was already too old to hold his hand but she gave a little skip and her shoulder brushed his arm. She passed so close to me. Adorable freckles. In another year or so she would begin to hate them. For now though she stopped before my window to adjust her reflected ponytail. I held still so as not to startle her. Imagine if instead of her face she saw my own, congealing from air, older than she'd ever imagined. She would shrink against her father. She *should* shrink. Marjorie had no one left to shrink against and somewhere inside Riverview Frostmouth was presenting her with tulips. How pretty, from your daughter-in-law, Frostmouth would say, because a lie, once spoken, really begins to live. They should have let me see her. Because the tulips were worse. Marjorie with Frostmouth's words in her ear, how pretty, from your daughter-in-law. Your mother lying dead still and thinking *Barbra*. Barbra and her donkey laugh, rushing out of the ether, sudden, as if from a dark glass.

13.

Frostmouth hadn't lied. There was a speed trap after the merge. I was not pulled over. I have always been a careful driver. Even angry. Even seething. Even itching to be back home. I had paid to put in fine oak shelves. They bracketed the fireplace. My photo albums lined them: one per year, acid-free paper, meticulously captioned. Subject, location, occasion, and date. Last name and then first, and always correctly spelled. Frank liked to tease that the average architectural blueprint required less precision. It was kind of him to pretend it was the tic of a well-organized mind. But Frank knew me. He knew my tendency toward scorekeeping. He'd been with me in the parking lot. He had to see those albums for what they were: the marshaled evidence of a happy childhood.

I parked the car. I was deliberate and careful doing so. The townhouse garage was narrower than the double one I'd shared with Frank. I locked the car. I locked the house. I went straight for the photo albums. It would be essential to be meticulous. Chronological order. Pammie in coveralls, helping to paint her bedroom the lavender she'd selected. Pamela, barefoot, writing her name in sidewalk chalk.

Her senior year at Wash U, Pam and her roommate had hatched the Austin plan. Come graduation, they would move south. Neither girl had people in Texas. Not a job lined up between them. But they wanted someplace sunny and they wanted someplace young. Pamela'd met Blue her last semester and bailed on the endeavor;

I supposed I would always owe him for that. But the plan stuck with me. To pack up and move on a whim like that was strictly the provenance of the young. No one in my generation would have done so. Certainly no one in your mother's.

Pamela in water wings and a ruffle-bottomed swimsuit.

Pamela in an Endicott School Black Watch skirt and blazer.

Frank and Pammie and a fresh-caught trout, my girl eyeing the fish warily.

Your mother had no kin in these parts. But your mother, Clarence, had her reasons. Her words, Gatling gun in my mind: *you don't know what it is to be a mother*. Her words, and Barbra's: *my hand to God, that woman's favorite sentence is* I told you so.

Pamela's face painted red, white, and blue for an Independence Day parade. Your mother could've been any one of the thousand passing patriots. Tracking my sweetheart. Taking notes.

Pamela sans milk teeth in the second grade spelling bee. Onstage before a darkened auditorium where anyone could be sitting.

I peeled the parade photograph from the album. It came away with the sticky sound of flypaper. I would need to find Frank's magnifying glass and a very strong light. I would have to unearth Barbra's wedding album—thank goodness I'd vetoed Ma on burning it—because there would be Marjorie pictures in it to cross reference. I removed the spelling bee picture too. Somewhere, surely, I had Pammie's old school directory. I could phone other parents, ask for crowd shots from the inevitable reception after, put the magnifying glass to work once more.

Pamela in her Girl Scout uniform. The den mom had been Cynthia Somebody. I could look it up. The Internet would help. She'd have records of the neighborhoods where Pam had sallied forth to offload cookies; from there it would be a simple matter of cross-checking ownership deeds.

The pile of photographs grew: Sixth-grade graduation, Pammie in the Jessica McClintock she'd begged for, and who knew how many strangers milling about with sugar cookies and neon punch. Pammie and her bunkmates, parents' day at Camp Discovery. Pam at Ted Drewes with her usual cup of butterscotch–graham cracker. A dozen folks in the background, queuing up for custard. Pammie's first Cards game; Pamela, Frank, and I, in three of Busch Stadium's *fifty thousand* seats.

It was dark out, and late. I poured myself a bowl of muesli and took an idle bite or two. Pamela, about to board the bus for the all-state swim meet. Pamela, dolled up for dinner before her senior prom, where anyone with a reservation at Dominic's could have seen her radiant in the green satin she had selected, the one I'd said could either be low cut or figure-hugging or short, but or only, given her age, not *and.*

The piles covered the table. Loose photos. Yearbooks with their candids. The magnifying glass, though I wouldn't muck about with that until everything was sorted and I could tackle it systematically. I went to bed and slept very little. Morning came; I brushed my teeth. I remembered: only the nicest shots had made it into the albums but thank goodness we kept *all* the negatives. I knew right where the boxes were. Spool after spool. So many crowd shots. I wished I was still in practice; I'd have the light board I used for X-rays, which would allow for a proper look. Instead, I held them strip by strip to the window. Thankfully it was a sunny day.

I only realized it was afternoon when Pam phoned. It was Saturday and I had missed Kath's linner. I told Pam I had a touch of the stomach flu. She accepted this without question, so I must have sounded spent and very strange.

14.

And then it was Monday. Kath Claverie showed up at our usual walkabout time, bearing a Crock-Pot of chicken broth. Acid rain could come, and race riots, and the Mississippi could churn thick with nuclear sludge, and Kath Claverie would still arrive promptly and bearing chicken broth.

I hadn't eaten. The soup smelled delicious and I told her so.

"Parsnips," said Kath. "They make it taste like it's been simmering forever."

"I'm awfully sorry about Saturday."

"It was only linner. Where can I put this?"

My townhouse was deliberately modern in its layout; airy, well-lit, and, in its common areas, predominantly wall-less. Ma's old dining room table stitched kitchen and living room together, its warm wood surface buried beneath my weekend's labor. I watched Kath take it in: the piled photographs, the magnifying glass, the photo albums I had not returned to their shelves. The forgotten bowl of muesli, and thank goodness I never could stand the taste of it with milk. A legal pad, busy with brainstorming. The yearbooks. The inexplicable compass and butcher's twine that I did not recall bringing to the table.

"Put it in the kitchen," I said. "That Crock-Pot will need a plug." I opened the cabinets for a pair of mugs. I had a fine set of soup bowls, porcelain with dainty handles, but I was meant to have been ill and there is something inexorably soothing about clear soup and a workaday mug. I passed one to Kath. "I'm sorry about the state of things."

"You scrapbooking?" Another reason I liked Kath: the slant of her mind toward the active, contained, and neatly accomplishable. Kath sewed Halloween costumes for the grandchildren. She gardened. She dried flowers from her garden and twisted them into wreaths.

"Something like that," I said.

Kath gestured with the mug. "May I?"

"Just keep it in order. It looks like chaos, but—"

"Say no more." She lifted a picture of Pam carefully by its corner. Kath Claverie knew about fingers. About the oils they secrete. She went for a second photograph. "Just look at that gorgeous girl."

Pam hadn't been gorgeous actually, not in the lively, expansive way common to the Claverie grandkids. There was always a reserve. Had she had her mother's vanity, she could have sported a ballerina bun and cultivated an air of continental mystery. To Kath, I made myself agreeable, saying, "Just look at those eyes." Your eyes, Clarence. It has always hit me hard that her objectively best feature is the one she gets from you. Very early on I made a habit of praising them first. Better that than allowing the compliments of others to catch me barbed and unaware. I sipped. Kath's soup was rich and warming, just the slightest bite of salt. A surge of feeling cared for. Cared about. "I was looking for her grandmother," I said. I made my voice decisive. One of my mother's sayings: talk bites trouble in two.

"Renate?" Kath asked, picking up another picture. Ma died before Pammie and Blue ever met; Kath knew her name only out of kindness to our family. *Her* mother had been called Bette and her husband's, Maxine; odds were even between Kath and me on that front.

I paused a moment. I could speak my mother's name; with the name of my mother all would be smoothed over. I shook my head. "Marjorie." It's an ugly name, Clarence. No surprise it came out a croak.

Kath set down her mug. The whole enterprise seemed foolish. My townhouse, a disaster. "Marjorie," Kath echoed, tasting the unfamiliar sound.

"Clarence's mother," I said, confirming what Kath Claverie was far too well-mannered to ask.

"Okay then. Marjorie." She offered a tight, social smile. "She's . . ."

Kath was waiting for an adjective.

Instead, an adverb. "Here." I felt like a magician, producing a rabbit from a hat. A stringy rabbit, palsied, thin-haunched. Sufficient only for stew. "She's been here for years."

Kath waited. Naturally. A mother of four knows silence is best for chasing out the truth.

"I looked her up online," I said.

Kath whistled, low and long. "That technology's going to put PIs out of business."

I felt less on the brink, hearing her say that. This wasn't futile and it wasn't neurotic futzing. We were simply two women of a certain age discussing new technology as broth warmed the air between us. "We cut contact with her," I said. It felt clean to be telling Kath. It felt right. "I just found out she followed us here. She's in O'Fallon, just across the way. No reason but Pam for her to be there. So I've been looking through old pictures. Trying to catch her, sneaking in on the edges."

"Good Lord." Kath clasped her hands like a child at prayer. "I'd have had a tail on her from the get-go. She could've come after Pam or—"

"She didn't." How absurd, my taking your mother's part against Kath. Kath, who offered no judgment for the way we'd sloughed off a whole side of Pam's family. I should have been glad about that. I should've wanted to take Kath's hand. Instead, I felt cluttered, my house and person, my mind itself, too cluttered even to remember whatever saying of Ma's translated to *if you feel like you've got away with something it's because you don't feel bad enough for the wrong that you did in the first place.* The turn of phrase had involved corduroys. Patching them.

"I'm sorry," Kath said. "I don't mean to second-guess you."

"You sound like a girl detective. Putting a tail on her." I said this because it was true and because Kath *had* been second-guessing.

"Paperback mysteries," she said. "My guilty pleasure."

As if crime were a thing to be enjoyed from afar. Every cell of me soured. That crack of Kath's about hiring a PI; as if a single disaster had turned our family into the kind of people with an impulse toward the seedy.

Kath indicated the table. "Did you find her? What does she look like?"

"She's not there." I hadn't completed my inspection, but it felt true in the moment that I said it. "It was a silly idea. She has Pam's eyes," I added, remembering that this was Kath, who hadn't the least notion she'd offended, who'd brought me soup when I was down, who said ten times a month that I was family. "I'd appreciate it if you didn't say anything to her."

"Of course." Kath's turned back to the table. She honed in on the next-to-impossible pile. "You know what I'd do? Take a good look at all the shoes. Marjorie came up in the Depression, yeah? So you look for old-fashioned shoes. Especially ones that pop up year after year. I remember my mom. Women that age would sooner waltz down the street naked than pony up for a new pair of shoes."

I should have been the one to think of it. When Ma died, Goodwill scored pumps that had been re-soled two times, even three. Across the Mississippi, there was a Riverview closet and in it shoes that fit the feet of Marjorie Lusk. Thriftiness is a virtue—Ma'd had a saying about that too—but I couldn't see giving Marjorie credit. "It's not that they were any better than us with money," I said. "Those women. It's just that the shoes they bought were better made. They wore like anything. America had craftspeople then."

15.

Maisie, today I had a long hard think about never writing you again. I don't suffer cruelty any more than I have to, and your letter was cruel and it was careless and you admit that you lied to me. That's a waste of my time and you know that time is my only commodity.

Did you think I wouldn't break out sweating when you go on about dying? Next time, think on your words. I'm a full person in here. I was a full person before you were ever born.

I could tell myself, it's just because Maisie's a young one. No excuse. My daughter's your age and her letters are never so mean. It's a weakness that I'm writing to you at all. You know how badly I need friends. But if you're going to jerk me around, don't bother writing again. I can't waste what time I have left on a little girl who lies.

All that said, I am sorry about your father. I guess I'm glad you can talk about it with me. Maybe I'm getting a taste of the legitimate Maisie. Maybe you were sunshine sweet that first time because you couldn't own up to the bits of your life that are sad. Don't do that again. You forget who you're writing to. Every day I face things worse than you will ever face.

And don't go expecting me to patch over the hurt that comes from missing him. I don't know you much and frankly (I promised honesty) this isn't a patch job I have it in me to do. My own daughter says I make up for every grade school penpal she had who never wrote back. That's not the kind of heart-hole a father wants to fill. My wife's folks shrunk me down so small in her eyes. It kills me. So think about how your father would feel with you looking for a fix-up. I'd bet he was a good man (you seem to think so and your mother seems to think so). Don't punish him. Dying's the only thing he's guilty of, and that's a crime we all do sooner or later.

Or if you're looking for a patch, don't look my way for it. I've got a daughter already. Whatever I want from you, it's not to be a father.

Though now I'm going to act like one and give advice (my own girl's got her head on right, so it's rare I get the chance). Don't try losing yourself in "somebody else's story" as you say. Don't dribble your one life away. Think about it like this. Every morning at seven the officers switch on our TVs. Stemble gets five channels. You have to fill out a form telling them which one you want. We've got to pay for TV ourselves. No money, no TV. I've got the credits but I won't buy. Even the guards think that's strange. But think about all the things we can't be trusted with and then think about all the shards and wires a TV could be busted into even though they've got them mounted way up high on the wall. Think about why they're willing to chance it. My mind's just about all I've got worth keeping. I'm not going to let it die before the rest of me.

Maisie, this isn't a life you want to get lost in. I've got no windows. Only dirty light makes it in. It's always hot. My daughter says it's been cold in St. Louis. When you write back, tell me about the cold. I haven't been cool in years. Even sitting still I sweat. We're allowed three showers weekly and we've got to pay for our own soap. Twice a month I get a mop to clean my cell. Water pressure's just about drool. Toilets clog. Ventilation's shot. Fifty men in this cell block and you can't imagine the stink. Some of my best dreams are of ice. And cigarettes. You asked if I smoke. I don't anymore. This isn't TV jail where you can rustle up whatever you please and it's a nasty habit so don't you get started anyhow. The officers are a bunch of pricks. They know most of us would swap an appeal for half a pack so they come on shift reeking of it.

Every day in Stemble's the same. Food carts wheel in at four AM. Officers with goggles and flak jackets, like the food's actually worth protecting. They make all kinds of noise even though lights don't come on till five. At six they go cell to cell for first count. By the time that's done the food's cold (if it was ever hot). Trays come through the locked slots. If you've ever been to the zoo you know how it works.

Stemble rations are all starch and sugar. Men thicken up over the years. They gobble up everything because chewing gives them something to do. Not me. I eat half of every meal, exactly half, which was something my wife used to do whenever she thought she should be slimmer. Our utensils are plastic. We don't ever get knives. When meat comes it comes pre-cut, like I used to do for my kid. There's a guy eight cells down who they say licks his door between every bite to get that metal taste you get off a real fork. I don't know if this is true. The cells are laid out so you can't see from one into any other. Not that you can see through Stemble doors. No bars. Like I said, it's not the movies. Don't go thinking it's the movies. The door is solid metal, perforated with one hundred and twenty dime-sized holes. I wish like hell I was water and could pour myself out.

The guards make pill rounds starting at seven. You get a Dixie cup for water. They give us swallow tests. Lift that tongue. You need permission for aspirin eighteen hours in advance. End of pill rounds means only four hours need filling till lunch. By then it's eight o'clock and they count us for the second time. Two hours later it's ten o'clock and count number three. Lunch comes at noon. Also at noon (I don't mean to be crass here) Duane Pelly in the next cell pleasures himself when the weather girl reads her report. I don't have a TV so I have no idea what about her does it for him.

Afternoons are the hardest because that's the longest stretch of the day and it's when things happen that you hope for. All afternoon you hope it's your turn outside. They never give you a heads up because they don't want you able to plan. Count four at two o'clock. You hope there's mail. Count five at three o'clock. You hope that dinner will be edible (unlikely). The trays start to come at five and then there's nothing left to hope for until tomorrow. Six o'clock, count six. Eight o'clock, count seven. Nine o'clock and the TVs shut off all at once from the master switch. The silence is strange. It doesn't comfort and it doesn't last for long.

Count eight and lights out at ten. I can't sleep. I wait for the next sound. The longest stretch of quiet I ever counted was 269 seconds. When I sleep I sleep fitfully. The cell stays a sweatbox. They leave on enough light so that they can always see me. And in the near-dark I get to thinking that a man only gets so many hours of light (even the weak Stemble kind). It's a sin to blink in the daytime. I told you from the first that I'm afraid. It's not this life that scares me now, it's the mechanics of leaving it. Sometimes they can't find veins. They have to break out a scalpel and cut to tap them. I do exercises. I clench and unclench my fists three hundred times at every count and another five hundred before I sleep. It makes my veins puffy and very blue. If I'm going to go, I'm not going out a split job.

I'd rather be like I was coming here in '82, scared of everything instead of scared of that one big thing. And I do mean everything. After the trial my lawyer says, don't put a toe out of line, Mr. Lusk. (I don't think anymore that he'll be able to pull off a reprieve but he still calls me mister and that's worth all the money Mom coughed up and more.) He says it'll help for my appeals if he can sell me as a model prisoner. Keep thinking Clemency Board, Mr. Lusk, he says. Worst thing you can do is act out.

So I'm locked up in Stemble. Scared to death of breaking some rule. And I'm scared of the men here because they've killed people (even if I've done the same). More scared of them than the guards, even though with a policeman dead officers've got to be looking for my least little slip up. It's 1982. I'm still thinking in terms of months. I tell myself just don't screw up, just don't screw up.

Now there's a man in the cell to my left, Nuz, who wiped out a whole family because one of the sons slashed his tires. I see him only when he's taken out to the pens. Guy looks like a turtle. He starts to talk to me. Calls me Doc (he knows I worked in a hospital before here, knows I've had seven semesters of college). And even though I'm scared (eight victims, grandparents and everyone), I start to think some part of this world is like my old one and maybe a nickname means we're good. Nuz tells me who to watch for. Warns about this guard, Wethtin, who gets crazy if you don't call him "sir" and "Officer Wethtin."

Guy on the other side, Enright, just laughs and laughs. He garroted a woman my mother's age. I pretend he's not there, one wall away.

Thirty-eight days pass and I don't crack. I'm an idiot. I actually think I'm going to make it. My lawyer's going to pull something off. Day thirty-nine Wethtin shows up for contraband check. He cuffs me. He goes through my stuff. He sees a picture of my little girl and puts a check mark in his log. "You got a daughter?" he says, real cold.

I go, "Yes sir, Mr. Wethtin."

And he says, colder still, "Repeat that, inmate?"

I don't get why he's mad. My hands are cuffed, remember. I repeat what I said, louder, because I thought maybe he hadn't heard. Nuz gets really quiet next door. Wethtin swings his fist right into my gut. Nuz only starts making noise again once it's over. On the other side Enright's laughing like crazy. The guy's a panzer but he's got this tinkerbell laugh. "Guard's name is Westin," he goes, "w e s T i n. Guard's name is Westin and heth got thith lithp." Even pulling the trigger I never hated anyone like I hated Nuz and Enright and Westin then. I never hated anyone like I hated that little ball of myself in the corner because I got then that this was it. The rest of my life.

Crazy thing is, when they took Nuz, I cried. Cried like they were taking me.

They have a new guy in Nuz's cell. Young kid, about your age, Maisie. Duane Pelly, who likes that weather girl. He showboats. None of this has hit him yet. He's from a huge family and has one joke that he tells over and over to the guards, Enright, me, whoever. He probably told the jury. You've got four brothers. Matthew, Mark, Luke, and Duane. Guess which one ends up in Stemble. Everything about the kid's thin as gauze. The longer he goes not thinking, the harder it's going to hit him. So he's here a week and I start to talk to him. Watch out for Wethtin, I say. Enright laughs. I don't think I deserve to die, and people outside will say I've done a whole lot worse, but setting Pelly up like that's the closest I've ever come to feeling maybe the state's right.

No man believes in his heart that he's going to meet the needle. But in my head I know that things are winding down for me. And maybe that's why I'm taking the time (and just about crippling my hand) to tell you these things. A man at the end of his life needs the love of his friends. And I know through bad experience there's no love without honesty. So I'm telling you the truth about me, Maisie. I realize that you're not going to like this letter, and so I'll say this. It will always be your choice whether or not to write back, but not everything's your choice. Now that I've told all this truth, seeing me as something less than a feeling human is no longer an option available to you.

16.

Your letter arrived with the season's first snowstorm. Early that year. It was only November. Mid-afternoon but the world felt twilit. Outside the post office, headlights were milky with flakes. I had thought to have a ritual, that I would read all your letters at the café where I'd made all that trouble with the plate. But it was a vicious storm and Stemble issued such cheap paper. A flake or so and your words would bleed. And so I read it there, in the post office, at the vestibule counter where customers sort junk mail from things that matter. I did not remove my gloves, Clarence. It was slow going and clumsy, of course, but you can't imagine that was my primary concern.

I read. I secured the letter in my purse. I removed my hat, which was wine-colored and, according to Kath Claverie, framed my face becomingly. I removed the tartan scarf that was still in good shape after a decade. The belt and buttons of my good wool coat gave me some trouble and for the first time I regretted not buying the one with toggle closures. The gloves I tucked away in my purse. I left the rest of it behind me. I opened the door. It's beautiful—you wouldn't have seen it in ages—the air that fills an empty threshold. Snowflakes cut the space like television static.

"Lady," someone said behind me. "In or out. There's a storm on."

Out. In Stemble you were always much too hot.

I started walking. I liked my neighborhood plenty but it was not without its troubles. Someone who had real need would come along to claim my warm winter things. Light poured from the windows I passed, buttering the flurries. You had no windows. I clutched my purse across my chest. Your letter in it, folded and dry.

My daughter says it's been cold in St. Louis.

My own girl's got her head on right, so it's rare I get the chance.

My own daughter says I make up for every grade school penpal she had who never wrote back.

My daughter's your age and her letters are never so mean.

The wind yowled. I still had my shirt and slacks, my solid boots, but in this weather I might just as well be naked. Yet there was heat, too. The sense I'd swallowed live coals. Pamela, Pammie, Pam. Three times a year we let you write her. On her birthday, because it had to kill you knowing she'd grown. At the turn of the year, so you'd mark another of yours gone. And at the peak of summer when she only wanted to play outdoors. You always ended with jokes she grew much too old for: what did the zero say to the eight?

Nice belt.

They were right to keep you warm in Stemble. Cold air could scour anything clean.

And Pammie was a good girl. "I've passed notes in Geometry that matter more than this," she'd griped at sixteen, waving that thin, cheap Stemble paper.

I had hid my glee. "You shouldn't be passing notes," was all I said.

Pamela left home five years ago.

Your letters should have gone the way of curfew.

Only, the wardens couldn't stop you now. Not like they used to. Inmates can't write minors without their guardians' consent.

Pam hadn't been a minor in years. Simple arithmetic. She'd been living without me almost as long as she'd lived in your care.

I never lied to her about Arizona. Frank and I agreed that was the right approach. Four bullets made splinters of Barbra's sternum. Pamela had to know it. For Barbra's sake and her own. Three letters a year. You were meant to be a gadfly. She was meant to swat you away.

What did the history book say to the math book?

You've got problems.

I reached my townhouse. My clothing made a second, icy skin. I was glad my neighbors worked. One peek out the window and they'd be on the phone to Senior Services. I was fine though, cold but fine. I didn't fumble with my keys. My fingertips were bloodless white and the meat of my hands very red. I thought of Ma, that chestnut of hers about labor and virtue. Red hands like a washerwoman's, true heart like a saint's. I went immediately to the kitchen and ran the tap. Cold water is best for cold hands; the shock of hot is all too much. We taught Pamela these things, Frank and I. "He isn't a factor in my life," I said to the empty kitchen, echoing Pam's stock reply whenever asked about you. I said it loud over the tap, its pressure Niagara to your drool. I couldn't remember the last time I had heard her say it.

She said other things, Clarence. My shakes weren't cold now but panic; there was a chance that these were things you already knew: Pamela never swore. That was Frank in her. Bull sweat. Mother of pearl. I remembered her grade school cadence going over spelling lists. A fragment of the poem she'd had to memorize for that battle-axe who taught eighth-grade French. And of course that high school solace: *I've passed notes in Geometry that matter more.* We raised her polite. Maybe she just kept up the three letter habit. Maybe when you wrote back she felt obliged to reply. Only duty. She'd sent wedding thank-yous within a month of the ceremony, such a responsible girl. Never anything less than a high B+. She'd got the top grade in Geometry. What notes she passed must have mattered very little. They must have been rare, those notes.

I lifted the kitchen phone. Buttons cheeped. I wasn't going to confront her. I only wanted to hear her voice. 2:46 P.M. She'd be off at work but it was her voice on the answering machine. She was far more tech-adept than Blue.

But Pamela answered, breathy, on the first ring. "'lo, it's Pam." Not the way I taught her. Good afternoon, Stearl residence. Claverie now.

"Aren't you at work?"

"Lida?"

"It's the middle of the afternoon," I reminded her.

"I know. I've—"

"Are you sick?" She had always been susceptible to colds. Even in the Arizona dry. Barbra told me. Good thing she had, or that first winter I'd have been sure we'd fed her something wrong. "I have good oranges," I told her. "Remember? I told you at lunch? They're organic and I'll never finish them on my own."

"I'm not sick, Lida. I'm doing some paperwork from home. What's that noise?"

"I didn't know they had you on paperwork. I thought—"

"I'm serious. Don't you hear that hiss?"

I shut off the faucet. "I thought they always had you out with the dogs."

"In this weather?"

"It snows on the blind same as everyone."

"Well aren't *you* profound."

"I'm glad you're not out driving in this mess. I like that the center gave you the day."

"Flextime's *genius*. I blow off every Thursday to meet my dealer."

"Very funny, Miss." If it weren't for Barbra, who'd also blown off work at midday, Pam might have gone for the more obvious joke and said *lover*.

"That's him knocking now. Just a minute, Hector!"

"Pamela." A miserable fizz in my brain. Every Thursday, Pam said, quippy and unpremeditated, like it was true. Today was Thursday. The day she had blown off work and met me for lunch had been a Thursday too.

"Oh relax, Lida. It's just the soft stuff. You know I can't stand needles."

"Did Blue take the day too?"

"Nah. He's got this monster deposition. I'll see him maybe in May."

"You sound lonely. I can—"

"I'm fine, Li, but I need to go. Got to keep the line free for the center."

"Say hi to Hector for me." I wanted to see if the name gave her pause. It was an unusual one to come up with off the cuff. No one thinks *Hector*, voilá, unless a Hector's on her mind.

"I'll say hi to Hector and Blue both."

I made sure to hang up first. I was no longer cold. I felt it in my cheeks. I've always blushed easily; I got that from Ma. Pamela didn't. She was old enough now to have secrets. You were writing to her. She was writing back. Please let that writing be the only mess she'd got herself into.

Barbra didn't blush much either.

Barbra who played hooky from work in the bed of Lawrence Ring.

The apple never falls far from the tree. "Stupidest thing I ever heard," Ma used to say. "I've run an orchard. Any fruit worth keeping gets picked long before it falls."

But: all those work-free Thursdays of Pam's. Her throaty, casual hello. *Hector.* She'd been so young when she met Blue. She hardly dated before him. And it had to be tough going sometimes, all the extra that she did for him. If she strayed with some seeing man, at least she could believe him when he called her pretty.

And of course she was her mother's daughter. Barbra, who never shared much with me. Never shared anything. I could count on my fingers what little I knew about her lover.

He responded only to Lawrence, never Larry.

He had worked at Folsom High for nine years.

He stood five foot eight, only three inches above Barbra, and was nowhere near as handsome as you. So Barbra must have seen something there; she must have learned to look deeper. Before your bullets tore her, my sister had begun to grow up.

He was tri-county amateur table tennis champ. I pictured Barbra, paddle in hand, laughing. Her hair falls in her face and she brushes it back. The paddle, still in her grip, grazes her forehead. "Careful there," says Lawrence Ring. It helped to pretend his voice was like my Frank's. It made it easier to pretend the rest, that she loved him enough to turn what followed to a little bit more than a waste.

You wounded him first but he died after Barbra. He bled and lived to see her bleed. My younger sister passed from this world in the company of a man whose name she never saw fit to speak aloud to me.

Outside my townhouse, the wind continued its shrill. Winter had always been my most difficult season. In the summer it was simpler keeping track of Pam. I put her in flip-flops. Each step she took, a sandal thwacked against her heel. Pamela walked in such small steps through the house, across the patio, pad, pad, pad. Listen, Lida, I'm right here. Listen, you can hear where it is I'm going.

17.

Saturday came, and with it another of Kath's linners. The Claveries lived in Ladue, where the brickwork houses strove so aggressively for grand that even the snowdrifts couldn't make them homey. From the driveway, it seemed as though Kath had subscribed to that Realtor's adage about buying the worst house on the best block. A single story, imagine, for a family of six and in such a choice neighborhood. But that was just a trick of landscape. The house burrowed into the back of a hill, descending for two stories that were invisible from the street. Kath liked it that way. The modest roofline made her trees look taller than her neighbors'.

She was the one who answered my knock. Narrow trousers, dark blue but never denim, and a wheat-colored, scoop-necked sweater that, judging by the drape and the absence of sheen, was clearly real cashmere. The Claveries' was a shoe-free household, and I exchanged my boots for the wooly moccasins Kath kept in an entryway basket. Kath was in gym socks, bleached bright and not remotely grubby, but nevertheless not quite the thing. Little chinks like that were what made it possible to truly like her. "We're all downstairs," she said, fingering the ever-present necklace of grandkids' birthstones. A silent moment swelled in which neither of us brought up Marjorie, followed by a squawk from the basement. One of the grandchildren, summoning Kath. She left me to hang my own coat. I was family now. I knew the way.

From the looks of the closet, I was last to arrive. Jackets pressed close together, sleeves bulging. All the Claveries hung their coats that way, sleeves stuffed with whatever outerwear was meant to pair with them. A coping system for Blue, I guessed, so he'd never have to fumble about. I hung my own and went toward the stairs. I passed through Kath's kitchen, which was one of those extraordinary rooms that always *felt* yellow, buttery and sunlit, though the backsplash was done up in slate and the walls were the green-white of asparagus ends. I could hardly see Kath's refrigerator for the stick figures; the Claverie grandchildren were burgeoning artists. An inlaid bowl stood on the central island, a lovely piece that anyone else would fill with glass baubles or fresh fruit. Assorted nothings cluttered it. A rock with googly eyes and pipe cleaner antennas. A book of stamps. Three wrapped lollipops. A watch. A pair of sunglasses. Kath's keys with a tennis ball keychain. Four pencils. A pen lid. Kath's driver's license.

Her hair was brown, as mine was, though in both our cases some credit was due Patrice at Salon Carondolet, a small world coincidence we had discovered in the lead-up to Pam and Blue's wedding. I picked up the license, what luck. It said she was five ten. I was barely five four.

They probably wouldn't look that close at Riverview.

A nova of laughter from downstairs. I froze, though really, anyone who walked in would assume it was simple nosiness. I dug the rounded corner into the pad of my thumb. Kath likely misplaced it all the time, leaving it lying about. Or forgot about it entirely if she left the house in a rush. It was set to expire in two months anyhow and was right by the lollipops. Any one of the grandkids might dislodge and lose it, reaching for a sweet. A juvenile shriek from the basement, followed by a crescendo of babble. I pocketed the license, digging its edge under my thumbnail, not enough for pain but right on its margin. The first thing I had ever stolen.

In the Claverie house, the staircase never squeaked. Framed photographs of the Gs—Blue's sisters, Georgia, Genevieve, and Grace—and of Blue—who was himself a mutated G, Gene to Blue Jeans to Blue—lined it. The siblings grew younger as I neared the bottom.

"Halloo," I called, stepping into the living room, where fringed rugs, presumably hand-tied, helped to muffle the noise of the Claverie family and kept linners down to a tolerable roar. The room abutted a generous patio; a wall of glass panes and sliding doors let in the bald November light. And there they were, slant-lit: the lithe, linner-eating Claveries of St. Louis, blessed in their heights and speedy metabolisms. Blessed in their numbers. Four generations crowded the room. A dozen merry Claveries at least. I palmed Kath's license, laminated and smooth. Most weeks, linners were just the thing. Rowdy, bustling, and they filled the day. The Claveries, young and old, were invariably warm. But there was a catch, sometimes, and I don't think any of them had the least idea. The more rousingly they welcomed me the more apparent they made it that I was not of their same stock and was therefore in *need* of welcoming.

Pam waved me over. Georgia was the G beside her. Pam had told me once that all those Gs tripped her up too. Especially with Blue going by Gene professionally. When they first started seeing each other, she had sent a highly flirtatious email to the wrong g_claverie. Georgia greeted me with a bright hello and waxy kiss on the cheek. From Pam, I got a proper hug.

"You two sound like you're having a grand time," I said. The g_claverie incident was some comfort if looked at properly. Clearly, I was running away with myself. A girl who'd share an embarrassment like that with her old aunt wasn't a girl given over to secrets. "Dare I ask what's so funny?"

"Long story," said Pamela.

And Georgia, "Just a lame joke."

"I've got plenty of those," I said. An opening, and fast; I seldom got plum little social gifts like that. I wanted Pam to think of you, just a little. It had been a while. I wanted a reminder of what that looked like. I fingered Kath's license. My new good luck charm. "How do you make seven even?"

"Take away the S." Pam turned slightly away. She wore a low ponytail and a broad collar. Add her strong chin and her profile looked like Jefferson's on the nickel.

"Terrible," said Georgia, but she was smiling.

"Why was the little cannibal kicked out of school?"

"Oh! I know this one." Georgia pursed her lips. Her lipstick didn't quite suit her. "Is it something about Grade-A?"

That gray coin hardness settled deeper into Pamela's face. You'd sent her that joke and the previous one, Clarence. You always ended your allotted letters with jokes, an absurd bit of cruelty after the ending you'd made that was anything but one. Pamela kept her voice neutral. She delivered the punch line. "Because she kept buttering up her teacher."

Georgia shook her head. "You two. You should take this on the road. A family act." Her *family* came out garbled. Mother-daughter, she'd been about to say.

"Hardly," said Pam. "Unless by 'take this on the road' you mean 'take it far away from here.'"

"Anything's better than knock-knock jokes," Georgia said. "Nicky's going through a phase."

"We've got loads more," I said. "What did the cheetah say to the witch?"

"Save some for next week, Lida. Georgie, can I borrow my aunt a moment?" Pamela really was an extraordinary girl. Warm. Forthright without being blunt. Look at how she navigated that bit of social triangulation. I know perfectly well I'd have flubbed it, fumbled a hint to the effect of *Georgia, dear, doesn't your mother need help with the ham?*

Georgia peeled away. A pufferfish sigh from Pam. "Lida, what are you on about?"

"Lame jokes," I tried.

"My father's jokes," Pam said. My father's. Not Dad's. Don't think for a moment it escaped my notice.

"I know," I said, stalling a little. I had led us to this point, yes. I had done it deliberately. But I wasn't as canny as I sometimes thought I was. I hadn't the least sense of how to get us from where we were to where I wanted us to be. He's not a factor in my life: what she always said about you. Everything would be okay if I could only get her to say it. "They're still funny," I said.

A blue, assessing stare. "Not really. And you made Georgia uncomfortable."

"She didn't know they were his." Nothing bad had ever touched the Claveries. Aside from Blue's blindness, maybe, but they'd chugged domestically along, scarves up their sleeves.

"*I* knew," Pam said, palm at the base of her throat. "You made *me* uncomfortable."

I'd meant to, at least a little. I waited.

Pamela out-waited me. One of those slight, significant fulcrums I had no idea was coming until I got there: she had never out-waited me before. "It was the conversation," I said. "I was only trying to join in."

Pamela held my gaze. I didn't turn my head. Not at the hollow, rubberized thud of a Claverie grandchild's basketball. Not at the pipe-pitched shout of *keep-away!* or the maternal *Archer Claverie Graham, I told you not in the house.* Claveries by the score. I wished Pam had married into a petite family; I would never get used to her looking so small. "Okay," she said, and the coin-face melted away. "This is me, deciding that you're saying what you're saying."

"That doesn't make any sense."

"It does. It doesn't sound like it does, but it does. Listen. I'm this close to being worried about you." Her thumb and forefinger pinched a sliver of air. "This is me trusting that if something's wrong, you'll trust me enough to say it." It sounded like something her social worker would have spouted, ages back. Across the room, Kath Claverie fussed with a vase of flowers, three daughters in her orbit. Her father stood to join her. The flowers were heavy-petaled, bold, pink as sunburn. I knew nothing about plants. If I had to guess, I'd say they were marigolds. Gladiolas maybe. The names just sounded so chipper.

"Kath really has an eye for flowers," I said, pointing.

"Grace did them," said Pam. "She's taking that class."

I stood there, stalled out, trying not to unpack the implication: this is a thing I should have known. If I really belonged I would know it.

Pam said, "Whatever you're thinking, un-think it." She made her voice sonorous. "Lida Stearl, turn off thy head, go forth, and mingle."

18.

I sought out Blue. Most of the Claverie height was in the legs; seated, Pamela's husband didn't look much taller than any other man. Everything about him was streamlined and efficient. Borderline buzzcut hair. No beard. No stubble, even. Frank had occasionally nicked himself, and he was almost 20/20. I wondered how Blue managed such a clean, regular shave. He cocked his head at my approach. How he managed to hear my footfalls over the gibbering of his three nephews I would never know. Seshet, his guide dog, might have somehow prompted him. She hunched still and silent at his feet, saddled with a vest of orange mesh. Even the littlest Claveries knew not to pet her.

"It's Lida," I said.

"I know." He waved, arm snaking deliberately through the air, avoiding the semicircle of children before him.

"My turn! My turn!" one yelled. Nicky, I thought. Georgia's son, who was going through the knock-knock phase.

Say hello to Lida, Frank would have told him, were you raised in the zoo? But Blue Claverie only laid his hand on his nephew's head and scrunched. Fine blonde strands cropped up between Blue's fingers. "What's this?" Blue asked. "A mop? I don't need a mop."

The three children laughed. Nicky and Benny. Lace ringed the third one's socks. A niece. One of Genevieve's. Emma? Emily.

"Do *you* need a mop, Lida?" Blue tilted his face toward me.

I laughed. "A snow shovel, maybe." I gestured at the drifts outside before remembering who I was talking to.

"It came on fast," Blue said, rubbing his arms against an imaginary chill.

"I know." I was speaking too brightly and too quickly, penance for a gaffe he hadn't even seen me make. "Last Thursday it was almost fine enough for Pam and me to eat outside."

Something not quite affable shadowed his face. He didn't know that Pamela played hooky on Thursdays. I peeked over at Pam. She had drifted back to Georgia. In the middle of the room some Claverie child had got down on hands and knees and crawled, barking, in circles. At Blue's feet Seshet held her preternatural stillness. Pam had trained the guide dog well; Seshet had no idea those antics were the sort of things her species had rights to. I studied Blue. Tried to get a read on how much damage I had done. But I couldn't glean a thing from the unfocused patina of the glass eye, his left, nor from the hard-boiled-egg surface of his right one, under which his iris twitched purposeless back and forth like a quick dark trapped fish.

I forced myself to calm. Pamela wasn't the sort to step out. And even if she were, Blue was safe. Even if he wanted to, Blue Claverie could never harm her. No matter how she hurt him first. He couldn't see to aim.

"Uncle Blue," Benny whined.

"Nephew Benjamin?" The disquiet—or whatever it was—fell away when he smiled.

The nephew smiled back.

"You'll have to join us next time," I said, covering in case Pam needed me to, normalizing, making our one-off luncheon seem a regular thing. "For lunch. If you can make it. I know you're busy."

"Always," said Blue. He extended his arms like a B-movie zombie, though he'd never seen a movie or anything else and I had no earthly idea how he'd picked up the gesture. "Billable hours . . . billable hours . . . must . . . have . . . billable hours . . ."

The collected children shrieked.

"Billable hours . . . or, what's this? A bug?" Blue pinched Benny's nose, "Yes! A bumpy little bug. Take it away! I don't need a bug."

"It's not a bug." Benny's voice came thin, like a telephone operator's. Nicky and Emily shrieked.

"Are you sure?" Blue asked, putting on his stern attorney voice. The child nodded.

"It feels like a bug. A roly-poly Benny bug."

"It's a nose!"

Blue released the child with an exaggerated sigh. Knock-knock Nicky darted toward his uncle's hand. Blue cupped the boy's ear and wagged it back and forth. "What's this? Lida, can you tell what it is?"

I wasn't a Claverie. I didn't know this game. "It's an ear," I said, wishing I was the madcap sort of adult capable of guessing.

A bracing guffaw. "Lida's kidding. I can tell it's not an ear. It's a butterfly!"

Benny and Emily squealed for their turns. A fourth and fifth child joined the group, shrieking full tilt.

Blue went for Nicky's other ear. "Another one! Another butterfly!"

I stood there, mute.

Blue jiggled the ears. "Just look at all these butterflies." His grin spread, exaggerated, clownish. "Who needs butterflies? No one needs them."

Giggles. Not from me. Last Thursday, and this. The unreadable twist of Blue's mouth. Last Thursday, and this.

Benny grabbed his own ear. "Butterflies," he demanded, tugging with a free hand on Blue's sleeve.

"Butterflies," echoed Emily.

"Butterflies," repeated Benny, copying the copycat.

"Butterflies," the newcomers joined in with no small urgency.

Blue's hands traveled. Ear, nose, hair. "I don't need butterflies. I don't need little bugs. I don't need a mop. You know what I need?" His arms folded around the child's frame. My throat squeezed close, as if it was trying to force down a hardboiled egg. A bit of me would break to hear what Blue was sure to say: you, Nicky, you. You're just what I need.

On the center rug, the barking girl continued to turn. Whatever G she belonged to should have swooped in ages ago. Every time she—Addison? Tess?—made a full turn I caught some new feature of Blue's. The slight bump of the Claverie nose. The thin sharp eyebrows. That wide, unreadable mouth.

"Yoo-hoo!" Kath Claverie clinked a glass beside the buffet. Claveries froze: Georgia and Pam like cutout paper dolls; Grace and Genevieve, flanking their mother; Kath's father slumping hangdog over his cup; Addison—it *was* Addison—mid yelp; the snow-dusted children tumbling in from the yard; the card-playing G husbands; Blue with one hand on Ben's head, one on Emily's; Nicky beside him on one foot, making an exaggerated show of his struggle not to fall.

I held still too. Not one person in the room looked like me. Kath brushed her bangs out of her face. "Linner's on."

Claveries swarmed.

I slid a hand into my pocket, checking once more for Kath's ID. At this and every linner, she'd laid out a display of peanut butter at the far end of the buffet, satellite to the home-cooked spread—the ham, the salads, the red potatoes still hot in their skins. The Claverie children made straight for the sandwich section—a constellation of jars, chunky, creamy, and everything anyone could imagine pairing with peanut butter—to assemble their revolting concoctions. Popcorn, tortilla chips, cheddar cheese, bologna, and pickles took their place alongside marshmallow spread, cut apples and bananas, chocolate chips. At my first linner, there hadn't been any jam. I'd commented—just an aside, really, I avoided peanut butter, it caked in my teeth—and the next week five sticky varieties appeared, bright as stained glass.

At the grownup end, ham fell from the bone in spirals, sugar-crusted and warm. Something smelled strongly of pepper, and Kath had put out a bowl of strawberries, bold as rubies, and, in November, almost as expensive. I stood elbow to elbow beside her. I examined her neck. The skin was almost smooth beside the birthstone necklace she always wore—my own, I knew, sagged with lines. Someone had warned Kath and she had listened; the neck is as exposed to sun and air as the face. Unless moistened and buffed with the same diligence, it'll be quick to show age.

Kath caught me looking.

"You must have been in the kitchen all day," I said.

She shrugged. "It's nothing, really."

"At least the kiddos could try it."

"It doesn't matter." And because she was Kath Claverie, matriarch of a sunny clan never touched by terror or by shame, she was able to say in good faith what followed. "The whole point of family," Kath said, "is to make things easy on one another."

19.

The next morning I dressed for Riverview. Simple slacks and a well-pressed shirt, jazzed up with one of my better scarves. The suit last time had been an error, formal and conspicuous. Instead of Frostmouth, a man was at the desk. He didn't give me any fuss over Kath's ID. Nor did he glance at the logbook where I wrote her name, the K spiked and deliberate, as it was on the license signature, the T crossed on a slant. It was as I often said: Women are better with the detail work.

The Riverview carpet was the color of under-eye circles. Each door displayed a cutout turkey, inked with its occupant's name and a tagalong exclamation point. Each turkey had a tail of construction paper feathers onto which residents had evidently been encouraged to list the things that they were thankful for. Alice! had illustrated her feathers with fat crayons, her scrawlings as indecipherable as Pammie's kindergarten chickie-birds. On her lone yellow feather, Janine! had printed the word *steak* as bold as you please. Herman!'s bird had three times the plumage of any other and every feather was crowded with names. Showoff Herman! Aside from Kath's necklace I'd never seen anything so tacky. Marjorie!'s turkey was wordless, its feathers a symmetrical fan. Someone had completed it on her behalf. It had to have been a serious stroke then, if your mother wasn't up for the task.

I didn't knock.

The room was private but very small. You would envy her window, Clarence, though the blinds were drawn. They'd painted her walls for false cheer, wan yellow, the color of undercooked eggs. The television was on. The room flickered.

A gummy mewl.

Your mother sat erect, bolstered by pillows. Her mouth drooped, comma-like. She'd got heavier. Her limbs mounded under the blanket. She looked like a thing a child might sculpt. Her eyes, blue, like Pam's, like yours, moved toward me in tiny increments. First the television screen. Then a patch of wall beside my hip. They paused at the pleats in my slacks. They rose to my face. The live half of her mouth stretched to a thin slash. I listened for the hard *i* that would mean she was trying for Lida.

A low release of breath. A wet intake. A grist-ground series of ch-ch-chs.

The television advertised a brand of leaner cat chow. I switched it off. "I thought I should see you," I said. "Now that I know you're in town. We haven't really talked since the funeral."

A dull huff from the bed. Frank and I had kept our struggle close and private. The steady tattoo of too-short pregnancies, the paperwork and hope winging their way toward Korea. Barbra knew, and you knew, about our losses and our plans to adopt. The both of you'd promised to be discreet. It was possible that in the parking lot Marjorie hadn't known the full twist of what she was saying.

Another noise from the bed, a flat *gluck*.

It was still a wretched thing to say.

She was still your mother.

We were burying my sister. She'd had no right to intrude on our goodbyes.

Her eyes wheeled away from me. Time had yellowed the whites. Thick fluid accumulated at the tear ducts. It looked like Elmer's glue.

"Never mind me, Marjorie," I said. "I only came to look at your shoes." That saying of Ma's: know what you want and you'll never want knowing. I'd been a tangled, nervy mess at linner yesterday, scattered and reactive. Today, I'd be best served going after something simple: black pumps with visible stitching, squat heels in two-tone suede. Shoes that had popped up with Pam in repeat photographs. Shoes whose feet I had been unable to identify. I should've brought the snapshots along for a bit of compare and contrast.

A dresser stood below the TV, three faux wood drawers. The first held a stack of cotton smocks not unlike the one Marjorie currently wore. I moved the lavender one to the top so it would be next in line when the staff came in to change her. I had it in me to be generous, Clarence, and it was a shade most people looked well in. The second and third drawers were empty. The Spartan bathroom had no under-sink storage. I checked behind the blinds, even knowing that was preposterous, and under the bed, my knees protesting slightly. Clean linoleum. Credit Riverview with that much. "Marjorie. Where are your shoes?"

Her eyes drifted to her feet. They focused briefly. She was in there, still ticking, that mother of yours.

"Shoes, Marjorie." Their absence spoke volumes about her prognosis. No one at Riverview expected her up and about. "Shoes," I said again, and struggled to my feet, stepping out of my square-toed flats. I raised them high. Their soles were scuffed. I'd never seen them at this angle before. Marjorie wasn't looking. I clapped the shoes together with a delicious smack. "I need to know if you were watching us all these years. Sneaking your feet into our pictures. Reporting back to Clarence."

Your mother's eyes found me at that. Quick as a pip and twice as twice as sharp, right when I spoke your name.

"Oh. So you want to talk about Clarence?" I liked the sad, sparse room then, liked that there was no visitor's chair. "All right then.

Clarence. First time I ever heard of him Barbra told me he thought she'd left strands of her hair all over his pillow on purpose. You know, to mark her territory? Barbra thought it was hilarious." Your mother blinked fast—maybe that eye gunk was bothering her—but did not look away. I thwacked the shoes together. I thwacked them again, closer, when she didn't flinch. "It wasn't funny, Marjorie. I should have known then there was something wrong with him. Thinking a woman's scheming when she just sheds a bit of hair. Thinking she's that much out to get him." Instead I'd thought: typical Barbra. She'd liked the idea of shocking big sis with her collection of men, their collection of women. And me still blushing at the idea that Frank and my first fellow Martin Dorsey lived on the same planet. Those were an important ten years between us.

Your mother grunted. Her eyes wandered off again.

Her bed had sturdy guardrails. They reverberated, metallic, when I brought the shoes down. "I want to know why he thought he was worth the trouble. Mama's boy. Was it you who taught him he was worth all that?" I am not the kind of woman who loses control. But your mother had made an animal sound. Right when I spoke my sister's name.

From the bed, a slow, gluey blink and a damp and chesty wheeze.

The tricky thing, and your mother had no business knowing it, was this: I could see Barbra in your bed, pinching a single hair between thumb and forefinger. The split ends would have to go regardless, waste not want not. Barbra smiles, so lucky she's blonde. The hair stands out well against the dark pillow.

"It was you, wasn't it? It was. You taught him that. You raised him."

Her vowels swam at me through mucous.

"If I should have known," and I should've known, "then you should have known."

A pitchy lowing.

"I liked him, Marjorie." Better than that Bruce of Barbra's with his damp handshake. Better than that Chuck who dropped her for the blandest little drip in school. And that Stuart who tore up her midterm. Better than What's-his-sideburns. And What's-his-beard. Doctor What's-his-beard by now. The way he went on about med school, like he was the first to enroll since Hippocrates.

Another incomprehensible sound came out of your mother.

"You should have known. You're his mother. And you said *I* don't know what it means to—" The worst thing anyone said to me, ever. And at my sister's funeral. "Look what a job you did."

Her reeling eyes found my face and stilled. And then she spat. Actually spat. At me, though it didn't reach. Wet dribbled her chin.

I could have clapped her head between my shoes. I composed myself. I put the shoes on the floor and clasped my hands together to still them. I kept my voice calm. Light, despite the words. "You're disgusting," I said. When my mother and Frank took sick, their bulk fell from their frames. Their skins sagged like clothesline sheets. Nothing in the universe truly disappears. All their lifeweight had piled onto Marjorie. Skin flowed down her neck and her eyes looked like they'd been pushed in by a pair of thumbs.

She made a sucking noise. Air rushed in over teeth.

It would be better to go like Frank did, lightened at the end of everything. I moved toward Marjorie. Her gaze was unfocused and her pupils undilated. "Marjorie? Do you hear? You're disgusting." A drop of spit swelled at the point of her chin, gravity drawn, a small wet stalactite. Her face was recognizable despite its wrinkles. Yes, it out-pruned my own, but by a narrower margin than I'd like. If Pam had to get something from that woman, I hoped it was the skin. "Disgusting and weak," I said, leaning close. Our lawyer had drafted the agreement. No Pam visits for your mother, not ever. In return you got your three letters. In Marjorie's place I don't think I'd have agreed. "I'd have fought for Pamela," I whispered. "Skulking at the margins wouldn't be enough for *me*."

But your mother was no longer tracking the conversation; her mouth had gone slack. A thin column of saliva tethered her top teeth to her bottom ones. The strand broke; another fine trickle made its way down. Marjorie blinked. With her eyes closed she was just an old woman. Tired. Well, I was too. A chest noise from the bed, perhaps a damp attempt at words. I went for the Kleenex in my purse. Your mother was wrong, Clarence. I knew how to properly mother; it wasn't in me to leave that wet on her chin. Her skin was cakey and had a surprising amount of give, much like a good dinner roll. I crumpled the tissue. Riverview really should provide trash cans.

"Pam's grown up well," I said, stepping back into my shoes. The words would have felt supplicating if I hadn't. Properly shod, I was simply stating fact: I had done a better job with my charge than Marjorie had with hers. "She's turned out perfectly," I said, as if the words eradicated the possibility of Pamela stepping out on her husband, of her penpalling about with you, of whatever mad course her Thursdays had devolved into.

Your mother's eyelids fluttered. Blue Lusk eyes. Marjorie in the parking lot. Marjorie in her sickbed. The first one somewhere inside the second, waiting like the fuse of a bomb.

But Pam was Pam Claverie now; this woman had no claim on her. "She smiles all the time," I said. Pammie's plaster teeth rested behind my bathroom mirror, across the river, safe in the townhouse. Both sets. "She used to have the biggest buck teeth. The grownup ones that came in after Arizona. They should've come in straight. Her mouth had plenty of room. They went crooked from the pressure of her tongue. She pushed them constantly, year after year. Textbook case, Marjorie. The mark of a nervous child. We both know what made her that way. But her teeth are lovely now. It was me. I did that. They're beautiful." There was no point in my being here; I wanted to go home. I wanted to hold those plaster impressions. I'd done well; I had. And I would keep on doing it, keep her safe. Those molds. From the Before to the After had been the best work of my life.

Your mother needed ChapStick. The limp side of her mouth was practically scales. Cracks in her lips deepened as she made another word that didn't sound like anything. Another bead of drool budded. I watched it swell in silence. It pearled out beyond her lip; it toppled and dribbled down. I fumbled for my lip balm. I uncapped it and the room filled with the scent of false cherry and wax. I smeared the balm across her lips. So her skin wouldn't flake off, I ran in the direction of the chap. I hummed a melodic scrap of lullaby, properly maternal, a little song I'd sung to Pam. I capped the ChapStick. I wouldn't be keeping it, not after it had touched those lips. And of course they hadn't provided a wastebasket. I stood it, centered, on her nightstand. Her keepers would see it. Perhaps it would spur them to mind her better, pay due attention to their charge.

20.

Maisie, it was good of you to write again.

I know I was harsh last time around. Until mail call today I guessed you took it too much to heart. It wasn't a good feeling. Life's lonely here, and if I scared you off it would be worse than before and I'd have only my damn self to blame (a feeling that, believe me, I am used to).

If we were in the world, there'd be more to do to make it up to you. I've been away a long time, but I assume young women still take flowers and the like by way of apology. All I can send is an explanation (though I stand by what I said if not how I said it. I have to have the truth from you). Guy down the row's in for doing three girls in his neighborhood and a little college girl too. Rape (I don't like writing about this to you) as well as murder. He's dirty too. Most guys reek on the way to the shower. Harris you smell coming and going.

We get one phone call a week. Ten minutes, collect. And this idiot thinks it's a good chance to jump his guard. Manages to get the phone cord around his neck. Officers pull him off before the guard even blacks out. So Harris goes in isolation and let me tell you he doesn't win any popularity contests when he gets back. Because Warden Kimpton thinks the rest of us are going to start getting ideas. He takes the phone away. For the whole pod. Just like that. I miss three weeks of hearing a voice out there talk like I was a real person.

Add it up and that would be a whole half hour of at least my words escaping.

Maisie, you know I am an intelligent man. Another semester and I'd have graduated college. I should have forbearance. By now I should have learned it. The privileges they give and take don't make me human. They only make me _feel_ that way. I didn't have to act like less than a man. I am ashamed at my temper, especially as you only somewhat deserved it. You aren't the one who wronged me most, but you were there and so I chose you. You're right, Maisie. Your lies were largely omissions. A tiny insult, all is forgiven now. My world is small and so I gave it to you in one piece. Yours is enormous. It makes sense for you to give it to me bit by bit.

So give and I will be, as ever, your

Clarence

21.

Thursday came and I had a plan. I loaded a cardboard box into my trunk. Pamela's old yearbooks and report cards, a crumbly corsage that smelled more of dank than of roses. With everyone else, I'd been quick to de-clutter. But I had no way to guess what Pam might want again someday, and she had lost more than her fair share already. I would tell her I only wanted a head start on holiday cleaning, that I just wanted to drop the boxes off. Pam would be home. It was Thursday and she was up to something. I'd feign surprise. Fuss and palm her cool head for fever. A janitor was cleaning the lobby carpets. I had to shout for the doorman to hear me. Pamela answered his buzz right away. Lida? Her confused voice gritted over the loudspeaker. Sure, send her on up. The doorman nodded toward the elevator, as if I was doddering and hadn't heard for myself.

I didn't have to knock. Pam stood in the doorway waiting for me, haloed by window light. She held out her arms. I thought she wanted to embrace but she only lifted the box from my hands.

"Your doorman didn't offer," I said. She wore sweats and a messy ponytail. Not an affair then. Or perhaps her someone wasn't here yet. Perhaps he liked her as she was.

"Not his job." She shrugged. "There's a dolly in the box room if we need it."

Pamela and Blue lived on the tenth floor of an Art Deco building just blocks from Barnes Jewish. The night shrill of ambulances had kept her up the first month they moved in. Sometimes I weighed the good of that against the bad: proximity to a nationally ranked ER versus a neighborhood that needed doctors so adept with burns and bullets and stabs.

"Does he do security? Your doorman? He didn't check my ID."

"I told him you were fine. Gary does his job."

Now was the time to ask: and why aren't you at yours, Pam? She cocked her head, exposing the smooth plane of her cheek for a kiss. An easy-peasy, companionable gesture. Instead of speaking, I obliged.

She set the box on the coffee table and busied herself with its contents.

"I planned to leave it with Gary but it turns out you're home. What a treat." I sank into the nearest chair, a hand-me-down from Kath that I had helped Pam slipcover. "But not for you, I guess. Home sick? Or playing hooky?" Again, I didn't add. This Thursday, and the last, and the last.

"I'll be okay." Pam smiled, not lying, not exactly. She opened a yearbook. "Good grief. Look at Mr. Simon's ears. We used to call him Sugarbowl."

"I'll run out for ginger ale."

"What?"

"Since you're sick."

"My stomach's fine." She palmed her waistband. Barbra wouldn't have sounded so defensive. She was a much better liar, and even she got caught. "It's my head." Pam's hand rose to her crown. "My temples." Her index fingers rubbed small circles next to her eyes. Liar. I wanted to drop *knee cap* or *elbow* into the conversation to see if she'd palm those spots too.

"You shouldn't have buzzed me up if it was all that bad. Maybe we should take the phone off the hook."

"Put the phone back, Lida."

"But your head . . ." She might be waiting for his call. The name she dropped last week. No reason and from nowhere. *Hector.* Strong furtive hands like my first fellow Martin Dorsey.

"This really isn't helping my head." Pam crossed to the windows and shut her eyes like she had an actual headache. The windows were the best feature of their corner unit. They flooded the apartment with light. If the landlord was smart, he upped the rent. Pam must enjoy it, which showed how much Blue wanted her happy. To budget the extra for a view he couldn't share. The kids were just starting out and I hoped they could afford it.

"I'm making you tea," I announced, "and soup if you have the right noodles." Forest Park rolled out beyond Pam's profile. Gray winter trees spiked out of the ground.

Pam watched me cross to her kitchen. "I really have a ton of work to do."

"Not while you're home sick. They don't pay you enough for that." Pam's cabinets were better organized than most shops, everything stacked in tidy columns for Blue's fingers. The couple stocked almost as much tea as Green Mother Grocery. I pulled out blends for tranquility, good dreams, energy, concentration, cold, flu and PMS.

"Lida, I really don't need this." She stood in the doorway. She registered the PMS tea in my hand and looked away again. Still my Pammie. If she couldn't even think about her monthly with me in the room, this wasn't going to be a comfortable conversation.

"It's no trouble, really. It does me good to know I help—" I am not a stupid woman, Clarence. Her stance said plainly I wasn't wanted. Hector could be here right now. She'd shrugged into the sweats at the sound of the buzzer. Hector was in the apartment, hiding. "Maybe it's dust," I said. "An allergy headache. I could sweep out the closets, under the bed."

"I don't need you to sweep. Maybe you should go?" A dry cough, blatant. "Who knows if I'm contagious."

"If you want me to leave, I'll leave. You don't have to soft sell it with a fake cough."

Light caught the frizz of her curls. She didn't look like you or like Barbra. Simply her freckled self. As long as we held off speaking I could pretend she was still that quiet girl who had come into my care. She hadn't grown up at all; she'd only been stretched. Small divots appeared below her cheekbones. She ground the wet rolls of her cheeks between her molars.

"That isn't healthy for the skin inside," I said at last.

"Oh my God. You said you'd go—"

"You'll rub yourself raw and—"

"Lida, you can't be here. I've got work and I'm cranky as all get out and you can't just come here and have me drop everything."

That meant she had something *to* drop. Some*one*. Hector.

I ached all over, exhausted. And, simply, sad. I felt it heavy and cool in the pit of me, like a great bubble of mercury. Frank would've been better at all of this. So affable, so reasonable. So much the reason Pam and I didn't know how to argue. We care for each other. We never yell. When you X, I feel Y because Z. The formula didn't work without him. Sadness forked through me, efficient as veins. The silence between us was terrible and long. When the phone jangled, ending it, I was relieved.

"I have to take this," said Pam. "And you have to go." It wasn't Blue on the phone. Blue Claverie she would let me stay and hear.

A second ring. I left the kitchen. I stopped just outside the door, against the wall, where Pammie wouldn't see me. "I'm going to duck into the washroom," I lied. I hunched low so she wouldn't see me reflected in her windows. Piercing sunlight, wasted in winter. In the park, snow had to be melting.

A third ring. It was 1:58. Maybe they were meant to meet at two o'clock. He was running late. He'd bring her flowers. It wouldn't be suspicious. Not if he chose a kind Blue wouldn't smell. Light caught my watch and refracted. Pam used to leap after glow dots, clapping clumsy hands. And further back, Barbra. I'd forgotten. When she was just learning to walk I tricked her into chasing them.

In the kitchen, Pam picked up, a little short of breath. "Yes," she said, "I'll accept."

We sent her to sleepover camp the summer she was eleven. *Call if you need us,* I told her, *we'll come right away and get you. Here's a roll of quarters. If you lose them, this is how you call collect.*

Hector must be at a pay phone. At least they were being careful.

"I've missed you too," said Pam.

She sent us two letters in her two weeks at the camp. Just the two and they'd been meal tickets. No admission to the mess hall without a quick note home.

"No, you first. How are you holding up?"

A tenor fuzzed from the receiver. Not Blue, who could've sung Escamillo in another life. I drew my knees to my chest.

"Well, I *was* worried," said Pam, and then, "Yes. I know it's out of your hands."

My own hands felt jittery but at least it didn't show. I pressed my palms against the floor. They could stand to vacuum more thoroughly. Long strands clung to the rug. For Christmas, I would get them a cleaning service. Frank and I had always had one; it was easily the best way to avoid spats about chores. I should've thought of it sooner. More of the burden had to fall to Pam in this marriage; picture Blue wrangling a vacuum. No wonder she'd started looking elsewhere. She was due a bit of glamour.

"Here?" she said. "Not all that much really. The center's a circus. The new puppies finally came."

I knew all about the puppies. Born two weeks ago. My stomach roiled for Pam. Hector wasn't even making her a priority; if she was telling him now, she must not have heard from him in a long time.

If it *was* him. Cement grouted my ribs. The collect call. I knew and Maisie knew: they hadn't let you near the phone in a long while either.

Pamela wouldn't.

Only, when I called last Thursday she answered on the first ring. Like she'd been waiting by the phone.

Hector. What on earth had I been thinking? *Hector.*

Pamela said, "My boss wanted to name them all after all the Star Trek captains. Last time around it was kinds of red wine. And he was on a world mythology kick for a while."

Pamela would never.

"No, no. We always do the naming at the center. Lucky for the dogs it was my turn this time."

Never, ever.

But she *was* writing you. You had no reason to lie to Maisie about that.

"No, not really. They say it's to simplify our records, but I think it's to make things easier on the puppy raisers. When they have to give them back. Yeah, that's right. If you don't name a dog it's never really going to be yours."

You were the one who called the day Pam was born. Mother and daughter healthy. We're calling her Pamela Clare. I could hear you glow at the middle name. Clare from Clarence. I tried not to use it.

"Otto, Asa, Emme, Nan, and Bob."

Barbra collected palindromes. You were the one who talked her out of Anna or Eve.

"I know, I know she did. You told me before. That's why I chose them."

Ice all through me. I hadn't accidentally spoken aloud; Pam's voice was light, no hint of exasperation. And there was one other soul on earth who could've known to say those things to her. That was *your* voice in her ear.

In my lap my winter hands were pale as chicken cutlets. For weeks I'd worn gloves. As if they could protect. Pam or me or anyone. I had goose bumps. I gagged. Pam didn't hear. I pressed my tongue to the roof of my mouth. Its bumps were impossibly distinct. Skin and tongue. The whole of me was sandpaper.

"I guess you're right," Pam was saying. "Blue thinks so too."

A feebler woman than I would wait wet-eyed till her niece hung up. If she tried to stand her knees would rap together and she wouldn't know, as I did, to press them together and draw strength from that buttressing. She'd lack the will to even think of leaving. Or she'd look back at her niece and freeze. She'd see Pam only as the series of moments that led to this one: Pamela's fat tongue worming out of a baby tooth gap, Pam's ten-year-old panda eyes after a botched mascara experiment, Pam's painted toes at the edge of the diving block, chlorine reflecting the streamlined blade of her body. But I was strong—not so strong I didn't see small Pam inside the grown one—but strong enough.

I saw Pamela; she stood like a stork in her kitchen, exposing the dirty underside of her sock. Pammie could never stay still on the phone. She was like Frank, who paced and spun. She'd bound herself up tight in phone cord. It crisscrossed her chest, half pinning her arms. It was either great strength or great weakness that let me leave her alone in that apartment, your voice in her ear, her voice so trusting, her body so trussed.

22.

I went to Riverview. I brought Pamela's teeth. I signed the book and the weekend desk man waved me down the hall. The door turkeys looked rumpled and droopy. Your mother's room smelled of cleaning solvents and stewed carrots.

She hadn't moved much since my last visit. They had her in the lavender shift and she lolled a touch less than before. The staff had tucked her blankets taut, but her legs looked alive and willful. Only the bedding batted them down. A bit of top sheet sag and those legs might walk Marjorie clean out of Riverview. Your mother stared intently at her own hands. The paralyzed right one lay in her lap. The mobile left hovered above it, circling and buzzard deliberate. It darted down. It curled its crippled partner finger by finger into a fist. Fingers kept unfurling. She tried again. Her fist never quite set.

"Hello again, Marjorie."

Her right flop fist opened out, another failed attempt. She looked at me then. Energy had come to her trailing down mouth. No longer a comma. A comet.

"You look better."

She snuffed. No snot on her lip, needing to be sniffed up. I sniffled back at her in case that was her attempt at greeting. "I've brought Pam's teeth. Remember? I told you about those." The only smiles I was likely to get these days. I didn't say it aloud. Like Ma always said: pity's a coin that earns no interest.

Her left hand reached out for me. Her right made a sorry little half-twitch.

"Can you talk yet? I want you to try."

She blinked. She made no sound.

"I need you to tell me what you know about his calling Pam."

Both hands flopped about. She wanted the teeth.

"No. Not until you tell me. How long has this been going on?" Once she hit middle school, Pam was the one to bring in the mail. She'd had a very influential Earth Sciences teacher and wanted to make sure we recycled the junk. The bus dropped her home an hour before the workday's end. Plenty of time for a private penpal. Daddy, I'm worried about my history grade. Daddy, I want a dog and Lida says no. Daddy, I'm lonely and I don't think Lida will ever understand.

A rasp came from your mother, followed by a series of vowels.

"What does he want from her?"

Grunt. A low, sad sound, nothing vulgar about it. The effort brought a flush to her cheeks. Either that or she was blushing, ashamed of her disobliging tongue. Imagine that. She hadn't had feelings enough to color at the funeral.

She had small hands. Stubby fingers, inelegant, not like yours or Pamela's.

"Please, Marjorie. I don't know what to do." Hearing that had to make her happy. After all this time. I watched her face. It strained redder than ever. Her head bobbled with an attempted word. Her left hand reached out.

"I'll let you hold Pam's teeth, but only if you promise to try. I need you to talk." I pressed a plaster crescent into each hand. "I need you to tell me some things." Her left hand wrapped greedy around Pam's Afters. The fingers of her right twitched toward the Befores as if drawn by a magnet. "Don't just squeeze. Look at them. See how pretty? That's her now. Perfectly even. Careful. They're breakable."

She kept good focus once I asked her to. Her eyes drifted from left to right and back again. Saliva ballooned from between her lips. The room was quiet; I heard the bubble pop. The spit didn't go far, just a blot on her lip. A second bubble budded.

"Marjorie. Pay attention. Those teeth are Pam's. Now can you try and talk to me? What do you know about the phone calls?"

A third bubble came and some kind of chortle.

In a baby, maybe, it would be endearing.

A fourth bubble.

Your mother was old and twisted as a root. "Marjorie. Not while you're holding Pam's teeth."

A fifth bubble. No wonder she always needed ChapStick. Marjorie made a smacking sound and moved her left hand in a gleeful jiggle.

"If you can't listen and not spit . . . I didn't have to come and you know it. I didn't have to share." I snatched back Pam's smiles. There was no help for me here. I'd have to make do on my own. Marjorie's fingers jittered. I wrapped the teeth in tissues and tucked them into my purse. Her left hand rose in my direction. I took it and laid it down on her blanket. She hadn't got sun in an age. Her skin had paled to the point of glowing. Green veins forked. Not long ago they must have put her on an IV. It had left her badly bruised.

"Frank said IVs don't hurt as much as they look. When he was in the hospital." Everyone made soap-eating faces when I spoke of it. His sickbed was beside the window. Sun or storms made no difference. Nothing changed wan hospital light. "He died. Almost three years now. I don't know if you knew that."

Irregular wheezes rose from her chest.

"I'm all alone."

A grunt. Easier to bear in its way than generic, social sympathy.

"Except for Pam." The ugliness in the apartment wasn't any of Marjorie's business.

Her good hand flipped back and forth, dead white. That really was a terrible bruise.

"Frank could have been lying about the IV. For Pam. She hates needles. Even sewing needles make her green. She still needs me to re-attach her buttons." Though she hadn't asked in months. Maybe she'd learned to be less rough on her clothes. Or she turned to Kath now. Kath who wouldn't know Ma's secret: strong coat thread with the first pass, then delicate to cover.

Your mother's chest crested and caved. Another hiss. We both knew why needles threw Pam. Marjorie's left cheek dimpled slightly as she molared at the slick inside.

"Pammie does that too. It's not good for her cheeks."

Marjorie turned her palm back up, a little cup to catch my words. Her eyes—your eyes, Pam's—were very wide. The black beads of her pupils spread out, doing their best to draw in light. She didn't have any right to know anything about Pam. We had a deal, fair's fair. She gave up the right and so you got your letters. And you were getting more than that. Much more. Calls on Thursdays. The funny little lilt when Pam's words ended in *O*.

"All you Lusks are getting more of her than you deserve," I said.

Marjorie flipped her hand bruise side down, then bruise side up. She did it again, fascinated. Bruise down. Bruise up. No one ever listened to me. My bones felt brittle and I sank to my knees. They really needed to put in a chair. Marjorie made a fist with her left hand and released.

"There's nothing in that hand, stop it. I'm talking."

Her hand stilled. My fingers itched to trace the bruise.

"With Frank gone, I thought I'd have to watch out for the Claveries," I said. "There are so many of them and you should see these people, Marjorie, they're just like you were, so grabby for her. I never thought to watch out for Clarence. I thought he was locked properly away." Marjorie's hand rose. It carved the air in fantastic swirls. "We were good to Pam. She always came first. I didn't think he had a chance over me. But *he* thinks it. He's trying to take her." Hairs spiked the caverns of your mother's inner ear. There was no help for me in Riverview. My legs ached from kneeling. "I don't want him loving her. He was meant to love my sister." Maisie Keller was twenty-three and just ripe. If you had to love let it fall to her, Clarence. Twenty-three years old. I hadn't even heard of you then. I'd only barely met Frank. I broke poor Martin Dorsey's heart. See me now and you wouldn't believe it. But I had purpose now and a keen memory; I still knew how it was done.

Your mother sputtered. I stood. She pressed her thumb to her index finger. It rested there, brief as a kiss, and rose again. Her thumb moved and met with her middle finger, then ring, then pinkie. Along the row and back. Something like a smile came to her mouth and I turned away. I couldn't talk to Pam about the phone calls; she was smart; she would work out how I knew and what I'd done. I couldn't confront Pam, but I could be Maisie and distract you. We could protect Pam, Maisie and I. I turned from your mother, whose thumb and fingers were still touching then parting, touching then parting. The last thing I needed was the sight of Lusk fingers at that kind of work. Not when plenty of smart folks believe it's opposable thumbs and not our language or love or souls that makes us human.

23.

Pamela didn't call and didn't call and didn't call and didn't call. I returned from Riverview and hunkered down by the phone. The weekend passed and then the week. I told Kath not to expect me at linner. I invented a Saturday bird-watching society. I bookmarked an Internet list of credible birds to cite when we went for our walks. Pam didn't call. I feigned another bout of flu at Thanksgiving. Kath brought a cooler of leftovers the next Monday, foil-wrapped and Tupperwared. Pam and Blue phoned and Blue carried the narrow conversation: the state of my gastrointestinal system, the anise Pamela'd added to the cranberries instead of cloves. At Riverview, paper Christmas trees replaced the door turkeys and Pam didn't call. I bought another round of organic oranges and Pam didn't call. I did my Christmas shopping: a weekly cleaning service for Pam and Blue, though Frank and I'd only had a girl in every other week. Pam didn't call. A two-tone, modern brooch for Kath that evoked the shape of a crane. Pam didn't call and didn't call. For the Claverie children, sundry Legos. Every afternoon I went to the post office. I took my time walking. Pam wasn't calling and it would serve her right if she got the machine.

A letter waited in the post box. I didn't bother with gloves anymore.

My fat lawyer was here last week. No news. Do people still say "no news is good news?" In here no news is just normal.

What's not normal is a lawyer driving three hours to Stemble just to say "no news." Something's up. I see it in his face. Fat should wobble, right? When he lies his rolls kind of gel. His whole face goes stiff. I know they'll read him easy in court.

Maisie, don't let yourself beef up. It isn't healthy for one thing. They feed us grease in here. We don't get space to move. Most men pack it on pretty quick (no point staying healthy with what we've got ahead). And weight's more than weight. You could get so tired carrying yourself around.

And don't forget you're a woman. Things go much harder in the world for a woman the more space she takes up.

The things I could have told you, Clarence, about the world and the hard ways it goes. But Maisie Keller knew nothing. I keep fit, I had her gush, I walk and walk. The sky is beautiful. I think of you.

I told Kath that I had spied a Horned grebe. I told Kath I'd spied a King rail. I did not ask after Pam; I did not want it to seem as though we weren't in steady contact.

I went to Marjorie plenty. My mother would've had a pat, pithy saying to sum up why; I'll simply admit that I was lonesome and that it was a balm knowing your mother would be there, stable and waiting, exactly where I left her last. One afternoon she kept fidgeting her palm. For an elated moment or so I thought she was trying for hand-signs. *Does palm up mean yes?* I asked. She palmed up. *Does palm down mean no?* Palm up. *Do you want me to leave?* Palm down. No. I was sure she meant no. She wanted me; someone did. And then: *Are you Marjorie Lusk?* Palm down—no. *Are you healthy?* Palm up—yes. *Are you happy?* Palm up; so much nonsense.

The Tuesday before Christmas, Pam finally called again. I decided to be blunt. That saying of Ma's: blunt blades slice sharpest. "Pammie, who was that on the phone in your apartment?"

"What? Oh, that. Just Trish." Her college roommate. Telling, how she didn't ask *in my apartment when?*

"She's a sweet girl. I hope she's doing all right."

"Fine. Great. She's great."

"Not in any trouble?"

"Trish? No. Never."

"But she called you collect."

A long pause. "I didn't call to talk about that. It's in the rearview."

"You turned me out of your house."

"And the Oscar for drama goes to Lida. It was the middle of the day and I was unfit for human company."

"Are you sure Trish is doing okay?"

"No. She went back in time and accidentally stopped her parents from meeting. It's a whole space-time mess."

"You don't have to be so smart."

"Can you once in your life just relax? We'll see you at Kath's for Christmas."

I spent an hour at Papyrus, choosing Maisie's Christmas card for you. It had patches you could scratch for the scents of pine and ginger, pungent and patently false. The sense of smell is tethered strongest to our *actual* sense. I hoped the card cut deep.

On Christmas Eve, I joined the Claveries for seven fishes. Everyone was issued a new pair of pajamas. After presents the next morning they had pancakes. Frank and I always broke out the waffle iron, let the contraption earn its annual keep.

Cutout champagne flutes and then early Valentines replaced the trees on Riverview's doors and your letters came and came. For a man so shut away from the world you had a preposterous number of opinions about it.

Whenever I wish I could see you, Maisie, I remember my daughter's husband is blind and you can care so much for a person and never ever see her. It's good her husband's blind, I think, even though my daughter's plenty pretty. I've been a husband. It's better to go in knowing you're blind than to wake up and find out you are.

The closest you ever came to telling Maisie what you did, and why.
You ignored it, mostly, and dreamed.

Best job in the world has to be trucker. They get to always be on the move. Miles and miles of country to cover. Maybe I'd pick up a hitchhiker. Maybe she would be a lot like you. My daughter and I had a bit of a car trip that last day I had her. I didn't have a plan. I never exactly thought I'd be in that situation. My head was full up of all those other plans I'd had, before, with my wife. I didn't know where I should run to. Thing is, with all the planning the wife and I did, all the places we were going to get to someday, we never actually got around to getting the kid a passport. I wish I'd thought straighter. Still, I'd have to have been an idiot not to know there was a good chance I'd wind up in a place like Stemble. You can bet I paid attention. I remember the moon over the highway. Forget the pyramids. Highways are the most beautiful things man has ever built.

Maisie, it's getting harder not to pace. Duane Pelly's begun to. He does it day and night.

Every letter you wished your life was different.
I understood that.
Not once did you wish my sister back.
You couldn't have moved me if you did. If wishes were horses, Clarence.

February became March. Small brown birds returned from whatever warm place they had wintered. I kept Maisie busy. She told you everything. I gave her a haircut. (*I wish I could see that,* you wrote, *the before or the after. It's fair to say I just wish I could see you.*) Her boss promoted her to manager. And, because poor Maisie didn't know how jealous you could be, I sent her on a date and on a second and then a third. I named her fellow Lawrence. Maisie had known him a little in high school. He'd filled out well these five years since graduation. (*I won't stop you from doing what you want. You've got your whole life ahead and a beautiful world to live it in. I have no claim on you and I guess that's how things should be between us, since I don't have much of a claim on life either. Just please be careful. Don't fall too hard. I sound old now. I never want to sound old to you. But trust me. Nothing's worse than loving someone when they decide they want to do you wrong.*

And for what it's worth I've never met a Lawrence worth trusting.)

For her birthday, Kath threw a mystery wine tasting. She put out four bottles with brown bags over the labels. Everyone sniffed and oohed and wrote down words like *loamy*. Pammie was driving and wouldn't touch the stuff. "Besides, Trish would judge me forever if I wound up loving the Franzia." She lay *Trish* out like a lure I knew better than to snap at. I said only that I happened to *enjoy* Franzia's hint of charcoal and that judging by the strawberry wine coolers I'd spied in their sophomore dorm, neither Trish nor Pam was in any position to judge. Pammie laughed, and that was good to hear. All the Gs had secured babysitters for the night so we were able to properly converse. At the evening's end, Kath revealed the four bottles were exactly the same; one opened just before the pour, one two hours in advance, one four, one six. I'd enjoyed myself so thoroughly that it seemed clever instead of a know-it-all trick.

Cutout tulips cropped up in Riverview, patients' names inked down the stems.

It was spring in Stemble too.

You wouldn't believe the bugs in here. Ants and mites and roaches and whatnot. They lay their eggs in winter and every March there's a hatching. Stemble can't (or maybe won't) fix it. It's not bugs they're interested in exterminating.

This year Enright's started collecting them. He keeps bugs in his cup till he has enough for a trial. Judge and jury, a whole mess of roach lawyers. Pretty funny, I guess, since you know what they say about lawyers. But what gets me is that Enright's this brick wall of a man and he always picks the biggest roach for defendant. I hear him measuring. And every trial the roach's guilty. Enright kills it right away. Just a bug underfoot. Then he goes after the rest of them and the next day it starts all over, Enright filling up his cup.

We each only get the one. I wonder what Enright drinks from.

With enough time gone for the change to be believed, I told Kath I'd convinced the bird watchers to switch their meetings to Sundays. Could I drop in again at linners? I asked her Monday on a walk. She cawed and improvised a jig right there on the street. At the Claverie house, the children looked strange and half-starved, husked for spring from thick sweaters.

"Glad you're here," said Blue with his warm, unguarded smile. He was bound to be the easiest; I didn't have to meet his eyes.

"You've been keeping well?" Pam asked, like I was a cut of beef and apt to spoil.

"I've been busy," I said and I thought of Marjorie. The half of her mouth that could manage it smiled sometimes when she saw me. Every weekend. I'd had the desk man find a chair for her room. His name was Arthur, but Call-Me-Art. He said Marjorie was lucky to have such a good friend, and I didn't correct him. Every visit, I switched off Marjorie's TV. You were so dead set against the box and maybe your mother felt that way too.

"I'm glad," Pam said. In the softening of her posture I saw that she'd been tense. I hugged her. Everything would be all right. She was so much prettier when she smiled.

April came. I paid for another six months of post box use.

The linner after April Fool's the littlest Claveries flopped about, playing possum. Midway through the month, I filled out my annual petition to visit and mailed it to Stemble. You were plenty smart, Clarence. You'd be suspicious in its absence.

Call-Me-Art stopped asking for my ID.

When positioned by her left hand, Marjorie's right regained the ability to hold a weak fist.

Pamela's sunny self returned. Her laugh carried across the Claveries' backyard on Saturdays and across the tables when we met downtown for dinner. Every Thursday, when I called her apartment, the phone rang four times and went to voicemail. The first time I let out a small, undignified cackle. I'd never been so happy to be wrong. Either that or she'd chosen, Clarence. She was past you now and glowing. And still in Maisie's post box your letters came, two, three times a week, hungrier than ever before, desperate and pecking, like birds to bread crusts.

24.

Dear Maisie,

What breaks a man is thinking about the Death House. After that last appeal they move you there until they do it. I've never seen it. No one in the pods has. They built it out of sight so everywhere we look we're looking for it. It's coming and we don't know when. Not knowing where's another extra to keep us up nights. They designed it that way on purpose. They do everything on purpose.

There's a dirt track that runs by the pens where they put us "outside" for exercise. Rumor says it leads up to the Death House. Guards know, of course, but they aren't telling. They aren't supposed to talk about the "terminal proceedings." (They do though. Westin gets his rocks off telling us how Nuz was a foamer.)

Nuz used to tell me not to think about it. "Shut off that goddamn Doc brain." But these days I can't. Something's up. My lawyer's working up our oral arguments for the ninth circuit (realistically my last shot). No date's set but you can't keep things secret in Stemble and everyone knows it's soon. You can tell when they start treating you decent.

I haven't told you about the showers. We get stripped before leaving the cells and are marched down the pods in our cuffs and our briefs. Shower's a single stall that's too small to sit down in (I have no idea how they fit Enright in at all). No taps, just a spigot that's up way too high to reach. The guards control the water after they lock you in. We're supposed to get a full ten minutes. We hardly ever do. Some of them (this guy, Doer, he's the worst) flip the water off and on the whole time or crank it way too hot or wait till I'm all soaped up and stop the water so I itch like crazy until the next time.

Today was shower day. Doer was there. I got the regulation ten minutes. He even rapped on the pane with a two minute shutoff warning.

And last Sunday Chaplain Crowler made sure to stop at my door. Most weeks I don't even get a nod. This time he asks, "How are you faring, son?"

Now Crowler's the one who told me a few months back my Mom was sick. They cuffed me and walked me to his office and none of the guards would tell me what was going on. Crowler kept me waiting forever. Then he comes in and tells me Mom's had a stroke, that her doctor "isn't comfortable" with the idea of being on my call list and the home she's at now has a policy against collect calls, no exceptions. Crowler says all I can do is write. And pray, of course. But it was late in the week. I'd used up my stamps. He wouldn't let me buy even one extra. "Commissary's Tuesday, Inmate." Crowler had all these diplomas up in his office. Believe me, I get why he took the glass out of the frames.

And this is the man who started calling me son. It always happens this way. It happened with Nuz. Stemble isn't kind, not ever, but for Nuz's last few months officers were sons of bitches only when they had to be. Don't go thinking it's guilt for what they're going to do to me. They just know I'm about to spend a bunch of time with my lawyer.

Before they took him to the Death House ("transferred," that's what they call it) Nuz drove me crazy practicing his last words. Only when the TVs were on and he'd whisper. Nuz wasn't the brightest. In a place as loud as Stemble it's the quiet sounds that stand out.

Maisie, I'm afraid all the time now. I try to be brave with my daughter who I know has a lot on her mind. But Stemble's harder to take than ever now that I've begun to flinch at loud noises. I'm only going to say this because I feel that we have a closeness between us. If I am crossing a line with you please pretend that I never asked. I know I promised I never would, but my daughter has sent me a bunch of pictures of herself and her husband. I need some beauty in my life (and a flirt like you has got to be pretty; please don't be offended). Would you consider it? A good death would be old and in bed with the people I love around. The fact of it is I know I'll die bad. I'm not asking for pity, only for a chance. Please let me have what matters in my sight as long as I can.

25.

Of course Maisie would give you what you wanted. She was barely out of her teens, after all, and it takes most girls the bulk of their lifetimes to learn a proper *no*. The obvious course of action was Flamingo at Green Mother Grocery; I'd casually modeled Maisie after her in so many respects. I gathered enough groceries to make my visit seem legitimate. I stood in Flamingo's line. She'd cut bangs in her pink hair, very short and blunt across her forehead.

"Looking good," I said, indicating the hair. Though like her crooked teeth, it shouldn't have. "It suits you."

Flamingo nodded and finished ringing up the woman in front of me, banging the register drawer shut with a quick swivel of her hips. My own sometimes clicked now when I walked; I could go weeks without having reason to remember they were also hinged for side to side. The peaches I was pretending to need advanced down the belt. My favorite fruit. Barbra only liked them baked into pies. She was a funny kid. Hated their skins. She called them fuzzifruits. "You know," I said, smiling at Flamingo, "I was just telling my mother the other day how absolutely darling you were. Ma, I said: there's a checker at Green Mother Grocery who is just the darlingest thing." *Darlingest*. The perfect word, grandmotherly and benign. "Your hair color. What do you call it?" I tugged at a strand of my own, bottle browned.

"Pink?"

A businessman sidled into line behind me, his tie loose for the lunch hour. He unloaded his basket. One of those bento boxes they'd begun to promote and two cans of ginger cola. He caught me eyeing his purchases and set the plastic divider between us.

"Just pink, dear? I'd have said it was magenta. I was just trying to describe it to my mother. I said: Ma, it's just the richest pink. It didn't grow in that way, did it?" It's easy to get away with things when you're pretty, Barbra used to brag. We both know how well that worked out, Clarence. If she'd lived, Barbra would've learned. It's even easier when you're old.

Flamingo had the laugh Barbra should have got: airy, fragile, sweet as a meringue. "God no. It's dyed."

"Mine too." I forced a conspiratorial giggle. I laughed like I had no intentions, like there wasn't a Polaroid camera in my purse.

Bento Box coughed behind me.

"Bless you," I said and turned back to Flamingo. "You should get him on that echinacea you set me up with. I hardly coughed all winter."

Bento coughed again, this time louder than was fully necessary.

I ignored him. My best beam for Flamingo. "Pink dye! I'll have to tell Ma next visit. She's very old-fashioned. She just about lost her wig when my daughter pierced her ears again." I pinched my own ear way up at the top to show Flamingo where.

Bento gathered his lunch and switched lanes.

"My poor little girl. Ma's still going on about it. If God wanted an extra hole in your head . . . but that's Ma. I don't think she'd ever believe how pretty you look." Flamingo beamed. Her own mother probably nagged her about the hair. She didn't get compliments much. She might be the kind of kid a prettier sister outshone. She handed me a receipt.

"I wonder if you'd be willing to let me take your picture. You know how it is with mothers. I'm sixty-three, but I still love to prove her wrong." I set the Polaroid on the counter.

"I'm not sure if I'm comfortable—"

"It won't take a minute. Please, my mother's in the hospital." I wasn't thinking of Ma. I was thinking of Marjorie. "Bedbound. I take this camera everywhere so I can show her beautiful things." I could start to, actually. It might do your mother tremendous good. And I could tell it was a fine idea, practical and kind, from the way Flamingo wavered.

Her *okay* came so quiet I almost missed it. She tucked a pink strand behind her ear. No piercings, just like Pam. I wondered if she was also scared of needles. The light was imperfect, but the smile just right, lilting and coy. "Tell your mother Meifen hopes she gets well soon."

"Meifen," I said, like I was testing the pronunciation. Really, I wished she hadn't told me.

"It was my name at the orphanage." She indicated her fundraising jar. The find-my-birthmother trip to China. "The Lennarts got the idea it meant Willow so that's on my passport and diplomas and stuff."

I shook the Polaroid like that would wave away the memory. Another picture, much older: Hyun-Ay in my safety deposit box, ten times more bow than her dark hair merited. It sometimes bore remembering: even without you, Clarence, my life could have bifurcated badly. Our Hyun-Ay, grown and sour beside a tip jar, saving for the homeland we'd cut her from on the strength of our wishing. We'd decided to call her Lucille Renate, for Frank's mother and my own. It wasn't the prettiest name—though as a nickname Lucy had a sweet ring to it. We'd thought it would help her feel connected to the Germanic family that she would never look like.

I unclasped my pocketbook. Kath had read an article about the hackers and credit cards; our Monday walks now included a stop at the bank to withdraw cash for projected weekly expenditures. One hundred and eighty-six dollars into the China jar, along with a handful of change.

"No way," said Meifen, her shock more charming than formal thanks could ever be. I wondered if she was going to hug me; only Pam really did that anymore. But she held very still, eyes on the money in the jar. "No way." No smile. No exuberant flutter of hands. And I saw then that there was discomfort in her stillness. The camera and then the cash; she could tell something about me was off. I drew an uneasy breath. Meifen had got into the store's patchouli. I focused on the Polaroid. That hair of hers plumed into view, the brightest pink your life had left. Her form congealed from photographic fog, solid as the knowledge: for all your remaining days her picture would hang cherished in your cell. For all mine I'd drive out of my way to do my marketing; my bread would be white and wholesome as Styrofoam, my peaches mealy and bruised. I would bite the mush spots first, every blot a reminder. I could never go back to Green Mother Grocery. I had wronged a child born Meifen.

26.

The Mississippi ran high that year, a very fine spring on the heels of an adamant winter. I had to change my preferred Riverview parking spot; the car overheated quickly if left too long in the sun. In the hallway, a nurse peeled a flowering paper tree from Marjorie's door, replacing it with a sunglasses-wearing construction paper sun. All these visits and this was the first time I'd encountered the changing of the guard.

"Very cheerful," I said with a nod. There's a trick to small talk: to avoid awkwardness and fawning, simply make an accurate observation. Human ego will translate it into a compliment every time.

"Thank you," said the nurse. An enormous, appreciative smile. I supposed in her profession compliments were sometimes thin on the ground. I edged past her into Marjorie's room. Some nothing just to the left of the door held her rapt. Her tongue tipped out. It lolled and curled. She rippled it into a cloverleaf. Pam's favorite party trick. There's a gene for that, one that neither Barbra nor I had. I guess I knew now who Pam got it from.

"Marjorie," I said. I stood just inside the door. I liked to wait until her eyes fixed on me before approaching. It would be terrifying having me appear out of nowhere. I was very aware of the nurse in the hallway. No chart in her hand but plenty of colored paper. If something seemed off about me, she would jot it down for sure. I tried again. "Marjorie. Hi, Marjorie. Hello."

I must have sounded desperate and that desperation must have carried; the nurse joined me, popping from the hallway like a cuckoo from a clock. "Look, Margie." She pointed, something we'd been sure to instruct Pamela it was never polite to do. "Your pal is here. Your buddy . . ." She raised a prompting eyebrow.

"Lida," I said without thinking. Or rather, I was thinking *Margie, buddy, pal.* That and the paper cutouts. The woman sounded like she'd rather be teaching Montessori.

"Your Lyla came to see you!" Her own name tag read "Holland." Unusual name like that, she ought to have a bit more care with other people's. I stepped into the room as if to prove I had a right to be there. If Holland would just skedaddle, I'd show Marjorie Pam's teeth. We had developed our small traditions. Every visit we went through my purse. The stroke hadn't scrambled her completely, not by a long shot. Your mother was sharp as tacks. Some things she gripped. Others she let drop. She never held my house keys. Always your letters. Always Pam's teeth. Never things that didn't matter, pencils and pocket change. This week I'd brought Polaroids. Not Meifen, on her pink-haired way to Arizona. But things about town that had struck me: a funny fat pigeon, a woman in an extraordinary church hat, a tray of donuts frosted in outrageous pastels.

"Margie sees better 'round the other side," said Holland. Rows of fruit dotted her scrubs, marrying uneven at the seams. Apple to pear, banana to orange. She looked like a losing slot machine. Nurses used to wear white. The measure of a decent hospital was the way its staff gleamed.

"It's *Marjorie*," I said. Another conversational strategy; corrections can be an efficient way to regain territory. Your mother's lips were pink and unchapped, thanks to my weeks of balm. She could at least look my way. The vinegar in the woman. Making me think all those times that I was welcome. Holding my gaze.

Straining for smiles. Your Lusk mother, biding her time. Waiting for an audience before giving me the snub. "Marjorie?"

Nothing and more nothing. Something in my gut deflated.

Your mother's mouth stretched into a thin and concentrated line. A new trick. If she'd just look at me, I'd tell her I was proud. She really was much improved, Clarence. She'd lost that sheen of serious illness. She no longer looked like so many gobs of rice pudding.

"The nice nurse is going to think you don't like me."

Holland's voice from the hallway, benevolent. "It's not my business to think that." A better nurse would tell me not to sweat it. Of course Marjorie likes you. A better nurse would put her hand over mine and squeeze. Your mother kept staring at nothing. Her tongue flopped wild now, a fish flopping desperate on land.

"C'mon, Marjorie."

Holland said, "Try talking normal. Easier for her to engage that way, isn't it, Margie?"

If I were a proper visitor I could insist she leave. Instead, I followed instructions. Perhaps she would leave us if my normal talk passed muster. "You wouldn't believe the number of people here today. I had to circle and circle to park."

Marjorie's lips stretched and twisted like she was trying to work them around something that kept changing consistency and shape.

"The drive over was nice though," I said. "It felt like summer already."

Holland finally retreated. *Enjoy your visit*, she mouthed. I would have to keep up the chitchat. She'd be just the type to lurk at doors.

"I saw Pamela Saturday," I said, "she looked very pretty." Your mother's head jerked up as if on a string. Her shirt this time was peppermint striped, a pattern they hadn't put her in before. "Pammie had a new blouse too. Blue-greenish. Blue bought it for her birthday. Such a good color. It just about matches her eyes. I don't see how he knew to pick it out."

But Marjorie wasn't interested.

Clarence, you know I was a shy child, gawking about in my younger sister's wake. I've grown. I have more or less mastered it. But that's a question of tips and tricks and carrying myself with confidence. Conversation itself rarely came easy; I seldom knew exactly the thing to say. I knew it that afternoon in Riverview. Exactly what Marjorie would want to hear. And hiding Holland would think we were a proper family. The lie came easily. "Pammie says to say hi. She's sorry she couldn't make it this time."

Your mother's eyes snapped to me. Her lips worked furiously. Her tongue thrashed behind her teeth. "Careful there," I said. She might choke. The worry came on swift, too swift for me to slough off as something I *shouldn't* care about. She was your mother. Her tongue did its terrible work. Her mouth pinched closed like a drawstring purse. "I'm going to call that nurse back. Marjorie, you're—"

"Cassava," Marjorie said, "cassava."

A word. I was almost sure that was an actual word.

"Cassava," she said again.

Yes. A word. Clear. She barely slurred the *s*s.

"Cassava," once more. Some kind of gourd, I was fairly certain. African? Possibly. Marjorie looked as surprised as I was. Everything in her face shot up. Hairline, eyebrows, the doughy folds of her cheeks. "Cassava."

"Marjorie, I don't know why you're saying that."

"Cassava." Her teeth flashed white against her lip. Edgy wet in her eyes. "Cassava." Every cassava louder than the one before. Holland was clearly long gone. She'd have come barreling in at the first comprehensible word.

"I don't understand. Marjorie."

"Cassava." Her chest rose and fell. Short breaths, possibly panicked. "Cassava, cassava, cassava." She strained a little at the gut.

"Do you want to sit up? I don't know how to get you up . . ."

"Cassava."

"Good, good. Yes, cassava. That's a word. You're talking. But can you try something else?"

"Cassava." There was a thinness to it this time.

"Try, Marjorie."

"Cassava." Sad slippery word. Mystified, and not a little panicky.

"Mar jo rie." I tapped her chest. Aside from the lip balm I don't think I had touched her in all this time.

"Cassava."

"Maybe Clarence. Clar ence. Try it."

"Cassava."

"Try Barbra." The name my mind flashed to first, the name I associated most with yours. I hadn't set out to pain your mother. I swear it, Clarence. Not that time around.

"Cassava." She caught on the double *s*, a small click like a motor stalling.

"How about Pamela? Is that what you're trying to say?" I sat on the lip of your mother's bed. Its springs groaned. I plumped Marjorie's pillow. She wheezed and continued to cassava. She held a curved left hand up and stared at it. She looked astounded at its emptiness.

For the second time in one day I knew the exact right thing to say.

"You're back now," I said.

Silly thing to say, silly as cassava. Your mother had always been right here. Ridiculous to act as though she'd journeyed back from some long and distant ways away. But she was back in the wordscape now, no matter that she claimed so small a holding.

It was the right thing to say and so I said it again.

I began to stroke her hair. Riverview scrimped on conditioner. I'd have to buy her a bottle. Pam's lavender kind. How soft her hair would turn. *Cassava*, Marjorie said and I rolled her split ends between my fingers. *Cassava*, I answered back, grateful for the bed that bore my weight. I doubted I could stand. Everything about today was strange. Your mother's voice and your mother's word and the feeling that came with hearing her. Strange that I could feel it at all. Something that was almost hope. Something that was almost happiness.

27.

Cassava. Noun. 1. Equatorial or tropical plant (*Manihot esculenta*) or the tuberous root of this plant. 2. The starch derived from said plant through the drying and leaching of its natural cyanide. 3. The source of tapioca. See *manioc, yucca*.

What had I done before the Internet? I had a dictionary, yes, and the 1992 *Encyclopedia Britannica*, but without the Internet I would never have learned:

Cassava was a Brazilian subsistence crop. It thrived in bad soil and kept whole families going. Last year's yield had been threatened by fungus. The devastation had yet to be tallied.

Cassava was purportedly delicious cut thin, deep fried, and sprinkled with salt. The Web recommended fleur du sel, kosher in a pinch. Or try the traditional preparation. Boil in goat's milk and mash with lime.

Cassava-Cassava would open in August at Kauai's Hibiscus Grand Family Resort. A dance club for preteens with virgin coladas and hula lessons at the top of each hour.

Cassava Love Dudley, heaven help her, was born last week at Sanpete Valley Hospital.

Cassava and Crumpets could be found at 817 Whidbee Avenue in downtown Paulus, Wisconsin. Purveyors of fine coffee and bubble teas. The website offered a quiz: what kind of bubble tea are you? I was Bouncing Butterscotch. Spit welled beneath my tongue; I wanted butterscotch. The Internet's power of suggestion was staggering. Astounding that it wasn't better monitored.

I searched again. This time *Marjorie Lusk and cassava,* bounded by quotation marks.

Nothing.

I cut the *Marjorie.*

Still nothing.

Clarence and cassava, no.

Stemble and cassava, no.

Barbra Lusk murder cassava, Riverview facility cassava, mother cassava, can't stop saying cassava. No, gibberish, no, and a page that—inexplicably—advertised a cream that would augment my bust.

I swallowed. Before Riverview I had known your mother very little. She'd toasted too drunkenly at your wedding and Barbra quarreled with you that first year of marriage over whether Marjorie had the right to an emergency house key. You won. I should have seen it then. You were no good for Barbra. You got her to cave. At the time I'd thought that was a good thing. Her mouth could get that mulish set.

Woman with a stroke saying cassava. Woman with a stroke repeating herself. A fruitful search at last. I clicked my way through a series of stroke support sites. Perseveration, the web said. Not uncommon in stroke recovery. Marjorie was working hard to get language back. A first word had bubbled up from wherever the rest of them were stored. By chance, *cassava.* It could just as easily be *surgery, Realtor, postage stamp.* And that first word became the only one. Tuberous plug in her memory circuits, blocking every word that tried to follow. I read on: Perseveration was generally a sign of improvement. In patients, however, the onset of perseveration could be met with frustration and panic.

"Perseveration," I spoke the word aloud. It sounded a bit like *perseverance*, which I'd been raised to believe an admirable quality. And your mother had no monopoly on perseveration. Every soul alive gets stuck once in a while.

"Perseveration," I said again. Conscious this time of the grit in my voice. It sounded a lot like *preserve* too. Another word I'd always thought meant good. Me and Ma, putting up cherries. We'll be lucky in winter. A little sweetness to do us good.

"Perseveration," I said again. Whatever it sounded like it meant stuck, plain and simple. Memory's sweet. It's like flypaper. We get stuck. We all get stuck.

We didn't tell Ma about all of them—she worried—but Barbra always knew when I miscarried. Clear across the country, she said, and her cycle would go all off kilter. She was probably lying; there's no kind of science to back that phenomenon up. But I loved her so much for saying it. For the zingers she'd come up with—scathing, I was much too shy to use them—for all our foot-mouthed well wishers. The things people say. At least you know you can get pregnant. It's nature's way of weeding out birth defects. Maybe you just aren't meant to have children.

Then Barbra was gone.

And people upped their earnest murmurs. I had nothing to say in response; I had the mental agility of banana pudding. At least it was fast. At least she wasn't in and out of hospitals. It's better for Pam this way, so young she won't remember.

I needed my sister.

I still needed my sister

I'm not stuck. I typed quickly. I was getting better at it; I have always been a quick study. Barbra would be inching toward her sixties now. She'd have aged irritably, like so many pretty women do. She'd wear flowing scarves and colors that no longer suited her complexion. She'd discover tanning beds and orange herself to leather. And I'd have felt petty and triumphant, aging better than her. I read the words on my screen as if they were actually true: *I'm not stuck.* I clicked. Foolish as Pam with one of those Magic 8 Balls she used to have, asking the same question over and over till she got the answer she wanted. Page after glowing page. The Internet was just like most people. Gadzillions of facts but it didn't know anything about anything.

Enough, enough. I turned off the machine and went to the kitchen. I still wanted butterscotch. The kind of sweet that grandmothers—doting and not responsible for the dentist's bill—carried in their purses. I went to my bag. Perhaps I'd grabbed a candy absentmindedly at the bank where they had them out in cheery baskets. I needed to thin my purse in any event. I spread its contents on my kitchen table, eye out for that glinting foil. Polaroids for Marjorie, credit cards, bank cards, checkbook and register, my driver's license, Kath Claverie's driver's license, a dozen grocery store twist ties I'd been saving up to give to Pam, Bic pen with lid, Bic pen without lid, Kleenex, tissue-wrapped plaster mold of Pam's teeth at eleven, tissue wrapped plaster mold of Pam's teeth at fourteen, a mess of photographs, eighteen receipts, lip balm—aloe and rosehips, the kind Meifen sold that I couldn't for the life of me find elsewhere—a whistle for emergencies, your six most recent letters, $1.89 in change, a set of keys, four American glassworks stamps.

I fingered the stamps. If they'd been the old lick-and-stick kind then at least I could get a taste of sweet. These stamps were yours; I only ever used them for you. But there was more to the universe than Arizona. I knew that, Clarence—I did. Somewhere, out beyond the townhouse, people used stamps like these to mail their bills.

But they weren't here—I was, standing at the head of a silent table, a silent set of objects splayed before me. I crumpled the receipts one by one. I could unstick. I left the coins out for the change jar. I could unstick. I would. I began to shunt everything else back into my purse. Maisie would let more and more time elapse between each letter. Eventually, she wouldn't write back at all. I zipped my bag with an efficient, decisive sound. It was my favorite, fine leather, well-maintained, lines and stitching that whispered quality. Good capacity. Kath liked to tease that the sheer heft of the thing could take out any mugger who dared approach. My sister had overstuffed her purses too. Just like our mother. Her saying about that: only the shipmaker knows why his ships all bear ballast. She said it cheerily enough, but it wasn't cheerful and it wasn't a mystery either. I knew how it went with any ship that bears ballast. She takes on all she does even knowing it will weigh her down. And, burdened, sets sail, hoping what she holds will keep her steady and above water long enough to reach some other shore.

28.

Thank you for the picture, Maisie. I've been looking it over every few minutes since it came. At lights out I take one last look and lie back, hoping you're familiar enough now to start coming up in my dreams.

I've been having Nuz dreams. He comes down the pods holding this jar like kids use for fireflies. But the jar's empty. Whatever was in there got out. Nuz looks the same as before, except for these holes all over his skin, just like the ones punched through my door to let in air. When I look close I can see they're all plugged up with ice. I think I told you how I like the ice dreams. This one I am always glad to wake from. I don't get back to sleep nights that Nuz comes. Men in here sleep loud. I try to blame their snores and grunts and all the like. I don't snore, in case you are wondering. Someone here would tell me. And my wife never complained.

I hope you don't mind my talking about her. You don't seem the jealous kind. She claimed she only snored on nights before rainstorms. But we lived in Arizona. She snored a whole lot more often than it rained. It's funny what a person remembers. I don't think she ever dreamed at all. But she'd talk big talk about it, all "I had this dream where you call if you're running late." "I had a dream you were the one who got the baby breakfast." "I dreamed you got the oil changed."

Life continues all by-the-book in here. Tomorrow I'll be seeing the medic. They actually gave me a heads up like they're supposed to. They told me at first count. My stomach's already all cramps but I am trying not to relieve myself. Tomorrow they're going to weigh me. And I figure they're going to have to check my Stemble file when they're calculating how much stuff to put in their needles. So I want to be as heavy as I can. My biggest fear (these days, until I come up with another one) is that they'll botch the numbers and their first try won't take.

<u>Later</u> (it's just about lights out now). I couldn't send this at mail call. I know it means this letter will reach you a day or so late. But I care for you, deeply. And I want you to think of me. But not this way. I didn't want to leave you between letters thinking of me dead and stuck full of needles or bowled up in here trying not to shit.

I have something better to leave you with now. I hesitate to write it. Still have some vanity left, see? I don't like reminding a pretty girl like you I'm old. But good news is meant for telling and I can't count on that much more to share. I've just heard from my daughter. If I can just hang on another half a year I'll die a grandfather.

29.

How I managed the linner drive without breaking my neck, I'll never know. I passed a playground. The playground where Pam once cut her foot on a bit of bottle glass. Every time I turned my back she wriggled out of her shoes. We'd swapped out the plain laces that came with her sneakers. Pamela liked the purple best. No use. She still wouldn't keep them on. Her cut foot bled and bled. She ran to me. I picked her up. Behind her, sticky footprints. Red proof: when Pammie hurt I was the one she came to.

I got on the highway. When Pam first learned to merge her shoulders shot clear up to her earlobes. It took a good half mile for them to slide back down. But her voice sounded as though she'd never been afraid in her life. A Barbra kind of calm. Stop that tapping, Li. There's never going to be a brake on your side.

Just off the highway—there—was the chain diner she'd go to in high school when midnight pancakes were the height of sophistication. Here was the exit to her little friend Meggie's. And her flute teacher lived just over there. Here was the exit for Blue's office. He had ten years on Pamela; timing was just about right for Blue. And the way they both got on with the little Claveries. But she would have told me, Clarence. She would have told me first.

Off the highway now. Slow driving in residential neighborhoods. I was nearing the Claveries'. Every block the houses got bigger. I'd taken Pam to a birthday party somewhere in this well-wooded grid. The first time a classmate invited her anywhere. I remember letting out a whoop when I saw the invitation. A pool party. Triumph and then the anxious twitch: I had no idea if Barbra had taught Pam to swim.

All the girls were Katies then. The birthday girl was Katie H. Funny that I still remembered. Pam picked the birthday gift herself. A lavender chain necklace and a starter set of clip-on charms, a snowflake in incongruous pink, a tennis racket with a ball molded to its surface, a blue whistle whose sound hardly traveled. So many objects of Pam's childhood were plastic.

I forgot to caution *don't run near the pool* when I dropped her off. A mother, a real one, would have remembered. For the party's three hours I drove past immaculate yards uneasy. And sure enough, at pickup, my girl was running. Barefoot, belly puffed out beneath Lycra, weaving between other children, the lot of them quick as ferrets.

"Lida!" A happy shriek.

I tensed. First I registered the volume, then the joy.

"I won at cannonball!"

Beside Pam a pigtailed girl scowled. Sour sport. "You call your mom *Lida*?" she asked.

Pam shrugged. Behind her Katie H's yard sloped toward a high fence. To someone as short as Pam it must have looked like the end of the world. "Everyone calls my Mom *Barbra* now," said Pam. She made *Barbra* sound solemn to the point of absurdity. Again the shrug. Everything in me clenched. A whistle blew. Katie H's ridiculous bracelet. Poolside, it sounded like a lifeguard. The sound stopped me in mid-motion and good thing it had. I'd wanted to wrest down those indifferent rising shoulders.

"Barbra," Pigtails said. "That's stupid. I just call my mom *Mom*."

Pam's hand went to the lace-trimmed pocket of her party dress. And then, impossibly, she had a gun. Purple and plastic, cheap. She pulled the trigger. A puff of water. Pigtails rubbed her forehead.

I snatched the toy away and Pamela gave a sharp cry. I'd been too quick, I thought, I'd hurt her. But Pam only wanted the gun back. She grabbed for it. What kind of parents had I left her with? To give out such prizes.

Pigtails began to wail.

"Pamela Clare, we never shoot. Not ever."

Furious pink filled in the space between her freckles. She reached again for her prize. "It's mine. I won it. It's my squirty."

"You know why we never ever shoot."

Pink became red and Pam's scowl grew. She pointed at me, her index finger, like Barbra's, nearly as long as her middle. The finger trembled. Above it, she cocked up her thumb. She jerked it back. "Bang, bang. You're dead."

My face so close I could smell the chlorine as it dried on her skin, the baby shampoo and Jergens cherries and almonds. Lusk eyes gleamed horrible. Birthday cake sugared her breath.

And here I was again, driving through the same neighborhood.

Shaking the same angry shakes.

Speaking with the same fever voice.

Speaking the same words I spoke poolside.

"You're a good girl, Pam, but there are things I would never forgive you."

30.

Summer linners were outside, no matter the heat. Kath's famous sticky cake wilted onto her picnic table, where whorls dyed in easy-wipe plastic attempted the look of real wood. At its foot a cooler stood open, ice cubes suspended in their own melt. Cans of soda bobbed. Unrestricted access for the junior Claveries, whose antics were not at all improved by sugar.

"Shoulders!" one of them yelled and his cousins lined up in pairs, pressing together at the shoulders and screaming the word over and over and over. One child remained unpaired and ran. The caller pursued. The grass they trampled had browned in patches where the sprinklers didn't quite overlap.

The unpaired child was tagged; he was the caller now. "Foreheads!" he called.

"Foreheads foreheads foreheads . . ." his cousins copied. They scrambled for new partners, repeating the word without pause. Foreheads knocked together. Someone was going to wind up concussed.

Pam wasn't anywhere. One look I'd know. Barbra had shown early. She'd carried it in her face.

"Butts!"

"Butts butts butts . . ."

"Language, Nicky." The adult Claveries hovered at the fringe of the yard. I quintuple checked. No Pam. They'd set up a croquet course. They had only two mallets between them.

"Patooties!"

"Nicky . . ."

"How about earlobes, Nicky-noodle?" Blue's suggestion floated from the shade, where he lay in a hammock strung between two tall pines. Pam lay with him. A gray sundress helped her fade into the cool. I knew that dress. For years she'd refused to scrap it. Cotton gone thin and soft as pajamas. It would show anything that needed showing. I crossed to her, dodging Claveries. They'd paired up without regard for height and struggled to stay together at the earlobes. Blue pumped his foot and the hammock swayed.

From nowhere, the odd child out zipped off before me. The girl with boy hair. Emily. An older boy—Benny?—raced after, gaining fast. A gruff whine came from the shade. My stomach fell to my shoes; for a moment I thought it was Pam. But Seshet was up and huffing on her haunches. I'd missed the dog before; she lurked so quiet beneath the hammock. Dogs know things. They track our movements way up above them like stars. Seshet was growling now, warning, imminent impact.

Pam and Blue ignored her.

Emily ran headlong.

"Slow down," I yelled.

She didn't listen. She barreled on toward where Pam hung netted.

I was running now too, to no avail. The Claverie girl would get there first. I called Pam's name at the moment of impact. Emily hit the hammock at chest level. She let out a sound like a bottle uncorking. Benny tagged her and wheeled off. She fell back on her bottom and made another cork noise. Pam and Blue hardly swayed. A little bit like Emily couldn't hurt them if she tried. I was a foolish woman. I needn't have run. But I had run, and so I saw: in the moment of impact, where instinct should have thrown them out as braces before her, Pam drew her hands in to her stomach, fingers splayed in wide protective fans.

She told you first. She told you first. She told you first. She told you first.

Blue's hand searched out Emily. "Steady, Bumpercar." He knew her height by heart.

If I were a believer, this is what I'd pray: please, God, fossilize me. Put all this eons behind me. "Emily?" Astounding I could speak at all. "Call out *patella*. Means the knee. They'll take so long figuring it out that you can tag anyone you want."

Pamela sat up. Even without your letter I'd have noticed the chub in her cheeks. Emily chugged off, screaming "patella." "That was really sweet of you, Li," Pam said.

"You're a natural at Siamese tag." That was Blue. It was he who stood to hug me, not Pam. "I wouldn't want to go up against you."

"You couldn't have anyways. The running . . ."

"Of course I can. With all that patella patella patella? Easy to hear who's where." He tugged his earlobe. "That's why Grace invented it."

I don't think I ever made up a game for Barbra; of the pair of us she was the more imaginative. I could have been a better sister. She'd sounded nervous, ages back, telling me about the cell-clump that would eventually be Pam. She knew the rawness of our wanting and her voice was like a stranger's, reading lines. I told her I was happy and I was. But also that old feeling, familiar as bedsheets. How easy life came to Barbra. "You're going to be fine," I'd told her. "Think about it this way: I've probably used up both our shares of bad luck."

I actually said that, Clarence.

All over the lawn, Claverie children shrieked. Ribs, ribs, ribs, ribs, ribs, ribs, ribs. They zoomed erratic as gnats. I asked Blue if he'd actually played in that meat grinder.

He nodded, then winked. Some G must have taught him all about winking.

"You're lucky you don't have a face full of stitches."

A finger to his chin. A fine, white kiss of a scar. "Georgia got me good when I was nine."

Pamela lounged back in the hammock, arm lolling. Cleopatra on her barge.

I looked right at her. "Lucky thing there's an even number of cousins. Off numbers would wreck the whole game." Pam didn't blush or blanch. Ice in her veins. Well. She came by that honestly.

"They're smart kids." She stood. "They'd manage."

"You look different," I said. This was Pamela. My good kid. Sixty-three must seem ancient to her. Forbidding. Maybe she didn't mean to shut me out. She might just be shy of admitting to sex. "Good, I mean. You look good."

"I remembered to brush my hair for once. Come on, I'm starving." She shot off toward the table. She'd taken off her shoes. Grime coated her heels. She'd been in the hammock with her husband a long while. Its ropes left hatch marks on her calves.

Kath stood at the table lamenting her cake. She prodded it with a rubber spatula. Gone all to gobs. "What a disaster. Four kids, four in-laws, my own father, eight grandbabies and not one of you warns me." She counted family on her fingers. She needed a second hand.

"You forgot Lida," said Blue. If only it had been Pam speaking. But your daughter only cozied up to Kath, making mollifying sounds.

A bee hovered near the plate. I said, "I thought it was supposed to look like that."

"Lida!" Kath rubbed her throat like she was trying to massage out a laugh. Around her neck, those mismatched gems threw back the sun. A second bee appeared. Kath had more family than she had fingers. If nothing else, I should be told before her.

A third bee joined the pair. That cake must be pure sugar. Pam grabbed a plastic knife to assist with the reshaping.

"Nothing to do but eat it quickly. Hey, everyone!" Kath yelled. "Dessert first!"

Claveries came from across the yard, little ones running despite the heat. One G noticed and insisted her children rehydrate. Another swung a croquet mallet in careless circles. The third stood arm in arm with Kath's father. Pam passed out paper plates. I counted a fourth and fifth bee. I wondered what Pamela would do if I let them swarm me.

"Since I have the knife," said Blue, "anyone who wants cake had better listen up."

The Claverie children quieted faster for Blue than they ever had for any G. Their treat at stake.

"Since we're having dessert first," he continued, waving the knife, "I figured we might as well overload on sweetness." What a family. I was the only one worried about the blade in his blind grip. "Because Pam and I have some pretty sweet news ourselves."

No.

I wouldn't be told like this. In a herd. Like I was nobody to Pam. Like I was another countless Claverie. I opened my purse. "Kath! Kath! You'll never guess. I found your driver's license today. It was in one of the lawn chair cracks." I waved the ID hard, as if it could waft away Blue's cloying coming words.

Kath mouthed her thanks; the card passed from G to G.

"More good news!" Blue chuckled. Another of his ridiculous winks. "Thanks, Lida. But that's not what I was going to say."

I'd lost Pam to these people.

The ID disappeared into Kath's pocket.

If Riverview asked for ID again, I would lose your mother too.

"This is the best family in the world," Blue said, and raised a hand to quiet a smattering of claps.

"The best," Pam echoed. "Everyone here." She grinned so big she shook with it. She and Blue both had such round heads. Hand in hand they looked paired for Siamese tag.

"It's hard to imagine a better family," Blue's voice cracked. "But they do say that bigger is better . . ."

Another wink.

My mouth was rank. This was so public, so cheesy. If only my ears were made of wax. The Claveries pieced it together with ecstatic whoops. Slower children tugged for explanations at their parents' shirts.

"When?" some G asked.

"In about six months." Pam's voice was buoyant and not her own.

Kath's fingers found her necklace. She counted stone by stone. "July, August, September, October, November, December. Another little tourmaline. Oh, you two."

The family moved as one toward Pam and caught her in their net of arms. She did nothing to break free. Pamela was the only thing in the universe holding still. The Claveries took their sweet time unknotting.

Finally, she faced me.

"Well, Lida?" Pamela stood before me completely pride-lit, though all she'd done was lie there. A petulant flash I knew I was much too old for: my turn, my turn, it should have been me.

"I knew already, Pamela. I've known for ages. I raised you. There's nothing you can keep from me."

"Keep from you?" A girl with that pout was too young to be a mother.

"You've never been any good with secrets. There's no shame in it."

"It's not a secret. You just heard us tell everyone."

"You should have told me sooner. I could have helped from the start, if—"

"What? Did you want to hold my hand while I peed on the stick?"

The Claveries got very quiet. The best family in the world. They stared and I wished every one of them blind. Blue found his way to Pam, with Seshet in her harness.

"We told you with the rest of the family because you're a part of us." His voice a studied, courtroom calm.

"Pamela and I were family before she ever heard of you."

"No one's disputing that."

"I shouldn't even know you."

"But you do." He actually smiled. So much for the blind being able to read tone of voice.

"We're happy." Pam sounded the farthest thing from it. "Just say congratulations and stop making a scene."

Blue kept his fool grin, wide and sightless as a carved pumpkin. "C'mon. You know this is good news." He winked again. A gesture he had no sensible right to.

"Congratulations, then. What are the odds of my grandchild being blind?"

"One hundred percent, Lida. She's going to slut around and shoot people too. Genetics are a bitch."

"Auntie P said the B word," Nicky singsonged. He perched at the edge of the picnic table and swung his feet in time. No Claverie tried to shush him. Not one move to defend their Blue. Best family in the world lumped around like potatoes in a bag.

"If your uncle could hear you say that to me—"

"He'd agree. Frank would be happy for us. He knew how—"

"I'd be plenty happy if you weren't so set on hurting me."

"Hurting you? It's a baby. A baby."

Never had that word been so sour.

"A baby I had a right to know about."

"A right? It's not like you're my mother."

I felt held together by grout. "Thank god I'm not your mother. When you turned out just like her."

As if my heart cued him, Nicky began to wail. He bolted from the table, right hand waving frantically, spread wide. Sobs came jagged as a saw. He was the only Claverie who listened.

My throat throbbed. I tasted iron. If I spat now it would hit the ground red.

Pam stood mute, Barbra rotten.

Nicky's hysterics built.

Those should have been my sobs.

Pammie turned away, head shaking, hands shaking. I wanted the sun to fall from the sky. Blue knew to follow her before Seshet even moved. He gave a stiff wave. His aim was off; he looked like he was taking leave of a lawn chair.

Claveries unfroze. They knotted about Nicky, blind to Blue and Pam and what had passed between us. They fussed over the welt on his palm. His cries began to dissipate. We'll get that mean old bee, some G promised. Looky here, some husband said, it killed him to sting you. So guess who's worse off?

The Claverie child was nothing like me, already cosseted and calm. While I blistered inside and envied that bee. One small barb against the world. But he could use it and never have to wrestle with an after. He stung; he winked out; he turned in an instant to quiet mash.

31.

Congratulations. Grandpa. (It's okay to call you that, isn't it?) That's just super-duper about your Pamela. Yeah, I know who she is. It's so easy to find things out these days. They probably haven't told you about the Internet in Stemble.

You always say how smart you are. Maybe if you're really smart you'll use your Thursday call to tell your lawyer all about it. You know he'll want to use this. What judge wouldn't spare a man waiting on a grandbaby?

Unless His Honor knows that when he died three years ago, Lawrence Ring's father didn't have a single "survived by" left in his obituary. It's been a long time since you shot his son. He could have had grandkids by now too. Maybe His Honor will hear how the cop you killed died so broken his only donatable organs were the eyes.

Come hearing time I bet I know what you'll say. Yes, you bought the gun. You bought it and you brought it to her lover's house. You only wanted to scare them. You don't know how you let all this happen. Please, Your Honor, please.

Of course he'll understand. You just got carried away. His Honor can't help but reprieve a grandfather.

Well, you can hope. Grandfather Going, Going, Gone.

Did you think I'd be happy to hear you loved me? Your love kills. And not just Barbra and the other two. Your love is killing Pam. Clarence, I've found out all about her. She should be building a career, not mucking about with dogs. She should have a roommate or still be living at home. She married right out of college. Nobody does that anymore. It's your fault she's rushing. She wanted you to see her married. And the baby's the same. Rush, rush, rush. She wants you to die knowing she has one.

But Pamela's smart. She'll figure out one day that she missed being young because of you. She won't ever forgive that.

Knowing exactly what you did (and what you keep doing) makes it so much easier to write this next part. I am marrying Lawrence. I love him like no one could ever love you. He says it's awfully tenderhearted of me to keep writing to you for so long. I'm a nice person. You wouldn't know anything about that. I planned on writing till the end. But I can't do it anymore. I don't even feel bad telling you that you're the last person on earth I would ever care for.

You see how good I am at learning what I want to. Your daughter will give up on you one of these days and I will know all about it. I'll cheer. You're going to die one day soon, horribly and puffed full of poisons. I'm going to know all about it when it happens. I'll cheer when you're dead, Clarence, and I can hardly wait.

32.

First thing Monday morning I walked the letter to the corner mailbox. Pickup times at 10:30 and 2:30. I dropped it in and it was gone. I waited to make sure they carted it off. Commuters chugged along, busy cogwork of the world. Hot out already, and it was going to be humid, the day sticky as Kath's cake. No one noticed me standing on the corner. No one spoke. Another kind of body would be questioned for loitering. A frailer kind of body would be asked if it needed help. Pickup at 10:30 just as promised. I walked home. My reflection cast in shop windows, frizzled like a fancy garnish, the kind that gets oohs and ahhs then more often than not is left on the plate. Kath was waiting in front of the townhouse. She spied me from two blocks away. She stood. She raised a large disposable cup. "So. You walked without me."

"Kath."

"Better that than *hiding* in there." She jerked the cup toward the townhouse. A clatter of ice. My joints felt three times their usual size and never in my life had my throat been so raw. Kath said, "If you'd done *that*, I'd have judged you like hell for a chicken."

"I guessed you weren't coming."

"Well, guess again. And let me in. I drank this whole thing waiting on you. You owe me the necessary at least."

I unlocked the door, glad that I am one of those women who tidies when agitated. Washrooms especially. There's something about the tang of bleach. Kath zipped off toward the powder room.

I'd been walking a while and it was gummy outside. I downed a fast glass of water and poured myself a second. "Want one?" I offered when she joined me in the kitchen.

"Lord no. Are you fit for human company?"

"Based on recent events?"

"So that's a *no* then." Kath went to the living room and sat. The squashy cloud of a love seat where Pam had liked to study, the one I'd had to have reupholstered when her pen burst and leaked all over.

"Are you sure I can't get you anything?"

"I'm lovely, thanks." She said *lovely* in a formal way that put me decidedly outside the word and its warm meaning.

It needed saying: "I was awful yesterday."

"A harridan."

"Good word."

"I had time to think of it. I was waiting on your steps a long while."

I checked my watch. After noon. Your letter nearly two hours irrevocably gone. "Kath. I honestly didn't think you were coming."

"We're family."

I said nothing.

"Have you talked to Pam?"

I shook my head.

"You should. You can't let these things—Pam deserves a chance to yell at you a bit."

"I've been visiting her grandmother. She doesn't know."

Kath absorbed the weirdness of it. Too easily. I had said it because I wanted to shock her. I wanted Kath angry with me. I wanted her gone as forever as your letter. Gone as forever as the rest of it. But she only asked, "Did you tell her? It's good news once you let yourself get used to it."

"Tell Marjorie about the baby or Pam about Marjorie?"

"Either. Both. It's all family."

"Our family doesn't work like your family."

A beat. "I'm sorry. I know." Another beat. "You scared the pants off me when the kids first got together."

"Our family?"

"Yeah."

"That's not fair. Just because her father—"

"Not him. That's—I don't know." An indistinct motion with her hands, an attempt, I supposed, to indicate *very far away*. "I meant you. You and Pam. You're like—" Inarticulate hands again, a cupped palmed pat-a-cake. "Imagine trying to find a place in that."

"Is that why all the linners?" Because it occurred to me: the other in-laws were not as regularly featured. I was mirroring the gesture she'd made for me and Pam. Hands worked that way making snowballs, shaping basic forms from clay.

"At first. But I like you. And I like that you like us." She tapped her temple. "Ego. You don't put up with much."

I couldn't stand the kindness. "Pam doesn't put up with much either."

"What's good for the sauce—" The cupping motion, pat-a-caked.

"I wish I was the way you think I am. I wish we were."

"You know what Patrice calls you?" Patrice was our hairdresser-in-common and had been for years before we met. "Good Queen Hedgehog. Imperious and prickly but—"

"You know what Patrice calls *you?*"

"—there's a soft underbelly beneath."

"Kath. He calls you Kath. Because everything in your world gets to be exactly what it seems."

"It's a *compliment,* Lida. We like the underbelly. And the prickles are something to live up to. Lida, I—" she unclasped her purse. Her ID was somewhere in it. My passport back to Marjorie.

My thoughts sharpened to a single *how*. Kath rifled. A baby picture emerged. Striped hat and the face of a wizened old man. "Coleen. My first grandbaby."

I took the picture. Coleen was eleven now, maybe twelve. Acne and elbows. On the springboard of her awkward age, about to dive headlong.

"It's a lot to take in," Kath said. "When Genevieve first told me, I booked a consult with a plastic surgeon. It was unbecoming. I told her and Alec there was meat in my freezer older than the both of them."

"That scene at the linner—it wasn't vanity," I said. If only it could be so simple. Good Queen Hedgehog. I felt all belly then, or worse than belly. I felt inverted, a thousand Patrice prickers turned in.

"You'll fix it," Kath said, and it was shocking. Shocking, her faith in me. Shocking, her cheery can-doism. Shocking that she'd got this age without knowing when a thing is broken for good.

33.

I shut off the AC. Soon the air would be hot enough to peel paint. I got out my tape measure. I tested a length and released it. The tape snapped across my fingers and I drew them to my mouth.

Pam slammed her fingers once in her bedroom door. Frank and I had sent her to her room for sassing so she was crying to begin with. It took me longer than it should have to discover something new was wrong.

And she pinched those fingers in the hinges of her dollhouse. Four separate occasions. The thing was a menace.

She burnt a finger on that ridiculous crimping iron.

Mashed a thumbnail attempting to hammer.

And the paper cuts. Even I couldn't number those.

My kitchen chair measured sixteen inches in width. I dragged it to the living room. Its feet roughed furrows in the rug. The couch was scaled for the old house. Precisely ten and a half feet. I shoved the chair up against it, making a neat corner. Barbra would have loved this. When she was a kid she'd cobbled together houses out of chairs and old bedsheets, her face small and lovely in the cotton-filtered light. I suppose you knew that about her, in your own way, back when you had her, had sheets. A tender sheen where light met her skin. How you must have hated her to do what you did.

Your cell was eight feet by ten.

You must hate her to this day.

The sixteen-inch chair belonged to a set of four. Lined up they'd be five feet and change. Close enough, if I added a pair of wide lamps. I went to gather what I needed. By the time the L was done I was sweating hard. My hair snarled sticky at the scalp. No rest though. I had two more walls to build. A long one—four-foot coffee table, sixty-inch (with extra leaf) card table, a narrow lamp—and a short one—a pair of twenty-inch end tables, a two-foot wicker hamper, a wheeled file cabinet—completed the box. Just as well I lived alone. Building it I couldn't help a few unladylike grunts. I stepped into the box. I lay smack in its center. I was panting. I shut my eyes and rolled onto my stomach. Let my own steady weight still the heaving. In breath out breath. The temperature rose and rose. Any time I wanted I could leave. Your cell was smaller than this, eight by ten exactly, but then my crimes were nowhere near as large. My lungs quieted. I could almost breathe now without sound. I must stink to high heaven. I turned onto my back and mopped my wet skin. If only these rivers could pull more from me than salt.

34.

I didn't call Kath and I didn't call Pam and I didn't go to Marjorie though they knew me now at Riverview and I could likely sweet-talk my way past the front desk. I spent my nights in the couch box. I passed a fair chunk of my days there too. They slipped by one after another after another with the light across my ceiling. One morning it rained, or threatened to. I couldn't tell from the floor. The townhouse ceiling was all bumps. The townhouse floor was all bumps. Whenever I stretched, cracks snaked down my back. When a knock came at the door I assumed it was something new in me breaking.

Pam wore a Cardinals cap that did little to rein in her hair, gone electric in the damp. "I want to come in." Something clicked against her teeth. Hard candy. Likely for nausea. My mouth swam at the thought of sweetness. My own meals had grown increasingly salty. Ramen twice daily. Buttered toast. I let Pamela pass. Green apple on her breath, the same scent companies had begun to add to dish soap.

She pulled the door closed. She looked wan by indoor light. She locked the door. She slid the bolt across. She clicked the top chain into place. Overkill, but I didn't argue. All those locks would slow her if it came to storming out.

"You must be roasting alive." She passed her hand across the brim of her cap, a catcher signaling I had no idea what.

"Thermostat's shot. I've got a boy coming to look it over."

"You've got it turned off." She flicked the AC back on. "You've got to pay better attention." She sounded like a mother already, exasperated. She pushed past me to the living room. She took in its state.

"Spring cleaning," I lied.

"You're always spring cleaning."

"The time's always right to put the tick in your tock." Another Ma saying.

"I always hated that one." Pamela edged into the box.

I shoved at an end table. "Just let me get a few things back into place."

"It's nine-hundred eighty degrees. Seriously. Leave it."

Pam took the couch. I went for the neighboring chair. Our knees almost touched. I hadn't paid such close attention to the gaps between knees since my first sneak-around dates with Frank. Pamela unsnapped her purse. The good hand-stitched one Frank and I had brought her from the Scuola del Cuoio. Preposterous with her grubby clothes. "Okay, Lida. Here's me, officially concerned."

"It's only cleaning. I wasn't expecting company."

Pam sighed. Cellophane crinkled.

"Got another?"

She tossed me an orange candy, shot through with a creamy swirl. She unwrapped a second for herself.

"Crystallized ginger helps with nausea," I said. I'd heard Meifen telling another customer once.

"It's not the baby. I just like the taste."

"I don't exactly know how these things work, Pamela." I never once lasted three months. We hadn't told Pam about any of it. Imagine if she thought we wanted her to be not herself but some lost one of them. The same reason I tried to nix when-Barbra-was-your-age stories. Pammie was Pam; we didn't want her thinking in terms of one-for-one substitutions.

The AC grumbled on. Pam's fingers curled up in a quick white-knuckled fist. She shifted her legs. The gap between her knee and mine could be plugged with a nickel. "Okay, Lida. Here's the thing." She was sweating, pale with it. Usually it made her seem hearty and athletic. Baby was to blame, sure as if it reached a milky hand up her throat and yanked down on her uvula. "I'm going to talk now," she said. "I want you to listen, even though I'm going to say some things that you don't like. I'm going to talk and then when my turn is done, you can have your say."

Silence.

"Lida?"

"I thought I wasn't supposed to be talking."

"Starting now." She drew her knees to her chest. Another few weeks and she'd be done with that for the duration. She wrapped a hand around each ankle and settled her chin into the notch where her knees met. "Okay. So I need you to keep that thing of Granna's in mind. You know? Everybody's just people."

"It was Frank who said that."

"Lida, I'm talking."

"Okay. Yes. Sorry. But it was Frank. Ma's sayings were always more ba-da-da-da-da-da-da-da, dah-dee-dee-dee-dee-dum-dum-dum."

"Lida." Pam took off her cap. Until she ran her hands through her hair, I thought it was a gesture of respect. "I don't care who said the thing. I just need you to remember the thing. Everybody's just people."

A beat. Another. She seemed to want me to repeat it. I obliged. "Everybody's just people."

"Okay then. Good. Here goes. I've been in touch with my father. Don't be mad."

Silence. A fat bolt of it unspooling.

"You know what? I think I want you to talk. It's loads worse just waiting."

I said, "You probably thought he should know about the baby." Imagine if I hadn't created Maisie. Imagine hearing it with no warning at all. Even knowing it beforehand, I felt veiny and defenseless, a shrimp all unshelled.

"No," said Pam. "Well, yes. But—before that."

"Do you have another candy?" While it dissolved I could be quiet and think of what to say. I knew better this time than to tell her I already knew; I was stubborn, yes, but I was capable of learning. The candy this time was bright yellow, banana-flavored where I expected lemon.

"I needed to know him," Pam said. "You and Frank acted like I invented the sky. My own personal pep squad with, I don't know, gold-plated megaphones. Every swim meet or report card or time I cleared the dishes—"

"You were a good kid. You were such a good kid." Beneath my tongue, saliva welled, banana-sweet and sludgy.

"I was *his* kid. I knew what that meant. I knew that every single yay rah was code for thank god the *Clarence* isn't showing yet. You'd never know it—here I was this kid who couldn't even swear—but I'd get so angry. Every time I tricked people into thinking I was just some sweet girl I wanted to, I don't know, scream, or light matches, or bite their stupid fingers off. So I started writing. I had to, Lida. If I was going to have a shot at turning out different."

"You were never a thing like him, Pam." We kept everything. Doily and paste Valentines. B+ essays on cellular mitosis. But Pam got it all wrong. We never—not for half a second—needed proof that she was good. We needed evidence for us. A shoebox of seashells and another of chestnuts. A cassette player in the shape of a bear. Proof we tried for the childhood she deserved. "You shouldn't have worried about that. You weren't like either of them. I shouldn't have said—at linner. You're not a bit like her."

"Everybody's just people." She rubbed her eyes. "That's the terrible part."

If my furniture was laid out properly there'd be tissues within reach.

Pam sniffed. "Before I got the guts to write him I used to wish it would turn out I was really Georg Ring's."

"The policeman's?"

"The teacher's. Oh, God. What kind of person can't even keep her father's murder victims straight?" Her laugh was an eerie, unconnected thread of sound. I hoped the baby hadn't yet grown ears.

"How long?" I asked. "How long have you been writing him?" It shouldn't matter but it did. Not under my roof, I thought. Not under my roof.

"You're not going to like this."

Pammie at sixteen, waiting that extra beat before letting me into her room. Pammie at seventeen, schoolwork colonizing the kitchen table, a protective arm shielding her notebook. *Little privacy, Li? It's just SAT words.* Then eighteen and off to the dorms. "Honestly, Pamela," I said, "there's not a whole lot about this conversation I do like."

"Sophomore year, Trish got her hands on some edibles."

My confusion must have shown.

"Pot, Lida. *The marijuana.* But in, like, brownies, so it wasn't carcinogenic or whatever you're about to melt down about. We wound up sitting with this Psych TA who'd been after Trish all semester—"

"I'm starting to regret all those tuition checks."

"Very funny. And nothing *happened.* We were sitting at this construction site over by the law school and having this weird, pretentious conversation about recurring dreams and somehow I wound up telling them how I used to wake up screaming from all those horrible huge birds. So the TA goes, 'what do you think the birds *are?*' and Trish is all, 'who do you think *you* are, Sigmund Freud?' and he makes some crack about *zee fazzer* in this fake German accent and I just—"

"You just what?"

"I knew, Lida. I figured it out. The big dark nightmare bird was the cop we hit. Bam!" She drove a fist into her palm, then let it fly. "Off the hood."

"Pamela, I—"

"Let's have it be my turn. I was nineteen and still having this dream every few weeks. I figured it was stupid to pretend I was normal. It was time to write him. And so I looked up the address. I'm sorry."

"Sorry for writing him?"

"Hairballs, Lida. I'm sorry for everything. I'm sorry that hearing this hurts you and that I kept it secret so long. I'm sorry that we didn't talk about him more. Or less. Or not at all. I don't even know. I'm sorry I got to know him because he's going to die soon and I don't know how I'm going to feel about that. I'm sorry I'm not a nice enough daughter for it to just plain gut me and I'm sorry I'm not a nice enough daughter to do a happy little jig. I'm sorry I don't remember Barbra very much and I'm sorry she did what she did to him. And I'm sorry he's such a colossal fuckup, excuse my French. I'm sorry I lied to you, or misdirected, or whatever. I'm sorry I didn't think to let you get used to the idea of the baby before we told the whole family and I'm sorry it's coming into a family that's so messed up. And I'm sorry because I ran a stop sign on the way over here and I'm sorry for that time I was twelve and stole a twenty from Frank's wallet and I'm sorry for—"

"Did you visit?" Spring break, junior year: *I'm seeing Trish's family in San Diego.* Senior year: *a whole bunch of us are driving to New Orleans.*

"No. I never have. He asked, but it'd be too much."

"You should have come to me if you were afraid. We wouldn't have stopped you writing him. Right away you should have come."

"I'm here now. I'm afraid now." She fished in her purse again. I recognized that flimsy Stemble paper. She waved a single sheet, inked on both sides. "This came yesterday. I always wait to read them till the morning. Otherwise they keep me up nights. This is going to keep me up nights. This is going to keep me up forever."

"It's paper. He's a paper father. If he frightens you, just stop writing."

She shook her head. "He's got a girl. Here in St. Louis. She's gone completely off her nut. She's been writing him all this mushy-gushy stuff for months. I was glad, right? The more people he has the less hard it is on—"

"It's prison. It's supposed to be hard."

"Less hard on *me*. If he has other people I'm not the whole banana. But it turns out this girl's a complete wacko. He says her last letter was totally different. And scary. She took him to town for what he did and she knows way more than just names. She's crazy angry. She goes on and on about how she wants him dead."

Maisie Keller. "It's nothing, Pam," I said. "And if he was even half a father he wouldn't want you worrying. They have guards in Stemble. It's not like she could just waltz in."

"But she's *here*. And she's crazy. She knows all about me. Blue too. She's seen me around town. She's following me."

"Maisie never told him that."

Pam stared, jaw set. She shook her head. "He's not the only person in the world to have done a bad thing. You've got these blinders."

Relief. She hadn't caught my idiot slipup. *Maisie*. I was a fool. "He probably thinks it would be fun to scare you."

"My father would never do that."

"Nothing's going to happen to you."

"He says she knows where I live. He said to get out of the house. Get someplace safe."

And she'd come to me. Like she did when she was small. I drew her close. Her hair was batted down where she'd worn the cap. She'd probably put it on so Maisie wouldn't spot her. "You're here. You're safe. I'm not going to let anyone near you."

"I've been taking Thursdays off so he can call me. Don't look at me like that. You get to be right—*yay!* There *was* something weird that day in the apartment. I'm pants at lying."

"You could have said."

"It's only been these past few months. I told the center it wouldn't be forever. Only until—"

"Until it's over."

"Yeah. And he's going to want to know I'm okay if they let him call today. And I know it's crazy but I don't want to go back to the apartment without Blue and I don't really want to talk to him right now because I'm pissed as anything, beg pardon, that he let that girl—"

"We'll sort him out. We'll sort out both of them. But it's all paper, trust me, it's just paper." Nearest I could ever come to explaining. Maisie Keller cast no more shadow than the swooping birds of Pam's night terrors. "No way paper can hurt you."

"'Cept paper cuts."

I pretended I hadn't heard that wisecrack shell click back into place. I pretended I couldn't feel nerves or guilt or anything complicated. I held Pam. She'd hardly mentioned the terrible linner. I pretended I wasn't relieved. I pretended I wasn't triumphant. "I'll head over to the apartment for you," I said. "I'll be there in case he calls."

35.

"This is an AZ-D.O.C. authorized collect call from inmate: Lusk, Clarence, 58344. All inmate contact may be monitored and/or recorded. This is a call from an inmate. Do you accept the charges?"

"Yes. I do."

The longest click I ever heard.

" 'lo, Pam?" Your voice had a rasp in it that I had not remembered. "I don't know if you got my letter but you need—"

"This isn't Pam."

Beat. "Maisie?"

Fear in your voice. I hadn't expected that. I thrummed at the marrow. "It's Lida. Lida Stearl. Barbra's sister."

"Where's Pam? What's happened? Tell me she's okay."

"Don't you tell me what to do."

"I'm her father."

A pause. "If Pammie were hurt, if she so much as stubbed her toe over this, do you think I'd waste my breath on you? She's fine, no thanks to—"

"Thank God."

"Scared out of her gourd, but not harmed."

"The things I've been imagining, the terrible—"

"You always did have the nastiest mind."

"Is Pam home? Let me speak to her."

"Say please."

I heard you swallow. "Please."

"Pamela came right to me. I promised I'd come over and take this call, tell you she's fine though it's more than you deserve. She's safe at home."

"So put her on."

"My home. Scared but safe as houses. Unless you told your psychopath all about me too."

Click.

This is a call from an inmate.

Click.

"I never even told her Pam's name. I was careful, I swear. I'd never put my daughter in danger."

"Please. It's me you're talking to. Me. Not some nitwit cashier. You killed a man in front of your daughter. You ran down a cop."

"Pamela doesn't remember any of that. One of the only things I'm grateful for."

"She's always had nightmares about giant birds."

"I don't see what that—"

"Of course you wouldn't. You can't for a minute think how the world looks to anyone else. Tell me something. When you hit him, Georg Ring's arms jerked out, right?"

"I'm not talking to you about that. Not on the phone. Not ever."

"They jerked out and they jerked wide. Wide as wings, I'd bet. A little girl in the backseat would have no idea what that meant. Easier for her to see a bird. Huge and dark in his uniform, bouncing right off Daddy's hood."

"I said I'm not talking about it."

"You arrogant man. What you're saying is, I'm right."

"The only thing you like to hear."

"You don't know a thing about me."

Silence. Pam and Blue kept their kitchen very cold.

"I know you care for Pam. You know I do." You paused. "We should just talk—"

Murderer. "Don't you pretend to be reasonable."

Click.

This is a call from an inmate.

Click.

"Look, she's not some little kid for us to snap over. She's all grown up." Your voice broke a little. "She's having a baby."

"I know that. Of course I know that. Did you think she wouldn't tell me?"

"I'm just saying, since we both—"

"She told us all together. Everyone who was family. A real celebration."

"Everyone who could be there."

"We were all so happy for her. It was really something special."

"You're loving this, aren't you?"

"You don't know what you're talking about."

"It's your big chance, Lida. Swoop in and save. Do what you do best—"

"I'm a good woman to know in a crisis. And you—"

"Don't start."

"You risked your daughter on a handful of floozy letters."

"And you're the one who's falling apart because Pam's got her own life and you aren't the most important part of it anymore. Pam says—"

"I'm a whole world closer to her than you'll ever be."

"Maybe. But I'm happy for everything she's got in her life. She's okay—"

Click

This is a call from an inmate.

Click.

"—even with everything Barbra and I did to fuck over her chances. She's going to ride this out better than anyone. Pamela's happy and if you weren't being so nasty about it I'd say you did good by her."

"I did absolutely right by Pam. It's me, me she came to afraid."

"You aren't so right for her these days. She tells me things."

"You're in no position to judge me. You'll never be in a position to judge me."

"I'm not judging, I'm telling. My last appeal's coming up. I know how you hope it turns out and I don't much care that you think it. But before, during, and after, you better go easy on Pam—"

"Don't you tell me how to love her."

I shouldn't need telling, not from you.

I shouldn't need telling.

"What I'm telling you is how to treat her. I'd never tell you how to do the other. Not with the mess I make of loving people."

"You love Pam."

"More than breath."

"She was afraid when she wrote you."

"I know."

"She's afraid now."

"I'm sorry."

A fine lot of good your sorrys did. "She's right back where she started. Nothing with you ever ends up better than it started."

Click

This is a call from an inmate.

Click.

You said nothing.

"Was this girl of yours worth it?" I asked.

"No. Not ever."

"Did you love her?"

"I don't have anything in here."

"You had Pam, you greedy thing. You ruined her. She came to me shaking. She wore a hat to hide from your girlfriend. Tell me you at least loved her."

"I thought I loved—"

"You loved nothing."

"I loved that she didn't know me. She wasn't touched by any of this."

"Until you touched her with it. Young girl like that, no wonder she lost it. You stay away from Pam."

"She's all I have."

She was all I had, Clarence. I felt threadbare. "Did you love my sister?"

"I'm not going to talk about her."

"I could tell Pam you just made this person up. You were bored and wanted to see how bad you could scare her."

"You wouldn't."

"Did you love my sister?"

"Be fair."

"Did you?"

"Yes. Badly."

"You killed her. You shot her and she died."

"I did. Yes."

"I want to know why. No. I want to know what made you think you could." Could and did, could and did, singing in my head like a cricket.

Click.

This is a call from an inmate.

Click.

"This operator. It's hard to get a word in edgewise." The roughness dropped from your voice. It was smooth now, thick as cream.

"I'll tell Pam you gave your girl her address. I'll tell her you gave out her social security number."

"I don't know her social security number anymore."

"She doesn't know that."

"You're only going to scare her worse, Lida. You really make a mess of loving too."

"Go to hell."

"I don't believe in it."

"I wish I did. Tell me."

"I'm never going to. Some things stay between a man and his wife."

You hung up on me. You actually had the gall. The dial tone blared like any other dial tone. Now every disconnect would jerk me back to this: Pam's kitchen, my chest tight, my own mute sense of smallness building with the dial tone like a siren in my ear.

36.

Pamela answered that old nature or nurture question, and thoroughly. Like her aunt, Pam proved a good woman to know in a crisis. She and Blue updated their cell phones. They insisted I go in on the plan. As long as that psycho was loose, everyone was to check in when they were going someplace and to touch base again when they got there safe. She and Blue started house hunting. They would need more space when the little one came anyhow and Pam felt safer doing it sooner. They found a three-bedroom condo in Clayton. Kath and I went in on new cabinets as a housewarming gift. On my advice, Pamela would use a P.O. box now to write you. On my advice, she would be judicious with what she shared. She said you understood. She had you send a description of the girl and you did. I wondered, briefly, why you didn't pass the Polaroid along. But only briefly. Meifen was lovely and you didn't have much in Stemble to look at. Pam circulated your description—Asian girl, slight build, pink hair, not too tall—at linner, nudging everyone to be aware and to be careful. All this fuss over a girl I'd designed to have no mettle. I couldn't say it though. I couldn't comfort. I'd accrued a wealth of things I could never say. I was glad none of the Claveries frequented Green Mother Grocery.

And then one linner over sherbet, Kath told me she was worried about Pam's grandmother. "With that girl about, somebody ought to warn her." Kath hadn't a clue Pam was in earshot. Kath was a friend, Clarence, so that was something I absolutely believed. But Pammie heard. She was in fine spirits. The doctors said all was healthy and the unexpected violet she'd selected for her new living room worked well with the blond wood after all. She sidled over, voice buoyant.

"I don't think there's anything she can do to her," Pam said, thinking of Ma, naturally enough.

Ma never had a saying for *if you're about to get caught in a whopper, own it first, and loudly, and fast.* Still, that's the best way to comport oneself. "Kath means your father's mother," I said, giving Kath eyes that would mean *quiet* in any language. "Her name is Marjorie. She was unkind at the funeral. Kath and I have talked about it. I don't always like to bother you with these things."

An inscrutable look from Pam. I worried she'd seen the *hush now* glare I'd meant for Kath.

"It was many years ago," I said. "I don't even know if she's alive."

"He never mentions her," said Pam. And then: "It's weird actually *talking* to you about what he does and doesn't say."

"I'll see if I can track her down," I said.

Behind Pam's back, Kath Claverie mouthed *sorry.*

I let two days elapse before announcing I'd found Marjorie. Any less and Pam would be suspicious. Any more and she might poke around for herself. That was so fast, Pam gushed. Lida, you can do anything. You were wasted in dentistry. You should have been a superspy. Pam laughed at her own jokes more than ever before. It had to be the hormones.

Pam wanted to visit which I supposed was inevitable. And a part of me was glad. It's a funny old world. I wanted your mother to know about the baby. I only hoped that Call-Me-Art at the desk was a professional, that he wouldn't greet me with *Kath!* or *long time no see*, that he'd be aware that no one visiting Riverview wanted commentary on how infrequently they stopped by. Waiting for Pam and Blue to pick me up, I practiced my shrug in case Call-Me-Art was indiscreet. In case your mother had more than *cassava* to say.

A second word could be disaster. If it were *Lida*, maybe, or *no*, or *leave*. I practiced my shrug once more. It's hard to look mystified instead of defensive, but I think I had it down. It's all in the casual tilt of the head. Pam and Blue were three minutes late, then five. They were seven minutes late all told. They'd already installed the baby's car seat. Between me and it Seshet had very little space. I'd printed directions to Riverview off the Internet and I read from them aloud. Another reason they'd believe me when I insisted I had never been to the facility before.

Pamela parallel parked in a space that would have taken me three tries at least. We unloaded. Pam wasn't showing yet, not really, but she wore a maternity castoff from the collective Gs, collared by a floppy bow. Blue fussed with Seshet's harness. He took her leash in one hand. Pam took his other one. She held mine too. Seshet led us forward, proud, like she was the superspy that had found Marjorie. Between my last visit and this one, Riverview had installed great stone urns to mark their entryways. They erupted with plastic geraniums.

We went in. Pam let go of my hand to fuss with her bow.

"Nervous?" I asked.

She shrugged.

"It's just your grandmother." That Blue. Earnest as a child. "Of course she's going to love you." Pammie hadn't let go of *his* hand. My life would be so much better if I could only notice less.

Call-Me-Art waved, cheery, but Pamela wasn't thrown. For all she knew he was merely exuberant. I waved back with Miss America enthusiasm and Pamela cringed beside me, embarrassed, like she was thirteen again. "The Claveries are here to see Marjorie Lusk," I said.

Call-Me-Art nodded. Pammie looked irritated. She was a grown woman. She didn't need me speaking for her. But grown or not, Pam had no idea how clever her old aunt was. I couldn't outright lie, not with her standing there, but it was hardly my fault if Call-Me-Art kept right on thinking I was a Claverie too. And Blue could only help matters. Call-Me-Art was a good kid; he had to be, why else would he take a job ushering people in and out of a nursing home? He wouldn't pay any attention to me, not when he saw there was a blind man here to help. "I presume it's okay to bring his guide dog in here," I said, just to make sure he noticed.

Of course it was allowed. They probably had laws about that. Call-Me-Art handed over his clipboard; we wrote our names. I signed even more illegibly than Blue. No one would ever be able to conclusively prove that it did not, in fact, say *Kathleen Claverie*, the name I always wrote before. I asked Call-Me-Art to get the door for us before he could ask for our IDs. He held it wide. I had to remember to meet with my attorney, draft some sort of assurance that if I ever fell ill I would recuperate in a much more secure facility.

The doors were decked out with little sailboats now. Senior scribbles in the sails, names spelled out across the hulls. Blue and Pamela followed me and I made sure to stop and read each door so it wouldn't seem like I knew exactly where to go. Janine!'s sail was crowded with concentric tracing; at the door that had once been Herman!'s a new tag read Saul!. A single dribbly *M* dominated Marjorie's sail. She could hold a marker now. More than. An uneasy gut roil. Acidic. Tidal. Your mother was well on her way.

Pamela hesitated at the door, tracing her grandmother's name with manicured fingers.

"Marjorie?" I poked my head in. "It's Lida. Lida Stearl. Remember me? I've brought a surprise."

"Ppft." A new Marjorie sound, like she was pretending to be French.

"Well, look at you!" I said. Marjorie's face was inexplicably caked with makeup. "Did you do that yourself?" Not likely, considering her wobbly sailboat *M*. Maybe Riverview brought in beauty school volunteers. Your mother's lashes spiked up in dark clumpy thorns. Wide fevered circles blotched her cheeks and her eyelids were weighed down with cocoa-colored powder. Some steady hand had daubed her mouth the wrong red, too jazzy for a woman who hadn't been outdoors in ages. It faded in places where your mother had licked her lips.

"Marjorie," I said again. She wouldn't look at me. Her favorite game. And fair was fair. I'd been sound and steady and then vanished without a peep. She was sitting straighter than I had ever seen her. I had to pretend like all of this was new. I had to do this without seeming excessively strange to Marjorie. "I brought someone special here for you."

"Hi." Pam waved. Blue stood very tall behind her.

"You." Marjorie's hand flapped. The cosmetic volunteer had been a bit too enthusiastic with the nail polish. Violet blobbed like a series of nasty bruises.

"Me," said Pam. "And this is Blue."

"Ppft."

A frown from Pamela. A light little sigh.

"She's had a stroke, remember?" I turned back to your mother. "That really is her, Marjorie. Clarence's girl."

"A Clarence girl, ppft."

So. No more *cassava*. I had to keep calm. Remember the shrug I had perfected. It's the immediate response that counts most when a body's accused of wrong. "Pam came a long way to see you," I said. "She brought her husband."

Blue waved. I'd have to ask someday how he always knew the proper direction to face.

"Ppft."

Pam said, "We drove out from St. Louis."

Marjorie stuttered. An *s* sound, an *l* sound, a series of *t*s.

"That's right, Marjorie. St. Louis. You can do it." As long as she focused on *St. Louis* she couldn't let slip I'd been there a time or twelve before. "St. Louis," I said again, enunciating. "St. Louis." A baffled look from Pam. I supposed she was expecting me to be unkind. Or at the very least not in my element. She knows sociability does not always come easily to me. "Say hello again, Pammie," I said.

"Hello." She stepped all the way into the room.

Marjorie looked and looked.

"Clarence's girl," I said again.

A fast series of blinks. When the word came, it came perfectly clear. "Slut."

"Excuse me?" Pam brought a hand to her not very much of a belly. In the door frame beyond her, Blue stiffened.

"Ppft."

"It's nice to meet you too." Pam stepped closer. A glance my way. "I don't think it's the *stroke* that's the problem."

"Hey now." That was Blue. He joined his wife at your mother's bedside.

"Slut."

I said, "A stroke can affect the language center of the brain and inhibitions sometimes—"

"Thank you, Doctor Lida. And now my long-lost grandmother thinks I'm a tramp." She leaned close to Marjorie. "I only ever slept with Blue, thank you very much. It's *obscenely* quaint and I think we're done here." She stood, fast. She took a step back and nearly clobbered Blue.

"I didn't know that," I said. "About you and Blue." Even I'd had Martin Dorsey, an age ago, before Frank.

"Oh my god." A withering look from Pam. "Put me in a clown suit and it's everyone's worst nightmare come true."

Blue lay a calming hand on her shoulder.

"Slut."

"A rubber clown nose." Pamela tweaked her own. "Right here."

"A slut girl a liar." Marjorie's words were horrible and perfectly ungarbled.

We'd been very forthright in our sex talks with Pam; it had seemed the appropriate and healthy thing to do. But she'd guarded her worry so close, her fear of turning into you. And she was Barbra's daughter as well. Afraid of following her path too, more likely than not. "Pamela, I know that you'd never—"

"Please, Lida. I just want this conversation to die."

"Your grandmother doesn't think you're a slut."

"Evidence suggests otherwise."

"She thinks you're your mother." *Clarence's girl*, I'd said. I should have said *daughter*. "Pamela, the stroke—won't you please sit down?"

"This family." Pam shook her head. She sat though. Blue's hand hung in the air briefly, shaped by her absent shoulder.

"Marjorie." I bent toward her. The greasy smell of discount makeup. "This is Pamela. Little Pam."

Your mother brought her thumb to her front tooth. She ran it back and forth, remembering, I was certain, the dental impressions I'd permitted her to hold.

"That's right. Pam. Clarence's daughter. Not his—not my sister."

"The little . . ." Her voice caught midway through the word.

"Pam." I rubbed my thumb along my teeth.

"Come," said Marjorie. The word came garbled, like she had twice the normal amount of tongue. Pamela scooched the chair forward. My Pam in her wide green dress, bright kite reeled in.

The reluctant scrape of Pam's chair. "Hello again. This is really weird, isn't it, Marjorie?"

"Grandmom Lusk. You used to call her Grandmom Lusk."

"Lida, please." Pam shifted. "She's not about to pop out of bed and bake us oatmeal cookies."

Blue jostled from one foot to the other, hands deep in his pockets. Barbra should be here. She was so good with uncomfortable meetings. When I first introduced her to Frank his shirt was missing a button. He noticed halfway through their conversation. He was nervous. I said he shouldn't bother. She was just a little sister after all. I was nervous too, even if I didn't tell him. Barbra bratted that she'd never like anyone as much as my first, Martin Dorsey. Frank's fingers kept picking at the spot where the button belonged. Without once stopping her chatter, Barbra pinched the button at her cuff and twisted it right off. She gave it to Frank and he liked her from that moment on.

"Close," said Marjorie. "More close." She paused. "Closer. More."

Pamela leaned in. They shared a profile. Marjorie might have been as pretty when she was young. I had to look away. The sickroom blinds cut the sky outside to ribbons.

"No. Close. Come close. More."

"Grandmom Lusk, this is getting silly."

I heard a hiss. I heard a gag. A muffled *wh*—. I whipped around. Marjorie had jammed her hand in Pamela's mouth, her fingers going piano keys over her teeth. Pamela grunted and arched back. Blue stood perfectly still trying to figure out what had happened. His hands were out of his pockets and ready to help. Hard noises came from Seshet's throat. Pam jerked away so fast not even spit linked her to her grandmother.

"What are you doing? What the hell do you think you're doing?"

"Pam," said Marjorie.

"Hands off."

"She's only checking your teeth, Pamela." The plaster sets were in my purse. "She wants to be sure you're you."

No one could blame Marjorie for thinking I'd pull such a sorry switcheroo.

"Well she can't. I didn't say she could."

"Pam," Marjorie repeated.

"I'm not a horse. What's her problem?"

"We're all okay here," said Blue. With his inflection it might have been a question.

"Your hands better be clean," Pam stood. "I think we should go. We can warn them about pink girl at the desk."

"Pam," Marjorie said again. My sister shouldn't have named her such a sad little sound.

"What, so you believe I'm me now?"

"Long. Time," said Marjorie. She turned to me. Her left half smiled. Gratitude. Please. Let it be that. I had found her, after all, I had brought Pamela to her side. "Long time," she said again.

"I guess so," Pam agreed, edging away.

"Long long time. I call you . . ." She opened her left hand to Pam and pulsed it, waiting. "I call you . . . call you . . ."

I wished Marjorie had more than present tense back. It made her sound like an imbecile. It made it sound like everything that had happened to her was happening still.

Pam looked at me, confused.

"She means a nickname, I think. She wants you to remember what she used to call you."

"My *Granna* used to call me Pamcake."

"Chub chick, chubchick," said Marjorie.

"I've got a lousy memory."

Your poor mother. I knew how it felt to get Pamela's ice voice.

"Ppft." Marjorie paused, strained, and copied Pam's word "Lousy. Lida." She grunted, eyes fixed on me. "Lida. Ppft."

A sharp hiss. From me or from Pam, I couldn't tell. "That's my aunt you're talking about."

"Ppft, Lida." Marjorie glared, unblinking. I was the one who got Pam out of all of this. Every recital, every kiss goodnight. I'd hate me if I was your mother. So what if I brought tulips, a bedside chair. Teaching Pammie how to read a map. Unscrewing the training wheels from her purple bike. I'd hate me if I was you. "Lida, ppft. Years, ppft. *Years*."

"Lida's the one who brought us here in the first place," Blue broke in. The only whole soul in all of Riverview. "If you don't mind my saying."

"Years and years." Marjorie clawed at Pamela. Her nails shone by the light of her bedside lamp. She was going to get that gunk all over. "Ask Lida, ppft. Ask."

"Please don't talk like that." Pamela stood, a hand pressed to her belly.

Marjorie eyeballed it.

"Listen," said Pam. "This whole thing has been really weird. I'm sorry you're sick and I'm going to believe that's why you've been so nasty. I hope you get better. I don't—I don't know you, but I really hope that, okay? We're going to make sure they keep you safe here and I guess—"

"Chub chick." It had been one word in the funeral home parking lot. One word and just as desperate. Marjorie's hand, twitchy and curved to a permanent claw, rose toward Pam's stomach. "A baby."

An explosive sigh. "Yes. A baby." Pam's arms rocked back and forth, cradling air. "A deliberate damn baby with my lawfully wedded husband, with whom I am disgustingly, *blissfully* happy."

She was halfway to the door. "Pammie. Wait. Your grandmother's been sick."

"I don't care. I just don't care." A long pause between each word.

"I don't think this is doing anyone any good," Blue said.

"She's family. She hasn't seen you." I knew what it was like when Pam turned completely away.

"Lida, enough." Pamela sounded so tired.

"Wait," Marjorie's voice was lead-tongued. "The baby. A girl." There was something of a pronouncement to it, witchy and unyielding.

"We want to be surprised," Blue said, moving with Seshet to the door.

"Poor chub chick."

"I like surprises." Pam scowled, so tall over her grandmother. "I am way overdue for an actually *pleasant* surprise."

"Your family . . ." A click from Marjorie's throat. "Nasty girls."

We should never have come here.

I should never have come here.

"You're a girl in my family," Pam's voice was lethally bright.

"Ppft. Nasty. Lida, ppft. Barbra, ppft." Your mother had got back all kinds of things to say. Your mother had re-learned how to point. She pointed right at me.

Marjorie didn't get three letters a year. Marjorie didn't get one. I took Pamela. It was my right to take her.

"Don't you talk about my family." Pamela at my defense. It should have warmed me more. My stomach felt gummed through and through. Pam leaned close to your mother. In a photograph she'd look like she was about to kiss her cheek. In another life. "I want you to apologize. To everyone here. To my husband. To Lida. To the dog."

Ma died four years after Barbra.

Frank, nearly sixteen.

I fought hard for Pamela. Dirty. My sister's daughter. Of course I fought.

Without Pamela I would wither just like your mother. My right half dying, then my left. They had your mother on medicine to bust up clots. Which meant her blood flowed easier now. Which meant that somehow she still had the heart to pump it.

"It doesn't matter, Pamela. Not to me. Not a bit. It's just her way."

"What's wrong with you?" Her lip curled down. "You aren't this woman's punching bag." Pam's arm arced back. She swung wildly at the bedside lamp. The room brightened with the ceramic thud. I'd never in my life seen her make a fist. On her way out she took a swipe at the blinds. Light danced horribly. Seshet whined. When his wife stormed past, Blue drew his arms in close. Pam tore the sailboat from Marjorie's door. She made confetti of it. She threw it at the wall, hard, and made a terrible gut-in-the-throat noise when it drifted instead of making impact. Blue and I followed Pam down the hall. I took no leave of Marjorie and she couldn't have been surprised. The two of us were clear in this much: my fealty would always be to Pam. She stopped at the lobby water fountain. Drank. Spat. She dug her knee into its base. It gurgled, horrible and metallic. She pushed hard at the front door. Its panes reflected Pam's face as the door swung out. I wished they hadn't. The human heart is only meat. A blue gaze like that could jerky it. Pamela kicked a geranium urn. She howled. She grabbed her toe and sank to the ground, rocking with pain.

Blue was there. He found her and—somehow—got her to her feet.

"I knew it. I just knew it. Of course she wouldn't be happy we found her. This family. Of course *my* grandma would be a B I T C you know the rest." We were at the car. She couldn't find the right key. Pam leaned against the window. It was late July, midday. I could almost hear flesh sizzle. "No wonder he never told me. Not a word. When we found her I thought that was strange. Since she was so close by and all. But he knew what she'd be like. He had to know. She raised him. She's got to be the reason why he's such a—"

"He couldn't tell you, Pam."

"Sure he could've."

"We had an agreement." You'd actually honored it. Both you Lusks had. "He got to hear from you now and again so long as she never, ever tried to contact—It wasn't kind, I know—I was afraid she'd try and—She was so grabby with you at the funeral."

"They went along with that?" Blue asked. "Really?"

"He wanted to hear from Pam. Marjorie's his mother. I guess he got her to go along."

Pam's head went back to the window. It rested there, sweating. "He's not the *least* selfish man ever, is he?" she finally said.

I didn't agree. I couldn't. Not when I'd had my part in the bargain making.

"You knew that about him, Pam," Blue said. "You knew that all along."

"And I guess I know now he comes by it honestly," said Pam. "That woman."

"Your grandmother's all alone in this world," I said.

"Just her and her puritanical Barbra hang-up."

"It's not a hang-up."

"Oh, please."

"It's not." What Marjorie felt for my sister—for me—was bigger than that sporty little word. What the pair of us took from her. I knew the feeling. It blinded her. And even that wasn't enough. It blinded her and then presumed to guide her way.

"Were you even in the same room as me today?" Pamela lifted her head. Her freckled skin warmed just the barest bit pink.

"I was there. Absolutely."

"Oh, ppft." The sound was bitterer when Pam made it, and sloppier. Spit flew.

"Ppft," Blue echoed. Just like Marjorie. He probably did a spot-on Aunt Li too, when they were alone.

37.

Dear Mrs. Stearl,

There's been a rules change. We can't keep Polaroids in Stemble anymore. Turns out they're made up of a zillion paper layers and it's easy enough to stash stuff between them. Enright got caught at random check with a half dozen overstuffed pics of his grandma. He crammed them full of his own nail clippings. Bit off. We can't be trusted with clippers to do our own.

I've told you all about Enright, Lida Stearl. Lida, you have to be impressed he had the brains to figure that trick out. But wasting it like that is pure Enright, wouldn't you say so, Lida? So thanks to him I have to trash this picture or return it. I've been meaning to send it back regardless. Seeing as she wasn't ever really mine. I'm embarrassed to say I don't know my sister-in-law's street address. You should get this anyhow, if you're still checking box 4770.

I told you I was smart. I've been telling you all along. But you are not so very smart, Lida. You forget I've got plenty of dead time to pick over our conversation. That and reread all those very friendly letters. You slipped up, Auntie Li. I'm not going to tell you how. I know you, Big Sis. Trying to work out your mistake should just about kill you.

It was good talking you, Lida. Really, just great. Fantastic hearing your voice. I could tell just by listening you really don't want to say a word against me at my clemency hearing. You've had such a long time to think things over. You've had a massive change of heart. You want to stand beside me. Say we're all human here and forgiving's the best part of being human. You could say it a lot better than that, of course. I had a penpal once. She had the prettiest way with words.

You don't know me very well at all, Lida Stearl. You don't know how badly I want to keep all this from Pamela. Like you said on the phone, you're the one she comes to when the shit hits. I can only imagine how learning something bad about you would gut her. I hope I don't have to tell her. You don't know me, but I bet you understand me.

I thank you, truly, for the use of the enclosed. I got a lot of mileage out of it. Whoever that pink girl was, she is very, very pretty.

38.

The baby wreaked havoc on Pam's nose. She couldn't stand the scent of her own hair. One week she said it smelled of boiled cauliflower. Another, of envelope glue. Then came aerosol cheese. A really wet sweater. When a series of shampoos—including the hypoallergenic bottle I bought special—failed to fix it, Pamela had all her curls hacked off. You look so modern, I always made sure to coo. That, or: it must be a blessing in this heat. Never: Pammie, you look good, you look cute, absolutely darling. You might tell her about Maisie at any time. I couldn't afford to tell Pam more lies. I panicked every Thursday, knowing you two would talk. My stomach only settled after I got her Friday-on-the-way-to-work call. It didn't help that Pamela got steadily crankier. She even snapped at Kath. Pregnancy swallowed her face. She hardly looked like anyone I knew.

She was in her twenty-sixth week when the Supreme Court—as we all fully expected it to—declined to hear your certiorari review and remanded you to Stemble Complex, Arizona State Prison for death by lethal injection. My lawyer phoned with the news. The State of Arizona gave you one week to prepare for your clemency hearing.

I hung up the phone. I had to get to Riverview. I nearly forgot to lock my front door. What I would do was kneel. Right by your mother's bed, as long as my poor knees could bear it. Kneel until words came. Marjorie, I won't be visiting for this next bit. I'm going on a little trip. On my trip I might be seeing Clarence. Probably, definitely will be seeing Clarence. Your mother might let slip some way around your threat.

Your mother might have some last thing she wanted you to hear. Call-Me-Art was on shift. He waved. His watch was a size or so too big. "We never see you Mondays!" He checked a master schedule. "Ms. Margie's in PT. You want to wait?"

"She's where?" All of these Riverview people called her "Margie."

"Physical therapy. She can almost stand on her own."

"Do you know everything about everybody? Right off the top of your head?"

"Just my favorites. She'll be done in fifteen, twenty minutes."

"I'm in a rush. I'm planning a trip."

"How nice."

"What if we took Marjorie along?" A good idea. I should have thought it sooner; I'd had all these months to plan. You would have to be grateful, Clarence, seeing your mother one last time. You'd owe me. Big.

"I'm not sure she's—"

"I know she'd want to come." I wouldn't have to be the one who told her. I wouldn't have to find something in that room to look at instead of her face. Her pale slack dough face. They never let her out in the sun. In Arizona I would be vigilant about sunscreen.

"You'd really need to talk to her doctors."

"It's a family trip."

"Even so. Do you want some water or something while you wait?"

"We're going to see her son."

"That's great."

I wanted to shake him.

I wanted to thunder his brain about his skull.

"It isn't great. It isn't. And you are lousy at this job."

"Sorry?" He blinked, confused.

"You haven't checked my ID in ages. What if I used a fake one? I could be anybody. I could be out to get her."

"Ma'am." That *ma'am* again. That word for women who were impotent as ghosts. "You're a regular. I always check out the new—"

"We aren't even family, Marjorie and I. We aren't even friends. You should have stopped me coming." I shouldn't be the one to tell her. I shouldn't even be someone who cared.

"You're here all the time. And the nurses say she's so much better days after—"

"Don't tell her that I came here. Don't tell her about my trip." Nobody cared in the world. Nobody was even smart. Nobody but me, and I was nothing but a coward. "Don't you say a word about her son." Call-Me-Art just let me walk away. If I ever came back, no one would stop my seeing her. All the fuss and bother about my ID, about Kath's. Nobody would have stopped me to begin with. No one would stop me, not now, not ever.

The way people got away with things.

I had to speak against you. My sister was dead. My baby sister.

You reached a long claw out to Pam. There'd be no getting her back if you told.

I couldn't speak.

I should.

I drove back to my side of the river. I spent the day on the phone. I booked three plane tickets, double-checking the airline could accommodate Seshet. I reserved a rental car to take us to Judith, Arizona, and two rooms at the Great Western Touristay. Last-minute rates didn't come cheap. The phone woman got a bit short with me when I tried to explain that Pammie was pregnant and would be so much more comfortable sitting on the bulkhead.

I went to the bank. It's generally best to travel with cash. But we'd be walking into a prison. Travelers cheques were a safer bet. I had the teller let me into our safety deposit box. Pamela and I might need our birth certificates to be admitted to the prison. I took Barbra's birth and death certificates too, and every scrap of paper associated with my legal guardianship, in the event I was called upon for proof. I fingered the photograph of Hyun-Ay. I had remembered the dimensions wrong. It was a proper shot, three by five. In my mind I had shrunk it to wallet-sized. The safe also held a velvet jeweler's case that for generations had housed the Haas pearls. My mother's mother married in those pearls, my mother did, and I did, and Barbra. We buried her in them. I never wanted them on the neck of another bride. I opened the case. The velvet thud carried through the vault. Against the old black lining, Pamela's baby teeth gleamed. I counted them. Each was still very white, with a brown poppy seed dot where the root had once dug in. I took the box away with me, Hyun-Ay tucked away amongst the teeth. I don't know what I'd been thinking, leaving them so long in the dark.

I packed underwear enough for ten days, toothbrush and floss, a sealed tube of paste. I transferred shampoo and conditioner into travel bottles. Estée Lauder had discontinued the lipstick—Plumflower—I'd worn at Barbra's funeral, but I'd hoarded my last tube. I packed nine unopened pairs of stockings, six black, three taupe. Summer slacks in navy, khaki, and gray. Blouses that matched the pants and were conservative enough to meet Stemble's specifications. A light jacket; the desert could be cool at night. Cotton pajamas and my thick robe. I needed a second suitcase. Deodorant. My three most comfortable pumps, my two favorite photographs of Barbra, the jewel case of Pam's teeth. A first-aid kit, complete with Band-Aids and aspirin, though Pamela probably shouldn't take one without a doctor's say-so. Two knee-length slips. A raincoat because one never knows. A sewing kit. A blow dryer and bobby pins. Travel alarm clock and extra batteries. Good black gloves.

My three execution suits, thoroughly pressed, got a garment bag all their own.

Kath volunteered as airport chauffeur. She came for me at the townhouse first. I sat behind her, leaving the front for one of the kids. Her shirt tag was turned out. A brand with which I was unfamiliar. Blue and Pamela had over-packed too, three full suitcases between them. Kath called Pamela her poor sweetpea. She kissed Blue on both cheeks. She told me that I went with love and, though it sounded like the earnest salutation of a yoga teacher, I felt it and embraced her. Kath insisted on unloading all our bags herself. She waited until we were well inside the airport before driving away. All the airport people stared. A blind man, a pregnant lady, and an orthodontist get on a plane. We'd make the start of a terrific joke.

Our stewardess had extraordinary silent film star eyebrows. Pamela claimed an aisle seat—the baby made her bladder ridiculous—and Blue insisted I take the window, saying it would be wasted on him. Seshet settled down at his feet. We were fifteen minutes waiting on the runway. Pamela studied the emergency instructions, rapt, like she expected her life would at some point hinge on them. She still read with a finger to guide her. It traced a line from one laminated disaster to the next.

I have never been an easy flyer. My breakfast rose a little during takeoff. The captain announced our cruising altitude. It would be a sunny ninety-two in Arizona. Only a few broken clouds.

"We had a swing set in Arizona," Pam said, apropos of nothing and with great authority.

"You barely had a yard."

"I remember swings. I remember him behind me, pushing me high. She was there too, in front of me, acting like she wanted to catch my feet and gobble them up. She was making faces. It's the only time I can think of that I remember them both at once. She had these shiny red apples hanging from her ears."

"Earrings." Silly things for back-to-school. A plastic worm wearing a mortarboard emerged from one of the pair. They'd gone straight to Goodwill. Of all the things for Pam to remember.

She shifted, grinding her back deep into her seat. "I know they were earrings. I haven't been going around all my life thinking my mother was a tree." Pam leaned her seatback down, squirmed a little, then popped it back into place. She took a swig from the enormous bottle of water Kath had pressed on her. Her bra strap slid down her shoulder and she shrugged it back up. I ordered tomato juice and the little stewardess brought me a Bloody Mary mix. The salt in it had me thirstier than I'd been to begin with. Blue began a very long and very boring story about all his childhood vacations. Kath never booked all her children on the same flight, just in case the worst happened. One Florida trip involved five separate drives to the airport. I liked Kath but would never understand her. Families would be so much easier if they all could wink out at once.

The stewardess handed out crackers and sweaty cheese.

The pilot suggested we look to the right for a clear view of Albuquerque. We were on the left side, but I looked anyhow. "I can't see the city, but the land is really brown. We're getting close." I said this more for Blue than Pam. We were all powerless, javelining through the sky. But Blue more than anyone had to sit strapped and trust that we were going where we were meant to.

They sent a different stewardess to collect our wrappers.

"I see the highway," I said, "we're nearly there. I see trucks."

Blue nodded.

"We're passing over something green. A park. Pammie, maybe your swings were there. No, it's a golf course. There's a sand trap. And there's a track and some bleachers. A high school." Maybe it was Folsom High, which had been in one of the northwest suburbs.

Could be, if the plane had circled a little on its approach. That parking lot behind the bleachers. My sister and Lawrence Ring leaving separately for their clandestine lunch. How many times had they done that without a hitch? Barbra's voice in one of those classrooms. What you do to one side of an equation you have to do to the other. Her hands at the end of the day, wiping chalk dust on her skirt. "Ooh. We're flying over a rich neighborhood now. Everyone has pools. And that looks like a shopping center. The lot's almost full. Wait. It's airport parking. I see people with their suitcases, going back to their cars." When we took Pam home from Arizona she had a window seat. I told her to keep an eye out for the arch. She squeaked and pointed when it appeared. She spoke for the first time that flight: I see the arch, I see the river, I see houses, the road, cars. I see somebody down there, I see a person.

Then she stopped talking.

Barbra was dead only sixteen days. This was the first time I let myself hope. Her daughter would come out right. Pam's counting game ended with people. There was nothing worth tallying beyond that; people were her base unit.

So I stopped speaking at *people* too, though I knew everyone down there had their purses and wallets, their house keys, their cares.

We were flying the same airline as last time. And here I was, echoing Pam, like her words had waited here all along, ready to be spoken again. But life isn't bookends, not unless you make them. And this couldn't possibly be the same plane. With all those souls we trusted them to lift up, surely airplanes were retired at the barest hint of age.

39.

The Great Western Touristay was the better of the two motels in Judith, Arizona. Thirty-odd tourist cabins horseshoed around a swimming pool, its water so blue it seemed to steal whatever color had originally been allotted its surroundings. Every building stood squat and square, adobes, dust covered, or at least the color of dust. We parked. Pam had insisted we get a second rental car, in case we were needed in different places. She and Blue followed me the whole way to Judith. Only I had thought to plot a route in advance.

The girl who checked us in had very blonde hair that fell past her shoulders from a very dark center part. She didn't ask if we were having nice days. She knew better. Stemble was her town's principal source of revenue. For an extra nineteen bucks a night she'd sign us out a microwave. For an extra twelve, a hot plate. When we declined, she recommended the Gecko Canteen. Her little sister waitressed there. We should say hi for her when we went.

Pam asked if we had any messages. The strain of all this had rattled out her common sense. "He won't know we're here yet. And the Touristay's not on his call list," I reminded her as gently as I could.

The polite dimensions of the desk clerk's smile did not change in the least. But something uncomfortable had come to it. This bleached girl—who had a sister of her own—knew now why we'd come to Judith.

She handed over actual room keys, not those new programmable passcards. I reminded Pam to check under her bed. To pat down the curtains and make sure there was no lurker in the closet or the tub. Standard precautions, but triply important in a prison town. I watched her room till I saw curtains rustle. She'd listened.

My own room would be serviceable enough for the duration. A thorough inspection yielded nothing more threatening than soap. It smelled vaguely of dust, bright flecks of which were suspended in the light from the window. I tied back the curtain. I saw Pamela come out of her room. She went straight to the pool. I didn't even know she owned a maternity swimsuit, let alone had the foresight to pack it.

My AC unit was beneath the window. I turned it to blasting. We'd phoned in a reservation; they really should have cooled our rooms in advance. My suitcase zipper snagged. I'd overstuffed. My suits were already rumpled. A clever little ironing board hung over the bathroom door. For the life of me, I couldn't find an iron.

I walked out into the shimmering heat. Blue had joined Pamela at the pool. There were no patio chairs, so he sat right at the edge, pants rolled up, one foot in the water.

"Pamela, did you find an iron in your room?"

Blue answered. They hadn't, but they hadn't looked. Beside him, Seshet didn't so much as try to drink the pool water. Even for her, the color was much too much.

"We need to look neat for tomorrow," I said. "It's a court of law. How would it look if we can't manage to dress ourselves?"

"Lida, will you please just be quiet? You're throwing off my count." Pam flipped over for backstroke. Her stomach bobbled with her like a buoy. It's not a vacation, I wanted to say, what do you think you're doing in this pool? I watched her swim a few more laps, then went in to the desk.

The clerk was busy with another customer. He hulked over the desk, blocking her completely from view. The dark stripes of his suit might just as well be wallpaper, they covered such a vast expanse of back. Even with the air conditioning I was sweating in my cap sleeves. With that jacket he must be fairly drowning.

The clerk peered around his arm.

"Iron?" I asked.

He turned. The thick stack of extra towels she had handed him seemed little more than washcloths. He bowed, slightly. The gesture was not in the least deferential. He wore all that weight like it was some new kind of armor.

Well. I couldn't rightly expect a paid attorney-at-law to bunk down at the Sleep Rite.

"Six bucks," the clerk said, "a day."

"I'll need one for tomorrow." I looked right at him. And, Clarence, I didn't blush at all. Your lawyer moved toward the door, jangling his room key. I refused to step aside for him, though at his approach I felt puny as a doll. I asked the clerk her sister's name. I asked her loud enough for him to hear.

I watched him stop at the pool. Blind man and pregnant girl, how many pairs like that could there be in Judith? I stood at the glass door and watched him introduce himself. I stood silent. And I thought for a moment that maybe *silence* would be enough for you. You'd let me keep Pam. I just wouldn't speak tomorrow. Not a word. All would be well, and it wouldn't hurt Barbra, not much, Barbra who was far beyond my helping.

I saw Pamela slosh out of the water at his introduction. He looked smaller at the pool with no furniture around to provide a sense of scale. He gave Pam a hand up. His grip turned to a proper shake. Pamela's wet limbs glinted. And it wasn't fair, him with the full heft of pinstripes and her in that Lycra bubble of a maternity suit. The swerve of her body, the shine on her skin, she looked blown from glass.

The hell with stillness. I was out the door. Across parking lot asphalt gone tarry in the heat of the day.

Pam didn't hug him. The hell with silence. If she was all that caught up in your cause she'd hug your champion, never mind the drips. I saw your lawyer palm her stomach. Pamela bristled, like she would for just about anyone, then reached out and patted his. My girl. He shrunk back, point taken. He had her beat on the belly front.

I watched him leave. Even with all that weight he moved quickly. I expect he knew he had hard work ahead.

"Who was that?" I asked.

"Don't pretend you don't know. It's insulting to both of us. That's Peter Kershaw. Dad's lawyer. He says you met in the lobby."

"I saw him. We weren't introduced."

"We're meeting for breakfast. To go over things, tomorrow. I'm taking the second car. Then I'm visiting *him* at the prison, before the hearing." Pammie went back down the ladder. Dad's lawyer, she said. Dad's. She began to swim again, her strokes keener. Blue said something friendly, trying to fill the air. I stood frozen quiet. Pam was on breaststroke now, her pregnancy visible only when she turned. If I let my eyes blur I might be able to trick myself: we hadn't got to this point after all, that stomach was nothing but the water's distortion.

40.

In the prison town of Judith, scrubland goes on for miles. You could see it from Stemble like I could see it from town, the open palm of land so uniform it didn't matter that we looked across it from opposite directions. I saw plants though, up close, plants you couldn't reach from your guard pen. Tangled branches, rain greedy, growing more out than up. On Judith plants, leaves sprouted sharp, like nettles. They were parched and gray up close. From a distance they looked soft and green; anything would, against a background so red.

In the Judith phone book no names I knew were listed. I checked for that guard of yours, Westin. But your keepers were a good deal smarter than you gave them credit for. No Chaplain Crowler listed. No Warden Kimpton.

The general store in Judith stocked cartoon cereals in fun packs. I bought some to munch dry the next morning, the morning of your hearing, the morning Pam would spend in strategy with Peter Kershaw. She'd see you tomorrow too. I bought a sorry-looking grapefruit. It would taste sour after cereal, virtuous.

I took a test drive out to Stemble. I went alone. Neither Pam nor Blue wanted to come along; we could meet up for dinner, they said, and they could follow Kershaw tomorrow in the second car. The road unrolled uncurving to the prison, the land so much the same on either side I might as well be driving along the base of a mirror. The buildings were gray and solid, large enough to hold their color against the desert. Guard towers looked absurdly like air traffic control, but none of you were going anywhere. All around, barbed wire coiled in ring after ring. It doubled up in patches and looked like the human genome.

In Judith proper, though, no one used the stuff. The municipal pool had a white plank fence; the library, chain link; the schoolyard, tall cacti twined together at angles. In front of the school a jumpsuited janitor lowered the flag, unhooked it, and began to fold. At the Gecko Canteen, the menu advertised "Last Request Pie," a peanut butter, Milk Duds, and a caramel concoction that wouldn't be out of place at Kath Claverie's table.

41.

We had an uneasy dinner the night before your hearing. Pamela ordered a club sandwich but was only interested in the bacon. She nibbled the pink and laid aside the marble fat. I opened my mouth to tell her eat up, hard day ahead, and you need the energy, you must be wiped out, all those laps. I got the *eat up* out but then my mouth went dry as dust. The Gecko door opened. I saw the widow walk in and I heard the blood beat in my ears.

The widow had been married to the cop you killed. Newspapers preferred her picture over Barbra's, despite the widow's unsubtle nose. My sister was very beautiful, but the press loved the cop factor. I should be grateful; Ma used to say it kept Barbra more ours than the world's. And the articles that glossed over Barbra tended to be kinder. They called the late Lawrence Ring my sister's colleague.

The widow scanned the Gecko. I wanted to wave her over and I wanted to hide like a child beneath the table. The hostess led her to a free booth. When she moved, the widow glided like a nun.

On breaks at your trial she used to knit, a funny, old-fashioned habit for someone as young as she was then. I never saw her leave her seat at the courthouse, not even for the ladies' room. Whenever she dropped a stitch she cursed. Before I figured that out I thought she had some kind of condition. She pressed a ladybug sweater for Pam on me a few days before I flew home. The strangest, saddest gift I ever received; in those days none of us were thinking sensibly.

I thanked the widow but was glad to see the sweater was much too small for Pam. I put it in mothballs right away.

Her name had been Arceli Ring. She stitched a *Handmade by* tag into Pamela's collar. Five years after your conviction I read that she'd remarried and I felt peeled and mashed. I dug out the sweater, snipped off the tag, and ground her name down the kitchen compactor. I continued to write my annual checks to the Georg Ring Foundation, increasing them in direct proportion to my income. But I always addressed the envelopes to *Mrs. Arceli Ring*. I had no business guessing what she'd done about her surname.

Pamela shunted a leaf of lettuce around her plate rim. Arceli was coming toward us, four booths away, now three. Blue asked if we were ready to go. He was a nervous eater; he'd completely cleaned his plate. I nodded. I knew he couldn't see me, but if I spoke my broken voice would draw the widow to us like a fish on the line.

Perhaps she wouldn't recognize us. Pam couldn't wedge a toe in that sweater now.

But if she didn't, I would only ever sit with Arceli in two more rooms. The hearing, the witness box, and then the open rest of the world.

Arceli Ring passed by our table. She stopped. Turned.

Arceli Whoever.

"I thought that was you," she said and gave a courtly little bow, just like your lawyer. I couldn't see why everyone was being so polite.

"Hello," said Pam, hand extended, just like I taught her.

Blue stood, hearing it was a woman's voice, just like—I'd bet— Kath taught him.

Introductions all around. Arceli gave no last name. "I'd like to sit a moment. May I?"

Pam knew who she was, I could tell. She shot me a pleading look. Tomorrow morning she'd see you for the first time in years. Whatever Arceli had to say Pamela didn't want to hear. "I'm tired," she said and she sounded about two years old. If only she were and I could tell her: put that lip away. Unless you want the pouty bird to perch on it. "Go on ahead," I told her. "I'll catch up."

"I'll get your Mom home, don't worry," promised Arceli.

Aunt. The widow of all people should remember. I wanted to leave but Pam and Blue were almost to the door already.

Arceli called me Mrs. Stearl, just like she did on foundation thank-you notes. Her whole family was staying in town with a friend of a friend's cousin. Everyone was being so kind, especially Henry, who was husband number two and supportive as could be. But she needed air, she said. I wondered what kind of woman needs to get away from that kind of love. She continued to speak, but I held up a hand. Wait. I watched Pam turn the rental out of the lot. Too far away to tell if they'd buckled up. "Sorry," I said.

She'd seen where I was looking. Arceli was beautiful, nose and all. Her wrinkles looked right and wholly natural, like she was carved from wood and they were merely its very fine grain. She said, "Your girl's grown up."

"I should think so. This has been a long time coming."

"That it has. She looks good. She happy?"

I could still hear my heart. "She's fine. She's safe. She's happy." Beat. "Or she will be. She got to know him." Beat. "I didn't mean for that to ever happen."

No wonder the papers loved her. Arceli's eyes got very wide. When she blinked I could tell those eyes were very good at making tears. "I think about her sometimes. She was such a cute little thing. When Georg died it used to help thinking he died keeping her safe.

Getting a little girl back to her people. Not just chasing down some nobody who shot up his cheating—"

Beat.

"Sorry."

"No," I said. "You're right. She did cheat."

She toddled after me everywhere when she was small.

She had fat grabby baby hands.

She cheated. She should have known better. She lied. She should've been taught.

"And I'm sorry," I said. "I am so very sorry."

"You didn't do a thing."

My family wrecked hers. My wrecking ball sister. Barbra's bad blood. Barbra's and mine.

And so I told the widow. I opened my mouth and out it came. Just like that. I didn't know it was going to. What I'd never told Barbra, and never would tell Pam. What I kept from Frank our thirty-five years of marriage. It was the widow, here, now, or no one. I kept my voice steady. Nothing draws eavesdroppers like a whisper. "I cheated too. Ages ago, but still. It was wrong. I should have been better. Our mother raised me to be an example. I already had a steady boyfriend when I started seeing my Frank." Martin Dorsey. At Pammie's age I broke his heart. A punched-out look to his spade-shaped face. We were supposed to get married. We'd planned it since high school. I'd been sneaking around on him with Frank for weeks. Martin's hand fiddled with his watch. I gave him that watch. College graduation. I saved and saved. I didn't have the right to tell him anything, not anymore, but I wanted to say no, don't look at what time it is, Martin, don't look or twice a day forever you'll remember.

No one knew, save the widow now, and Martin, wherever he was, and me.

I lied to my sister about when I'd met Frank. I put off introducing him for nearly a year. She was ten years younger than me and clever. I was afraid she'd figure out what I had done. She'd adored Martin Dorsey, who used to tease that he was just waiting for her to grow up.

The widow smiled. A gentle smile, like she actually understood. "Your old boyfriend, he didn't kill three people when he found out though, did he? None of this is on you." She couldn't have said a kinder thing. In the moment of my unburdening it felt like a slap. After carrying it quiet all these years. After thinking—irrational, superstitious, no matter—that that was why we couldn't—the doctors knew the problem wasn't Frank, it was me, and an insomniac voice whispered it was what I deserved for hurting Martin. And it was worse after Barbra. Because that wasn't irrational, wasn't superstitious. The other was just biology, but this, this I might have changed. The kind widow. Her kind words. They felt like *so what*. "I shouldn't have said that about your sister," Arceli said. "Nobody did this but Lusk."

I wished I'd ordered coffee. I could sugar it, add creamer. Do something with my hands.

"Georg would want me to remember that. He'd have hated knowing how much I thought about him saving your little girl. He believed in the law. He said it like *the law*. He sounded like church. And he died defending it. Getting her back was just dressing. Still. I'm glad you say she turned out good. That's something."

"She is good. She trains guide dogs. Her husband is blind."

"I saw."

"They're having a baby."

"I saw that too."

"She's younger than I'd like but she's always been responsible. They're happy about it. They'll be great parents. And her in-laws adore her. Everyone does. She's a good girl. I want you to know that." Barbra would never be worth any of this. Not to Arceli Ring. But there was Pamela. "I want you to know that because she's speaking for him tomorrow."

I wished Arceli had brought her knitting things. The silence between us could use that clackety-clack.

"Well. I'm glad he has someone."

"He killed your husband." Her old wedding ring had been silver or possibly white gold. The new one shone yellow. "Your first husband."

"You don't have to remind me. But Georg believed in the law. Lusk's gone through the whole process. He's got better breaks than most. And I want his fancy lawyer and his sweet little daughter fighting for him with all they got. Even if it's more of a chance than Georg Ring had. More than your sister too. That's hard to swallow but the law's the law and the law allows it. So let him have his hearing. Let him speak. And when we're done here and things come out right, nobody can say after that Lusk didn't get his fair shot."

"But you don't know how they'll rule."

"He was condemned in a court of law. Georg would want me to trust in that. Georg believed in the law," she said again. She said it like he must have. The Law. "He always talked about going to law school, maybe part time. When I think how he didn't get his chance it helps remembering he died for something he believed in. Whatever happens tomorrow, Lusk won't be able to say that. Hardly anybody can. No one's really a hero anymore these days."

"I understand you," I said, and I did.

The Georg Ring Foundation awarded scholarships to policemen who wanted to enter law school. Gold into straw, Frank used to tease whenever I cut the checks. Arceli's conversation had a practiced air. I'd bet she lifted scraps of it from foundation speeches. She had her share of insomniac nights, lying awake with a silence of her own to atone for. Arceli and her silence, thinking how safe her husband would have been behind a desk, a Georg Ring, Esquire, nameplate on the door. Thinking she should never have blanched at tuition, a second mortgage. What she wouldn't give to have said *I believe in you, honey. Kids're in school now. It's no trouble me going back to work. It's for both of us in the long run; I know that; even if it's tough going, together, we'll find a way to get by.*

42.

I was up before the sun. I watched it rise. I stood at the window and ate my little box of Froot Loops. Pam used to sort them by color. She put off eating her favorites for as long as possible. Every color tasted the same. My window reflection looked old and tired. Combing my hair would help. I knew exactly where I'd put my brush but did not move to get it. I stared out at the desert and worked my fingers through the worst snarls.

"My name is Lida Stearl," I said. My breath fogged the window. I smudged it away. "I am sixty-three years old." I didn't know who exactly made up the clemency board. Membership couldn't be a full-time position. The world wasn't in so sorry a state as that. The board would arrive in Stemble soon. Past the gates and down the halls. They could be en route even now, somewhere beyond the Touristay out in the scrubland.

"My name is Lida Stearl," I tried again. I had to get beyond that point. Pamela's rental car wasn't in the lot. She was off with Kershaw. She was off with you. "I've been waiting almost twenty years for this. For people to care about what I say." I cleared my throat. It wouldn't do to allow my voice to catch. "I should say first that I am not any good at speeches. I've got to stick to the simple truth." The desert splayed out unvarying before me, but I had been to Stemble. I had seen it, solid. Your clemency board would be solid too, its members in their dark robes. "We're here today because my brother-in-law, Clarence Lusk, shot and killed my sister and two other people. You're hearing a lot about him today"—I assumed they *would* hear a lot about you today—"but I think it's only right that you hear about who isn't here today, my sister." I gave a terrible speech at her funeral; I was giving a terrible speech now. I wasn't meant for this. No one on earth is meant for this.

"Barbra was ten years younger than me and very smart. She smelled of clean cotton and for a while after she died it was hard for me to even do laundry. She would have teased me about that. She'd have laughed. She laughed a lot, which could be annoying to a serious person like me, especially because her laugh had a grating sound to it. But I like to think of it now because the sound— because Barbra herself—was so happy, so unselfconscious. She was never timid, never cautious"—though how things might have gone if she'd learned to be, even a little. "She loved life. Clarence took that from her. Life, love. He took everything. I'll never get to hear her laugh again. Her voice. Please think about that. He took that life she loved and he took her from a family that loved her. He took two more lives after that. He killed my sister and he killed two good men. What you're here to consider . . . it shouldn't even be a question."

The sun was all up now. It burned the parking lot and pool, the road, the dry and dust beyond. "I've come before you today to speak for my sister." I was wearing my good bathrobe. I smoothed it like it was the skirt of my suit. "It's an easy thing to say, she loved life. Everyone says it, but Barbra really did." There wouldn't be enough time to tell them. Barbra tried and tried but never learned to whistle. Barbra went barefoot when she drove. "You know she was a teacher. Part of the reason, I think, is that she wanted to pass on that spirit, that love. She taught math." I could have been describing anyone. Barbra, barbarian. *Barbaros*—one who isn't Greek. A stranger. I felt the sun on my face, even through the glass. "She taught math. She wanted her students to think it was elegant, the way equations balanced. I've been thinking about that a lot today. But that's not why you should put her killer to justice. It's not about restoring balance. She was my sister. There was no one like her in the world. I'm not saying this right. The sentence has to stand. Not to even out some equation, but because there's no way to make it even, because after what Clarence has done, balance can't ever be restored."

I couldn't do this. I had to.

Everything I said came out so much nonsense.

Exactly as I felt hearing the news. Barbra dead. Pammie mine. Nonsense. I couldn't do this. I had to.

Nothing had changed, not in twenty years. In the motel window I saw my reflection cast faint against the landscape; I saw Arizona run right through me.

43.

Everything in the hearing room had clearly been ordered from a government catalogue. Avocado-colored chairs lined up in rows. The only nod to pomp was a gilded eagle perched on top of the flagpole, and even that could be found in any elementary school auditorium.

Pam was up front on the left beside your lawyer. She had on the same dress she'd worn to meet your mother. She filled it better now.

"Pammie's off to the left," I told Blue. He'd been quiet the whole ride over. "I'll help you and Seshet."

He shook his head. "I thought I'd stick with you."

Pamela turned at his voice. A quick, sad smile.

"She put you up to this, didn't she?"

"Pam knows this isn't easy."

"I don't need babysitting."

"It makes Pam happy," said Blue.

I introduced myself to the prosecutor and he checked something off on his yellow pad. Blue and I sat. The hard chairs were a good sign; they couldn't expect this to last long. The room filled. The temperature rose. I was in my black gabardine. It stuck to my skin. I envied Georg Ring's widow, who wore something caramel-colored and silky.

The room had two doors. The wide double one I'd entered through and a narrow, knob-less one up front. It opened and the board filed in. Four men and one woman. She wore a pantsuit, which was much too casual, frankly vulgar, considering these proceedings. All around me people shifted. We didn't know if we were meant to rise; it was like attending someone else's church. I stood. Pam did too. It was as I had taught her: it's seldom wrong to err on the side of respect.

The board members carried manila folders, slim ones, considering what was at stake. The chairman waved us down into our seats. He identified the case by name and number, outlined the proceedings, and kindly asked the observers for their respectful silence. He nodded to an officer I hadn't noticed before. A door opened.

You came in with the guards like the five spots on a die.

You were older now.

Your scalp patched pink through gray.

You had that good Lusk skin, sesame marked but barely wrinkled.

Your hairline retreated in deep fjords.

You had entirely too much forehead.

One row in front of me, the widow hissed.

You smiled. Your eyes didn't. Your teeth barely showed. Pale lips faded into pale skin.

They'd chained your hands before you. You moved like you wanted them there.

Next to everyone's court wear, your jumpsuit looked like pajamas.

You blinked fast, like the light was too intense. Pam's blue eyes, of course. "Those eyes," I remembered Barbra's voice. She was giddy. She'd just met you. "Those cheekbones, that chin he could use to cut things."

You'd managed a good shave, considering you couldn't be trusted with a razor.

You were weasel lean.

You hardly cast a shadow.

Clarence, you were not so tall as I remembered.

When the lawyers spoke—ours first, then yours—they referenced the manila files. The woman was the quickest to find the right pages. In another life Peter Kershaw could have been a newscaster. His voice was thunderous and reassuring and precise. He reminded the board: your record before these tragic events was unblemished. Everyone agreed you were a model prisoner. From the start you cooperated with the authorities in every particular.

The widow choked down the sort of noise I'd come to expect from Marjorie Lusk.

You showed true remorse, Kershaw said. You suffered, he said. Anyone could see you suffered deeply. It was right that you suffered, no one in the room would dispute that, but to take your life as punishment, because of a checklist of exacerbating criteria, because of the occupation of the unfortunate Officer Ring, because of a father's instinct to keep his child near in a life gone hopelessly awry, that was arbitrary, that was vengeance, that was us at our worst.

We spoke in turns. There was no swearing in. Anybody could have been anybody. A young man in a suit had a letter Lawrence Ring's father wrote while he was waiting to die in a local hospital. *And will you tell Mr. Lusk from one dying man to another that my son he killed was a good man and that I'll be seeing him on the other side when I get there. And if we see Mr. Lusk there even if I don't think in my heart that we will, then I will try my best to forgive him, just like I've tried in my life. God forgives but I can't find a way to forgive Mr. Lusk or to forget what he did. If God finds that a failing in me then He will understand it just comes from how I loved my son.*

When the widow spoke, she gave her full name, which was Arceli Velasco Ring-Berzon. She raised her right hand, though there was no bible in sight. She turned from the board and she looked right at you. "My husband Georg was the 'unfortunate Officer

Ring.'" Arceli's scare quotes looked like talons. "When you ran him down, you ran over my life." There was none of that Gecko Canteen coolness, none of that hushed legal reverence. Tears came. An older man—husband number two—passed her a proper handkerchief. I'd only thought to bring a pocket pack of Kleenex. "I had three kids," the widow said, "and I had no husband when they acted out." Arceli drew a fat fan of photos from her purse. "Look at those kids. Look at the grandkids Georg never got to see." She named them one by one. She cried so hard now it sounded like an accent. I wondered if she'd had any children with Berzon. If they'd even considered it. Her new husband stared at her, just stared. His hand went into his pocket, looking for another handkerchief or for anything that would actually help.

His wife turned from you, giving her salt-striped face to the board. "Remember that Georg Ring was a cop, so if I think of all the people he could have helped—the other officer with him? He left the force, after. So you think about the difference that makes, when you decide today, in terms of other people in this state. And think about the three themselves and the family and . . ." She sat. The squeak of chair on floor her only punctuation.

So it was my turn.

I'm sorry. I don't have the composure. Please, I couldn't speak now. Please, may I speak later?

They shouldn't have allowed it. If this room was half what it should be they'd never. If this floor beneath me were marble. If the board wore robes. If those robes put their elbows on mahogany. Anything but their conference table. Any natural grain at all.

You looked right at me while the board considered my request. You mouthed four syllables. Mai sie Kel ler. And then you smiled again. You put your eyes in it. It gave you mump cheeks.

I almost stood then. I'd rehearsed the speech in my room. I'd been rehearsing it for decades.

I would've but you whispered to Kershaw. We'll allow it, he said. He could use this. I heard it in his voice. See, he might say, I told you he's cooperative. Or maybe, later. The hearing went out of order. My client didn't get his full fair chance.

Again I almost stood.

But Pamela stood instead. She rose pale like the moon from behind Kershaw. Her new weight filled out some of the sharpness of her face. She was lovely. You saw it too. You looked and looked. Your head like a balloon straining its tether. The back of your neck was very red; I could see it from across the aisle. It couldn't be sun. Laundry rash, perhaps. Nervous scratching.

Pam took a deep breath. Pain twisted across her face. Even though it was much too early, I thought: the baby. Bad luck to even think it. Worse still that something in me hoped.

But if anything would stall her. If anything would keep her mine.

"I'm, um, Pamela Claverie and this is my father."

I had no way to stop this.

"I, uh, I grew up more or less without him, which considering why we're all here, um, that was probably the right thing."

One, two, three ums. I counted. The only way to bear this.

"I was a happy kid. You should know that, and I want him to hear that about me. I have, um, only a few solid memories of my mom." Four. "And I'm sorry for your loss, ma'am, but I never saw your husband."

A stifled sound from Arceli Velasco Ring-Berzon.

"I never saw my mother's, um, friend either. She kept me from all that. She was a good mom, and from what I remember my dad here did a good job too. After, um, uh, she died my aunt and uncle still let him send me letters. It's probably important for me to say today that I hated getting them. My stomach would get all knotted every time I had to read one. I was a mess, scared he'd come and get me if I was ever bad. But I was safe with Lida—that's my aunt—and Frank and I knew it, and they said I always would be. Didn't matter. I was still scared. But I'm stubborn. That's, um, another family trait. So when I was older I wrote him more, to force myself to face it. By then I was scared that I'd turn out like him as much as I was scared *of* him. But I'm not like him, not very. I can say that now because I got to know him. I can also say that if I could forget about what he did—which I don't, and I want you to know that too—I'd actually like him. He cares about people. He has all these penpals. I know they sent you letters. He's smart too. He's always thinking and trying to learn things, even though it would be easier for him to, I don't know, atrophy. And he's funny. Not like strange, funny. He tells good jokes."

Pam had a tissue in her hand. She tore it in half, then in half again.

"I'm twenty-four years old and I'm still scared every time I get a letter from him. Part of it's that he's my father and I know him and I'm afraid *for* him, but part of it's that I'm scared to death this time I'll really *get* him, that I'll understand how a person can do what he did."

You hadn't moved since she started speaking.

I'd barely breathed.

"I'm sorry," said Pam. "I'm trying to say this in a way that makes sense. I'm trying to be as clear as possible."

Arceli Berzon was still sniffling. By now a bit of it had to be for show.

"I don't get my father. I don't get how he could do what he did. Even if he was hurting. I just don't get it, and I hope that I never do. But we're all people here and I'm sorry, but I don't get how we can think of doing the same.

"You all can probably tell that I'm really, really pregnant. And except for getting to know my father this is the scariest thing I've ever done. I'm not looking forward to telling this little one about his grandfather."

His?

"But what scares me even more is that I might have to tell him how everyone in this room did the same sort of thing, even though we had a chance to show we were so much better.

"I hope I don't have to tell him.

"I hope that my father will be able to see this child.

"And I hope that I'll be a good parent and that this child will grow up knowing I love him, even if he acts a way I don't like or does a thing I can't bring myself to understand. As for my father, well, I guess I want him to hear the same thing too.

"One more thing. As far as his trying to take me with him counts against my father and complicates the charge, please listen when I say that I wasn't hungry or hurt or even frightened and that I know he meant no harm by doing it. Thank you."

They told me it must be my turn now. If I was to speak at all.

I didn't know till now Pamela was having a boy.

I stood. Blue put out a hand in case I wobbled.

You were too much a weakling to look at me.

Clarence, I didn't wobble.

I licked my teeth. Smooth and straight and slick. I had spit enough for that.

Barbra laughed for two years solid when I wore braces. When it was her turn she lost her retainer twice. She told me you'd lost yours three times. I can't imagine that went over well with Marjorie.

"I am Lida Stearl," I said. "I used to be an orthodontist."

Which was neither here nor there.

Silence. No one in this room cared a fig.

I licked my teeth again.

Barbra, Clarence, me, even Pam. All our teeth moved the same way. Slowly, I used to tell my patients, like continents. A silly analogy, I knew, every time I spoke it. No mouth has room for tectonic showiness. No quakes or buckles, nor cruel range upthrust.

Teeth need constant, low grade aching, guiding them imperceptibly into place.

"I am Lida Stearl," I began again. I had to concentrate. I had to do this right. "I am sixty-three years old. I've been waiting almost twenty years for this. For people to have to care about what I say.

"I should say first that I am not any good at speeches. I've got to stick to the simple truth."

The whole room was listening. All I had to do was say it.

The truth, simply.

"And the truth is I loved my sister, Barbra.

"I love my niece over there, my Pam.

"I didn't have children. Couldn't. And so I didn't expect to raise any. When Pamela came to us, my husband and I, we came up with a system. We called it 'you pick, we pick, I pick.' For if she acted up. The first time, she picked the punishment herself. The second, one of us would pick with her. Third, fourth, and so on, she got no say. I picked alone. Only it never got to that. Pammie—Pam, sorry, Pam—never pushed that far.

"I've been waiting a long time, waiting, which is only half a way to live a life, and here it turns out I don't know the least thing about punishing.

"All I know is I loved my sister, Barbra. So much that I've done my best to fight back any memory that's not a shining one of her. And fighting's no way to keep what I can of her alive. My sister wasn't . . .

"But that's not why we're here. She wouldn't want me airing her business anyhow.

"I love Pamela. And I know this life of waiting and fighting, it can't have been easy on her. I'm sorry for that. The living matter more than the dead. I know that's not a law, but it should be. Either way, today we're done waiting. And I want to be done fighting too. I love my niece, more than anybody, as much as these things can be measured. I know my sister loved her, and Clarence, Mr. Lusk, sorry, I guess he does too. So I think my sister would forgive me. If I say don't do this. Don't do this thing that would hurt Pam."

I shut my eyes.

A sigh or so, but no wailing, no sharp intake of collective shock. Papers rustling.

I opened my eyes again. The widow stared at me like I was sludge. The wood-faced woman I gave Martin Dorsey to, his shovel face, his wet eyes on his graduation watch. I could remind the widow: Arceli, you wanted him to get his fair chance. But I didn't care if she hated me. Barbra had known I was saving up for Martin's watch. She offered to crack open her piggy bank. The widow should hate me. I deserved it after everything I had done.

You stood. You began to speak. Nothing I said had mattered. Before you got two sentences out the chairman loosened his tie and I knew how it would go.

44.

For the rest of my life any chop-splash, chop-splash would be Pamela wet and silent at the Touristay. Laps till dusk. She swam freestyle. Her stomach dragged deep like a rudder. Blue said she'd want space and went inside. I waited. My shadow grew longer on the pool bottom. Line up Pam's laps and she just might get far enough away.

Every few laps she slowed enough to speak.

"Not good at speeches, Lida? Are you off your nut?"

Three laps.

"Every time you open your mouth it's a little mini-speech."

Six laps.

"Sorry. I don't mean that."

One lap.

"Thanks. For today."

Two laps.

"I mean it."

Five more laps.

"What are you standing here for?"

The next lap.

"Pamela?"

A lap later.

"Yeah?"

"I didn't know you were having a boy."

Eight laps.

"I don't know. But I've *decided*. The moment Grandmom Lusk said it would be a girl."

"That's not how it works."

"Please, Lida. Today's *exactly* the day for you to tell me where babies come from."

"Do you think we should have brought her here? Marjorie, I mean."

One fast lap. I had no stopwatch but would guess it was good enough for back in high school.

"That woman? She's mean. And she doesn't know her hat from her heinie."

I let her go a dozen laps. This spoon-sized pool. They weren't a quarter the length of proper laps.

"We could've brought a letter," I said. "Or written one and said it was from her. For Lawrence Ring they had a letter."

"I didn't know till just now we had a *we*." Pam hung on to the pool's tiled edge and let her legs float up.

"You should tell him we'll look after her. He might want to know. Tomorrow. When you see him. Tell him she'll be walking soon."

Pamela began to swear then. She started her laps once more. An ugly word each time she touched wall, reliable as the widow dropping stitches.

I left her to her swimming. On the table in my room the phone blinked red. The message was from Kershaw. *He's agreed to see you tomorrow. 8:00 A.M.*

I felt weary and grit-mouthed. I had to brush my teeth. Upper left quadrant. We the people of the United States. Lower left. We the people. I began to shake. The brush ping-ponged about my mouth. There'd be tomorrow to get through, and then tomorrow night, when none of us would sleep. Then there'd be the Arizona dawn, the desert hour when your guilt would pass with you from this world. They said it would take seven minutes, less time than it took to fry up an egg.

45.

Once again I was up at dawn. Your next-to-last sun lit up a desert that looked too soft a place to have you in it; mellow in the morning light, fake and dewy, watercolored. I pressed today's execution suit. The oldest of the lot. I got into the skirt through the good grace of control-top hose. I put on my watch. Sometime today some medic would prescribe the drugs for your tomorrow. I put on earrings. Simple gold studs. Stemble forbade visitors in hoops and dangles, anything that could be grabbed, along with jewelry in any visible non-lobe hole. I still had a pair of little silver bells—Barbra's favorites—squirreled away for Pam. But she never pierced anything. That lifelong fear of needles. Stemble allowed me just one ring. My solitaire was lovely but I set it aside. I thought of Frank. It was my plain gold band that sealed us.

I did up my eyes. I powdered my skin. I daubed on lipstick, a dignified rose. *Why don't you put on red?* Barbra asked. She was always ten years behind. She liked to watch me put my face on. *Red lips are cheap, silly.* We sat up in my room before a high school dance, some spring or winter celebration, I don't remember. I should have paid better attention. *Lida wears war paint,* Barbra singsonged. She whooped about the room. Barbra Barbarian. We heard the doorbell. *Are you going to marry Martin? If you don't, can I?*

Don't make me laugh. You're just a kid.

I won't be, not always.

She was always ten years behind. And then eleven, twelve, sixteen. Coming up on thirty now.

I applied a second layer of lipstick. I couldn't bring the tube into Stemble; I wouldn't get a chance to reapply. Good thing I knew the trick. A layer of rouge across my lips for staying power. I emptied my purse. Traveler's checks, address book, aspirin, my compact, a jewel case full of baby teeth all piled on the bed. I'd be back long before they came to change the sheets. My bag felt empty with just my birth certificate, license, and the single car key that Stemble allowed.

A Visitation Officer searched my car when I drove into the lot. In their yellow protective gloves his hands moved like a mime's. Some previous renter had left behind a map of New Mexico.

There was no line at the registration desk. The woman doling out the forms had lost neither her baby face nor her acne. She looked bored, bland as caulking, even when she read who it was I'd come to see. She took her time with my papers. She wore a studded rubber thimble to help her sort the pages. She spoke into a callbox. "One for sigh you."

"Sigh you?"

"SIU."

Special Isolation Unit. The Death House. A van arrived for me, large enough to seat ten. The driver wet his nervous lips the whole ride over. There were no seatbelts; a lawsuit waiting to happen.

A loud blare and I was admitted to the Death House. A long hall. At its midpoint a guard sat inside what looked like a tollbooth. I should have worn flats. My heels tapped as I approached. I passed my purse through the slot. He checked my face against my ID. I had a good five years on the photograph and hoped it didn't show. He returned my things without comment and nodded down the hall. Another door. Another clang. It opened on a long shoebox room.

Dull, flecked linoleum. Plain walls. It smelled of recent cleaning. Lit like a good hospital, except for the cages built around the long bulbs. Those fluorescents must be miserable to change. Two guards stood near a metal detector. One asked me to turn out my pockets. They were still sewn closed. He let me use my car key to pop the stitches. I stepped through the arch. Something buzzed, somewhere deeper in the building. I hadn't set off the alarm; I'd been careful getting dressed. I wore a soft cup brassiere, no wire whatsoever. It would only be a handful of hours, and no sense kidding myself. I was closing in on sixty-five. Whatever had a mind to sag was going to. The guard ran some sort of wand over me. The other officer had a leashed dog that never moved from its haunches. When Pam came through here yesterday she must have had a thing or two to say about the white gunk in its eye.

Another clang. Loud as a siren but only half as shrill. I was glad to hear them now, for practice. I wouldn't startle, hearing one, with your eyes upon me. The officers escorted me to a windowed door. A glance from the one with the dog prompted his fellow to speak. He scowled before opening his mouth. His face was scored all over with lines.

"You have one hour. I will be right at the door. Do not give the inmate anything." His scowl deepened; Stemble, I saw, didn't offer much by way of dental plans. "Keep two feet back from the glath at all timeth." The other guard choked back a mean grin. I stuck out my hand. Westin stared, oatmeal-brained, like his mother never taught him shaking hands is what people do. He stepped aside. The door clanged and I went in without having touched him, his hand that knew the way you crumpled at a fist.

The visitation room could fit in my kitchen. A floor-to-ceiling wall of glass sliced it in two, its panes shot through with bracing wire. The wires made a grid that looked like picnic gingham. The walls were pale but not quite bright, like the paint had been over-thinned then layered over a much darker color. A single bar of light screwed into the ceiling above me. The cage around it flaked tetanus red. I approached the glass. My reflection stood black-suited on the other side, amorphous in the dim.

Another clang and your door opened.

46.

You have to know that I spent years imagining this.

My brother-in-law before me, guard-flanked and hangdog. A ghost already, in his ghost chains.

Never once did I imagine you would come into the room laughing. If your chains—linked foot to foot to belt to cuffs— scraped over the floor your laughter masked the sound. You had a better laugh than Barbra. A good one in its own right. Rich and somehow damp, almost like gargling. That sound the wettest thing in all of Stemble. Still laughing, you raised your cuffed hands and wiped your forehead. You moved well for all that hardware. Your laughter stopped. You hadn't shaved as well as I'd thought before. Stubble roughed your skin in lichen patches. Gone mostly gray now, so I hadn't been able to see it at a distance. Your skin had a gray tinge too, as if it couldn't hide how close you were to being meat. You let the silence turn thick as stew between us. I adjusted the fall of my skirt. You grinned. One of your canines had gone red-brown as gravy. You spoke. "If you see her again, if there's some sort of afterlife coming, Little Sister's going to be pissed."

What I should have said was: at me?

Or: you are the one that killed her.

Or: say hi for me. You'll see her soon enough.

You know I didn't say that. I only said hello.

"You kind of sold Little Sister out."

I should have said: Barbra never was your sister. Or: don't think for a minute I did it for you. I stood before you like a lump, like the eye of a potato.

"Not that it did me any good."

"No," I agreed, "it didn't."

Sweat ringed your jumpsuit collar, bled out from the armpits.

"First courthouse this county put up they built over a burned-down brothel." You smacked your lips. "Goes to show."

The kind of thoughts you had, Clarence, when things didn't go your way. "That isn't true," I said. And here was another something for Barbra to forgive. Instead of my sister I thought of Georg Ring, whose widow said he loved the law.

"Well, you've got a whole life to prove me wrong. A whole damn life."

It would take half a shake to find out online. You had no idea. "I'll check it out."

"While you're checking things out, you might want to look up the law that says it's wrong to fuck with the mail. You might want to ask Peter Kershaw. His caseload's about to lighten."

You don't get to feel sorry for yourself. You don't get me to feel sorry for you. Quit your bellyaching, I should have said. Instead: "You were right about Kershaw. He really is one of the fattest men I've ever seen."

"*Maisie's* the girl I told about that." You were sweating in streaks now. You looked like you'd come from the sauna. You arched your back and I heard your spine crackle. Except for the hair, you were getting much less gray. "Maisie Keller. Maisie Fucking Keller. The wife always said you were too boring to live. She said you had to have this secret other life."

Barbra red and gummy lipped, getting into the basement cherries.

Barbra finding constellations for homework. Barbra, bored, inventing new ones.

Barbra wrestling a suitcase closed.

Barbra fever-handed with Lawrence Ring; Barbra touched the way I'd never again be touched.

What I should have said was: Trust me, Clarence. You don't want to know what she used to say about you.

Even if it would have been a buck-toothed lie. The last time we spoke Barbra imitated one of her students, who'd sputtered when she caught him fudging his midterm. Your name never passed her lips. I loved my sister, absolutely. But she was a cheat and I knew maybe ten real things about her.

"You never apologized," I said. Barbra was gone. There was nothing left for me to learn. "Not even a word."

"I never had anything to be sorry for. I never did a thing to Maisie."

"I don't mean to her."

Your laugh. It was getting uglier than Barbra's. "Maisie was a rotten thing to come up with." Nastiness brought your color back. No gray. You were the color of just undercooked poultry. You don't get to judge. Not me, not anyone. I almost said it, but you spoke first.

"I liked you better when you were boring. But Barbra would have been proud. So we're at odds. Maybe Pam can be the tiebreaker."

"Now wait. I did ask them not to, tomorrow." My tongue felt crusted over. Don't dither, I taught Pamela. If you want something, straight up ask. It's unbecoming to hint. "You heard me in that room." I was hinting. "You heard me. You were there."

"Cut the simpering, sister. It wouldn't even have worked for her."

I'm not your sister, I should have said.

Your smile grew and grew. You must have looked down on Barbra like that, wide and cruel-toothed. And she'd have looked up at you, bleeding. From the ground that iron smirk must have looked like a horseshoe hung for luck.

"Don't." Cowards beg. "Don't tell Pam."

"Say please," you said.

I should have said: that brown tooth is dying, Clarence. There's blood in the tubules. It's predeceasing you.

"Please," I said.

You stood before me luminous. It couldn't all be sweat. "Maybe." Your cuffs gave just enough space for you to crack your knuckles. You know I've never liked that sound. "It doesn't have a damn thing to do with you if I do. Knowing what you are won't do Pam any favors." Your voice slid into a whisper. "You know how it feels."

I almost didn't hear it. I was too cowardly to ask what you meant.

"Please."

"Keep your pleases. Just know I made you say them." Your laugh returned. "'Please' won't change a thing between us. If I let you off the hook it's cause I want Pamela thinking at least someone who had a hand in bringing her up was actually good."

Maybe I should have defended Barbra. Maybe I should have defended myself. What I said instead was the one thing in our conversation I'm actually proud of saying. I spoke my husband's name. "Frank. You forgot Frank. My Francis was unquestionably good."

A silence, and then: "I'm a lucky man. She loves me."

"She loves me too."

"She loves me knowing the worst I ever did." You smiled like Marjorie now, the half her face that could. Tired, not sure if you could quite manage it. "You'll think about that, Lida." My name in your mouth was thick and sweet as pancake syrup. "You'll think about that and you'll owe me the rest of your life."

"The rest of my life. However long that may be." I forced a grin of my own.

"Lida, don't try. You can't do worse to me than you've done already."

"It was letters, Clarence." Even if you loved her. "Don't be a baby."

Your face contorted. It broke like the yolk of an egg. "You got my kid. You came out ahead from all this. You got to be the one who made sure she turned out so good." Your voice cracked and soared high, like it was hormones and you were young and hadn't yet made this happen.

Clarence, I'll have the wide rest of my life to think of should've-saids. I've thought of them, words that could have wrung remorse from you like juice. You know I couldn't find them then. But even in that moment I think we both knew what needed saying.

Thank you, I should have said, for Pam.

And, Clarence, you should have said the same.

You didn't say it either. I watched you recompose your face. "You never got that kid," you said. "The one you wanted. From Asia."

"Korea, Clarence. Korea is a country. Asia is a continent."

"But they never gave you one. Pamela was it."

"Pammie was it. Is. Is it."

"You're sick in the head. You know what I thought when I figured out about Maisie? I thought—that pink girl—I thought it was part of your messing with me, making me *think* about my kid's sister just because you could."

"Maisie's twenty-three. You shouldn't have been *thinking*."

"I don't think you've got the moral high ground here."

A squirming, silent moment.

"They matched us. The agency. Right after—right after your trial. A little girl. We said no. We had to be there for Pam. She was everything. Everything."

A dry cluck, almost matronly. You were enjoying this. One of the last pleasures your life had in it. "Poor thing."

"We did *absolutely* right by Pam."

"I meant the other. Left behind in the rice paddies. Dirt poor." Your voice was fawning, lazy. A lover's voice. "Married off at—what, twelve, is that how they do it?"

"Korea is an emerging superpower," I said. "You've been away a long time, Clarence. They have the best free education in the world. American kids would kill for a spot in their programs. They're on the cutting edge of robotics and microchips and—and gene splicing. And they're leading the way in gender equality. Their last three prime ministers have all been women." You had shaped my life more than anyone else in it, Clarence. More than Pamela. More than Frank. You and your bullets, horrible but true. And here we were. You would die the next morning. We would never speak again. Of all the things I'd meant to say to you. I knew nothing about Korea. It would take a solid minute for me to find it on a map.

47.

Housekeeping hadn't yet come to my room. I picked up the nightstand phone. The Touristay was bound to bleed me for long distance, but such was life. Then one for out of state. The area code for St. Louis and the rest of Kath's number. Three rings and a pick-up click.

"I just saw him," I said. "It was awful. I hardly said anything right."

"Hello?" Kath's voice, confused.

"I'm sorry. I must have dialed wrong." I didn't want to discuss it after all. I hung up. I should have been the aphasic one, not Marjorie. I should have been *born* that way. I flopped out across the bed, right in the middle of the purse mess I had made that morning. You know what I am, Clarence, but at least there's this: I was glad there were the beds in forty-nine other states where couples stole each other's covers and didn't know what was to happen tomorrow in Arizona. I shut my eyes. Bright still pulsed behind my lids. I fumbled for the velvet jewel case. Pam's milk teeth rattled inside. I opened it. Eyes still closed, I put my hand in.

By its nubbed points I knew the molar she'd lost biting into a pear. A canned pear, all mush pulp. With a tooth loose we'd never have given her hard fruit. And here was the hard shovel shape of a lateral incisor. That one had gone the same day her little first-grade boyfriend lost one of his. Here was the canine she spat into my hand two years and four days after the death of her mother. And a molar she lost at twelve, saying, really, Lida, I'm too entirely grown-up for this kind of thing. I touched teeth lost at the zoo with Ma, lost in P.E. and recovered from the grass, lost in line for the ladies' room, lost while recuperating from strep. A whole childhood here, save three central incisors that had come out in your care. I should have thought to ask you. How they wriggled free, if Pam was scared, how much you put beneath her pillow. The fourth central I had. I tucked it into my palm. My little favorite, the first one we saw come out. Frank used a cotton ball to stop the bleeding, not knowing how the fibers would stick. Pam, just under a week in our home, worried the tooth fairy wouldn't be able to find her. I phoned the mothers of five classmates to best gauge the going rate.

I opened my eyes. I looked at the white little nub. It probably budged first on your long car ride. Pam's legs swinging. Pam safely strapped in, bored with landscape. She had her crayons, but this tooth was interesting. More so than the telephone poles she'd been counting, at least as high as she could count. Her tongue found the tooth again and again. It worked hard until the sirens came. And then, later, Pam in her best dark clothes. Legs still swinging, funeral benches much too high. Her tooth was still there, wet old friend. Her tongue wiggled, grateful. Not everything had changed.

I would wait outside for Pam. She would come straight to the pool. When they kicked her out of Stemble, Pam would come. I took her best tooth with me, pressing it into my palm. It was sharpest where it had attached to the gum. It didn't seem fair to Pam that in this hard world all her sharpness turned inward.

Great clouds of gnats swarmed the pool edge, drawn to its false wet. They'd brought in the evening. The ground bruised. The air purpled. I hoped Pam had brought sunglasses. Coming home from Stemble she'd be driving straight into sunset. No matter how hard I pressed, her tooth was too weak to break my skin.

You and Barbra didn't save her teeth. If Barbra hadn't died this one would have made its way into your trash bin then off to some arid landfill. In another life I would never have held it. In a better life, I suppose. I shivered despite the Arizona sun. Barbra should have lived. This tooth should have been lost here. Lost and thrown away. I had no business keeping it. I had a right to Pam now, yes, but something of hers would always belong in Arizona. I let the tooth fly. It entered the pool with a quiet plink. I bit down hard on my cheeks, like Pam used to. I watched the tooth's outripples.

I was right. Pam did come to the pool. Her face was still as a silk mask. It was a shame you would never get to see her with better hair.

"Pammie. What did he say?"

More than anything I envied you being there for her birth, for holding her new-faced and thinking, even for a moment, it wouldn't be complicated to care. There's no rational way to know this, but I believe: that silk face was the one Pam had brand new.

She stared at the water. Even knowing it was there I couldn't see her tooth against the tiles. Pam sank to her knees, drawn down like her child had only just discovered gravity.

"What did he say to you?"

"Goodbye, Lida. He said goodbye."

The gnats swarmed then. She'd knelt down in their low territory and they were drawn to her like sap. She didn't raise a hand to stop them. Whenever they landed or got near to landing, I was there. I brought my hand down. On her shoulders. On her neck. Swat against Pam's back. Swat against her arms. If the clerk looked up from her desk she'd have to come running. I'd look crazy, violent. She would think I was a hard, cruel woman, that I never loved Pam, not at all.

48.

ARIZONA D.O.C.-STEMBLE
   FORM SIU-014t
   Inmate: Lusk, C.D. 58344
   To: Inmate Services-Stemble
   Re: Last Meal Request
Following the dismissal of my plea for Executive Clemency and with the approach of my Execution Date, I request the items below for my final meal:

   Two (2) grilled cheese sandwiches
   Nine (9) strips of bacon
   One (1) tomato, firm
   One (1) bag Doritos chips
   One (1) bowl tapioca pudding
   Three (3) cans Coca-Cola
   Three (3) cups cubed ice
   Three (3) cups crushed ice

   I have read and attest I comprehend the following:
   1) That my Final Meal Request will be considered in conjunction with the items on inventory at Food Services-Stemble and 2) that Inmate Services shall make a reasonable *but not exhaustive* effort to procure items not available in prison stores provided that such items are 2a) locally obtainable and

2b) not prohibitively expensive and 3) that my Final Meal 3a) shall not exceed reasonable portions as outlined in ASPM section IV-023 3b) shall not include tobacco products 3c) shall not include alcoholic beverages 3d) shall not include any foods to which I have a documented medical allergy and 3e) shall be consumed within the standard allotted forty-five minute meal period and 4) that the SIU-014t form is my only and official means of conveying my Final Meal Request and 5) that form SIU-014t, once submitted, can not be resubmitted.

Clarence D. Lusk, Inmate 58344

Wallace F. Collier, D.O.C. witness

Cc: Food Services-Stemble

They left you with a copy. It came to Pam with your effects. Pink and tissue thin, like the triplicate sheet of an ordinary bank form. Even for this you couldn't be trusted with a real pen. The writing came through light as spider steps.

I know you, Clarence. Better than you'd like. *Some of my best dreams are of ice.* I see you, last tapioca pearl gone from your tongue. Coke taste clings to crushed ice. Into your dark mouth. If you had sunlight to reflect it, the cubes would glint like gems. In the cell's dim though, ice is just as rare. You grind your teeth down on the cold. Crunch. Your mouth fills with cool sparks. Chewing ice is the best way to splinter your teeth, but let's not pretend that matters. You take another handful.

You take a single cube and then another. You put them on the floor. Your shoes come off. You stand on the cubes. Cold shocked soles. Cold veins up your calves. You take a cube for each armpit and draw your arms close to keep in the slippery chill. You squat. Cubes for the pits of your knees. You passed a fevered final night. You felt embers in your joints. You slither a handful down your back and press against the wall to hold it. Your guards—you've had double watch non-stop since you came to the Death House—eye one another but say nothing. They try not to talk to you, not now you're off the pods. You've known these guards longer than you ever knew your wife. You take another ice cube and anoint. Forehead and earlobes, the crevice between ear and skull. Over your eyes like pennies. Into the well of your tongue for the ferryman. You slip it all around your groin.

You're quaking now, Clarence. A thought with all the force of prayer. Let the ice hold out. Let it be your last best shell. May the needle be frozen piercing it. May the poisons fork through you much cooler than blood. May you at least be cold getting on the gurney. May you believe the cold is why you shake.

49.

The guards let Pammie bypass the metal detector. I felt mealy inside because back at the airport I hadn't thought to insist on that. Her poor baby. A gloved guard approached her for pat-down. He used the backs of his hands. Pamela looked ill. I hoped the baby was a soccer baby. I hope he kicked the officer good and hard. Blue went before me through the search check. Seshet didn't growl at Stemble's still-haunched guard dog. Neither barked. Neither moved. They hardly seemed dogs anymore, we'd worked them so hard; neither knew it was meant to sniff the other's nether parts.

An officer ushered us into a waiting room. A second officer awaited us. No gloves. He introduced himself as Wally, our Special Operations Liaison. He was almost as tall as Blue. Whenever the walkie-talkie at his belt crackled, he answered with his full title. He probably didn't have one on ordinary days. A water jug with knobs for cold and hot stood in one corner of the room. The wheel-cart beside it displayed wax cone cups and packets of instant coffee. Pamela looked shaky. There were no chairs anywhere. By rights we could have gone into the victims' waiting room. They were bound to have a wealth of comfortable seating. Wally asked for our attention. We'd be joined shortly, he said, by two Media Witnesses and two Citizen Witnesses, chosen by lottery from approved petitioners. We should be assured that the families in Viewing Room A would be joined by the same number and type. The Media Witnesses were not permitted to ask us for statements while on prison grounds, though he was prohibited to interfere should we speak to them of our own accord.

I wondered how many times Wally had done this.

Four witnesses filed in. More guards. More gloves. I could tell which two were reporters; the citizens wouldn't meet my eyes. They all hovered by the beverage cart, but no one drank. The phone rang and I just about crawled out of my skin. It was ordinary, white, wall-mounted. It looked just like the one in my kitchen. Wally answered. Listened. Hung up. They ought to have communicated via the handheld. Somewhere in the Death House you had to be thinking of the governor. How you'd hope if you heard that ring.

"The condemned has been moved into the chamber," said Wally. Yesterday Westin called you *the inmate*. I wondered when they'd made the change. "Please follow me." A steady heavy sound. My heart or my steps down the hall. I walked close beside Pam. Her lavender conditioner and the aggressive mint of toothpaste. The witness room was laid out in three tiers, each carpeted in rumpus room brown. Five chairs per tier. They looked like ordinary folding chairs, except for the feet, which had been clamped to cement blocks that poked up through the rug. Each chair angled toward the front window, over which a heavy floor-to-ceiling curtain had been drawn. Pam took a chair up front. I sat on her right. Blue took the chair to her left. Seshet's rump hit the curtain when she settled down on the floor. It swayed but let in no light. Wally stood up front, flanked by the curtain cord and a telephone with a green light bulb screwed into the top. Pam's hands lay in her lap. She clenched and unclenched her fist. It looked like a beating heart.

I heard my watch tick. It was 6 A.M. The phone bulb flashed once, sallowing all our skin in its dull green light. Wally picked up the phone and listened. He replaced the receiver. "There has been no stay," he said. He was no longer slouching. Pamela made a weak mewl. Pump, pump, pump went her hand. Wally tugged on the curtain cord.

You lay supine on the gurney. A leather strap at each wrist and ankle. Leather stripes, in benign belt colors, marched up your body. A band at mid-calf and mid-thigh, a thicker one across the waist like a seatbelt, one across the chest and a last one at your forehead, where Frank used to wear his terrycloth sweatbands. Four guards stood around you, still as stalagmites. I couldn't tell if I knew any of them from yesterday. To a man they had great barrel chests. You probably couldn't see around their torsos to the windows paralleling your either side. From the other one I knew Arceli Ring was staring. To you those windows would look like mirrors. It's good you couldn't see. If you could raise your head, Clarence, you'd catch mirrors reflecting one another. You'd chase down a scrap of memory. You'd be younger, bored, at a department store, maybe. Marjorie slimmer, taking her sweet time. You'd remember your own face in the hinged mirror. The back of your head in its companion. The mirrors in those mirrors. The front and back Clarences the new mirrors caught. The unwieldy sight of infinite you.

You wore the same sort of jumpsuit as before. I hoped they burned it, after. Imagine if it cycled back through prison laundry.

You could probably see the clock on the wall at the gurney's foot. Either it or my watch was a full minute off.

You couldn't see the curtain by the gurney's head. The same green as surgeons' scrubs, with two plate-sized holes midway up from the floor. You couldn't see the door you'd come through anymore and you couldn't see the red phone beside it. Your eyes must have landed on it; they had to, when you'd been wheeled in. A short man in a blue suit—Warden Kimpton—stood beside the phone. Prompted by no visible signal he approached the gurney. He changed places with a guard beside your head. The exchange happened seamlessly, soundlessly too, like the men on your side of the glass wore submariners' boots. Kimpton produced a paper. The Death Warrant. He bent over you, reading. He was balding up top. He'd sunburned his bare spot. Pam's heart fist contracted, released, contracted, released. We couldn't hear a word Kimpton read. The warrant took a long while to get through. Pam got nearly two hundred fistbeats in before he finished. A guard stepped forward to reclaim the warrant. Kimpton said something and you nodded as well as you could. He produced a cordless microphone. He had to have got it from the guard when he handed off the warrant. I needed to pay better attention; this was happening; this was happening now. Warden Kimpton switched the mic on. It spat. He held it at an angle to your mouth.

Your voice sounded deeper than yesterday. Deeper than I remember it free. Your position forced your diaphragm down. More air inside you to reverberate.

"To my daughter that's here today, I don't want you hurting too bad. Remember you're the best part of me. I knew it the first day you were born. I wouldn't want you any different even if it meant I could've lived a different life." Blue laid his hand over Pamela's fist. It was still pumping. It made his fingers move. "To anyone my living might have hurt, I'm man enough to hope this gets you your peace, though I don't see how it can. To everyone else who thinks I deserve this, just know that I'm a person here you're killing, a person same as anybody, so think hard about what that means you deserve."

Wally's phone flashed. The light shone on Pam's face like fireworks when she was small. Wally didn't answer. He began to close the drapes. As he did I saw the curtain above your head rustle. Some Special Operations Officer was there, prepping antiseptic.

Only Blue's fingers moved, riding Pamela's hand.

Only Seshet breathed. Wet and meaty and sour.

The door opened. No warning. Every hair on my body came alive. Warm air in from the corridor. Peter Kershaw came in with it. He still had his briefcase, useless as a toy. He was weeping already. Tears without sound. Ordinary tears, ordinary sized. They should have been proportional. On his great griddle face they looked daubed on and delicate, salt pearls.

Flash. Wally's hand on the cord. The curtain inched back.

You were lucky, Clarence. That took hardly any time at all. They must have found a vein on the first or second jab. Your flexing worked. Or the alcohol they swabbed you with, less to prevent infection than to tease blood back to the surface, despite the frightened constriction of veins, worming out the ready blue threads of you.

A sharp intake of Pam breath beside me.

I layered my hand over Blue's. His skin was soft as a girl's. I looked at my own hand. I'd forgotten my gloves. Pamela's fist was still going. I felt her beat through Blue.

You had the room to yourself. A clear tube snaked out of each curtain hole and down into you. One per arm. The second tube was only backup, but it made the whole getup look cyclic, like it would be possible to draw back out what they were going to pump into you.

Your eyes shot quick as minnows from one tube to another. They should have at least warned you which side they'd use. We would tell your mother you died peaceful in your sleep. Unpredictable apnea.

They'd perched a heart monitor on your chest. It made it easier to mark your lungs' up and down. You worked them like bellows. Your lips moved too, like cilia, trying to usher in and out air.

I could feel my heart all through me. To the tips of my fingers. Blue must feel it in my palm.

Your eyes fixed wide on your left-hand tube. There. You saw it. Sodium thiopental began its downflow. Ten seconds to wink you from consciousness, sense by sense by sense. You struggled against four blinks but the fifth one took. Color—even the gymnasium shower hues of this last room—lost to you now. Maybe you felt the bands still; I watched your lung-work press against them. Perhaps you felt an itch in either forearm. Something under the skin that shouldn't be. If you heard your monitor's blip blip blip now it would be from a distance; you wouldn't think it had a thing to do with you. If you smelled you smelled leather and strident cleaning—they had to give this room a solid go-over, between times—or your own sweat, that and whatever other dampness you'd begun to let go. If you tasted you tasted dry sponge mouth. Or maybe your erratic breathing raised a last belch. There, in your mouth, a spit echo of pork fat.

They gave you five grams. The half-life of sodium thiopental is 11.5 hours. If they let you alone, you'd wake up in sixty or so.

I know my chemistry, Clarence.

They gave you 100mg of pancuronium bromide. It stopped acetylcholine from binding to its receptors. It stilled muscle fibers. I watched your chest jiggle and stop. Your diaphragm fell in like a cake.

Your heart kept on. Involuntary muscle. The heart is meant to keep on. One hundred milliequivalents of potassium chloride flooded yours. Hyperkalemia. Your heart was mechanical as anything. You couldn't depolarize. You couldn't contract. You tried; Clarence, I am sure you tried. Asystole.

Warden Kimpton was there to announce your time of death and over his voice I heard my own. *Cassava*, I said, *cassava, cassava*. The stuck word, the every word, the poison plant, the plant that keeps scratch farming families alive.

50.

I have a diamond. It hangs from my neck.

Rigel Francis Claverie came via cesarean into this world sixty-eight days after you left it, named for Orion's brightest star.

"But you can't even see the stars," I reminded Blue. Girl or boy, they'd have saddled their firstborn with Rigel.

"I know they're there. And I know they're wonderful," Blue said, which is just the brand of sentiment I've come to appreciate from him.

They gave me a diamond at the hospital, a bit shy of a karat and flawless, with the explicit understanding that they'd never catch me up to Kath. I was glad; Pam looked scooped out and mottled; she'd labored almost forty hours and been split like a melon. Kath got a fat tourmaline, Rigel's actual birthstone. She is still waiting for her amethyst.

Pamela and Blue don't know I've swapped out the stone. The price difference went straight into a savings account for Rigel. He may need it, later, with his parents going about buying up gems for old women. And besides, flawlessness is entirely too much to expect of any thing or one, even of Rigel, who is still so new. He can't tell if the diamond's a little smaller, a little rougher. When I hold him it sways up above him and he stares at it as if at a hypnotist's watch. If I'm still around when he meets the right girl, I will give it to him for her.

He's a smart boy. Just six months old and he can already flip himself over.

On the day he was born I stood by the nursery where Rigel was safe in his baby bin among rows of other safe babies. I touched the glass, as if my warmth could pass through to him. He had wriggled himself asleep; his hand formed a fist and he held it steady by his ear. It looked like some kind of fanatic's salute. The room was just a little larger than the room where I last saw you. Flat-backed behind glass. I needed ID just to visit the ward. They were vigilant checking. Wire enforced the nursery panes. Pamela and Rigel wore bracelets with bar-codes on them. I wanted them to hurry up and take the baby home.

So it seems this is my punishment: I still think of you. Clarence, I know you won't think that's harsh enough for me. You never were forgiving. Just know that it isn't easy, knowing what I owe you.

I apologize. I've never been any good at explaining myself. I tend to make a mess with words.

Rigel has a lip blister from how he drinks his milk.

Rigel can never stay awake in a car.

Pam and I take him to your mother most Thursdays. Family is family and we don't have much of it left. Pamela is tentative around Marjorie, but I have decided to like her. For one thing, I'm no longer the most difficult woman in Pam's universe. Call-Me-Art has never once looked at me askance. It isn't fair or right. I should be banned for life. I know what I deserve, Clarence, I know. When she returned to work, Pam opted to keep her off Thursday schedule. She was used to it and it meant more time with the baby. Pamela misses—not you but—your presence. We talk about it less than you would like, but agree: our life is very strange without your shadow. Your mother is speaking again. Whole sentences now. Paragraphs even. On some visits she knows who we are. Sometimes she thinks that Rigel's you. Her words sag out of her slumped mouth and sometimes her language is appalling, especially considering the presence of her great-grandson. Until last week her limbs were too uneasy to hold him. But Thursday we put him in her arms. Pam stood close by to spot. Rigel didn't know these arms. He purpled with rage. Your mother stayed calm. She handed him back. "Maybe later," she said, slurring just a bit, "He's little. He doesn't know he's not part of you."

I'm sure she meant physically, Clarence. Your mother drifts. She forgets you've gone. We don't remind her. Pam and I can't see the good of it.

So Barbra is a grandmother now, imagine. Her grandson doesn't much look like her. He doesn't much look like you either. Rigel's bright but still a few months short of speaking. When he does, he'll call me Granlida. Blue thought of it; he sees how Grandmother would feel criminal.

That Claverie Nicky has developed an affinity for Rigel. Every linner now the child comes straight for me. I have the wipes he'll need before touching the baby. My position in this family is secure, at least until Rigel learns to fend off germs on his own. I wipe Nicky's hands and caution him to mind the baby's mush spot. He eyes me so skeptically, a guard dog to be got past en route to the baby, like a level on one of his video games.

Today, at linner, Rigel discovered his own hair. It's come in thick, thanks to my side of the family. His fingers laced through curls and, curious, he pulled. He's new. He couldn't guess how it would hurt. He's got quite a little grip. He howled at the pain but was too startled to let go. Pam tried to unsnarl his fingers but Rigel just yanked harder, frightened at the noise and the way it smarted and the worry on her face. You can guess how it went. The more he pulled the more it hurt, the more it hurt the more he screamed, the more he screamed the more Pam fussed, the more Pam fussed the more that poor scared baby pulled and pulled.

Blue is a hero. Blue is so good with the boy. He took an ice cube from his cup and rubbed it on his son's hand. Rigel let go, hiccoughing a little. Kath applauded, and Pam's smile returned. She smoothed her son's hair and Kath noticed that Rigel had my ears.

Pamela agreed. "I thought you looked familiar." She made a big hammy face and tickled her boy under his chin. Then Blue put a hand to my ear and a hand to the baby's to see for himself and that Nicky who is always hovering shrieked "Butterflies!" Rigel flinched at the ruckus and I saw the roadmap of Blue's veins and you were there again, reminding me. Every moment with this family stems from your silence and from your sufferance.

"Butterflies," Blue echoed and let out a thick chuckle. He lifted his hand away from my ear. I heard laughing all around me and still couldn't forget that all this I owed to you. Blue smiled toward the warmth he knew was his son and told the boy, "Hear that, Rigel? Granlida's where you get your butterflies."

We got the call just as Kath was bringing her cinnamon dump cake out of the kitchen. Riverview, on Pam's cell phone. The next of kin should know. Your mother had a fall.

She was trying to stand alone. Her hip's smashed up. Eighty-seven years makes for brittle kindling bones. Kath fussed and dithered and would hardly stay quiet enough for Pam to write the information down. Kath's own mother didn't live a month after breaking her hip. She just sundowned. That won't happen to Marjorie, I promised Pam. They'll make Marjorie a steel ball and socket to match the steel rest of her. We'll get her at a linner yet.

I want that to happen, Clarence. Marjorie in her chair, cursing and sputtering, scattering Claveries before her like so many chickens.

Pamela's smile was uneasy; I'm not sure she wants that.

Riverview had her transferred to a hospital on my side of the river. Pamela left the baby at Kath's and came with me to see Marjorie. They'll operate in the morning. Marjorie's doped up for the pain, too groggy to tell she's been moved but lucid enough to try and hiss her roommate into the hall. "Where's my baby?" she asks Pam. Pamela's vague as possible, not sure if she means Rigel, or herself, or even you. "They're putting brass tacks in the bed," Marjorie says. "They take your jewelry when you sleep."

Pam hushes her. "Nobody would ever do that." Visiting hours are almost done. Pam tells your mother we'll both be there after the operation tomorrow, when the doctors wake her up. Your mother's alarmed; she's forgotten her own jigsaw hip.

I have my camera. The Polaroid I used for Meifen. With a baby in the family it's best to keep one near. I slip into the hall, which is long and clean and unpopulated. Marjorie's doctors will come for her with a stretcher in the morning. If the pain meds hold, your mother will be too bleary to know what's happening. They'll lay her down and she'll wheel along the hall.

She might not remember where they're taking her or why. She might cry out. There is nothing worse than being old and alone and afraid.

I crane my neck up. Marjorie will be terrified on her back. The doctors will wear masks, as doctors do. She might not hear the soothing things they'll tell her. I take a picture of the ceiling. The Polaroid spits it out. This much I can bring to Marjorie. At least the fluorescents will be familiar. The snapshot solidifies, a flat bland rectangle of light. I take four steps down the hall and snap another picture. This one shows bare ceiling, textured like a sponge. All the way down the hall I work. I keep the pictures in careful order; Marjorie will roll comfortable through this territory. My neck aches from the tilting. I knead it; I never can work a crick out like Frank used to. Kath tried—unbidden—to unknot me while we waited together endlessly on Rigel. They'd just decided on a cesarean. I shook her off. Kath wouldn't understand—only you could possibly—how this was the sum of my nightmares, old and new. Pam with an IV, with eyes that couldn't settle and lips flaking like fish scales, flat and in pain on a gurney, wheeling away.

She must have gone into the OR down a hall like this. I snap another picture. And you too, wheeled into your last room, even if your light bulbs were caged. I see you, Clarence, and Marjorie, and Pam. The bulbs are unfiltered bright above you, the space between throbbing dark. And you're sore and afraid, even if you are as strong as anyone. The light is raw. The light hurts. You fight back blinks, your eyes are dry as husks, but you fight. Your pupils constrict, black pinpoints in the blue. Your eyes start to water, there's no helping that; but as long as it lasts you'll never shrink, not from this, the light that comes at regular, blessed intervals.

Acknowledgments

First thanks goes to my agent, Ayesha Pande, and to teacher extraordinaire, James Hynes, for the longstanding enthusiasm for this book that at times outpaced my own. I can imagine neither *The Done Thing* nor my writing life without their advocacy and support. Thanks as well to Ben LeRoy and the whole team of fearless fictioneers at Tyrus Books/F+W.

To Jennifer Vanderbes for a conversation ages back that helped me work out this novel's essential shape. To V.V. Ganeshananthan, Leslie Parry, and Robert James Hicks for their friendship, advice, good humor, and for regularly asking after my characters as if they were actual people. To Sigrid Brunet for sharing a brain with me and listening to me whine. To Rachel Jagoda Brunette for sharing a brain with me and giving me lots of wine. To Melissa Duclos for reliable wisdom on writing, work/life balance, and wardrobe crises. To all members, active and emeritus, of my adored writing group, The Guttery, with special thanks to current critiquers Mo Daviau, Susan DeFreitas, Jamie Duclos-Yourdon, Cody Luff, Beth Marshea, Lara Messersmith-Glavin, A. Molotkov, and Kip Silverman.

I know and adore many, many lawyers; any inaccuracies regarding the law and how it operates are either mistakes on my part or fudging for narrative convenience. No lawyers were harmed in the making of this book. Similarly, my father-in-law, Jeff Alifanz, answered my many random questions about teeth. Any dental errors are wholly a function of the author failing to listen properly to the wisdom of her father-in-law; perhaps my mother-in-law, Susie Alifanz, to whom I always pay perfect attention, will put in a good word for me. My mother and father, B.J. and Steve Manaster, are unstinting in their support, as is my sister, Katy Manaster Strand.

Writing a book means spending a ridiculous amount of time cranky and in my own head and my husband, Marc Alifanz, handles that with remarkable aplomb. Marc, I hope you know that you make the world outside my head wonderful, as do our extraordinary daughters, Elodie and Adeline. Girls, you asked me to include a cheetah and a witch this time around. Please take a look at page 106, then put the book away. You are both remarkably bright. You astonish me on a daily basis. Nevertheless, this book is not appropriate for second graders.